KING PENGUIN

WINTER DOVES

David Cook was 'born into a working-class Lancashire family in 1940. He failed Grammar School Entrance at eleven, was sent to a Secondary Modern School, and left at fifteen, unable to spell and with no aptitude for arithmetic. As an adolescent, he held a variety of dead-end jobs in quick succession: in the storeroom of a slipper factory, unloading lorries for Woolworths and making bricks at a brick works.' At the age of eighteen he was accepted by the Royal Academy of Dramatic Art in London. After his training he played leading parts with the Bristol Old Vic and various repertory companies throughout Britain. He created the part of Trevor in John Bowen's *Little Boxes* in the West End; and spent a year as the host of a children's television programme, as the side-kick of a bear.

David Cook began writing in 1969, and has published three other novels, *Albert's Memorial*, *Happy Endings*, which won the E. M. Forster Award, 1977, and *Walter* (Penguin, 1980) which received the Hawthornden Prize for 1978. He has also written several scripts for television, including 'Willy' and 'Jenny Can't Work Any Faster', both of which were nominated for awards.

He lives in London and near Stratford-on-Avon, and does his writing in both homes and sometimes at the local Public Library.

D0808756

DAVID COOK

Winter Doves
A LOVE STORY

A KING PENGUIN
PUBLISHED BY PENGUIN BOOKS

Penguin Books Ltd, Harmondsworth, Middlesex, England
Penguin Books, 625 Madison Avenue, New York, New York 10022, U.S.A.
Penguin Books Australia Ltd, Ringwood, Victoria, Australia
Penguin Books Canada Ltd, 2801 John Street, Markham, Ontario, Canada L3R 1B4
Penguin Books (N.Z.) Ltd, 182–190 Wairau Road, Auckland 10, New Zealand

—

First published by The Alison Press /Martin Secker & Warburg Ltd 1979
Published in Penguin Books 1981

—

—

Reproduced, printed and bound in Great Britain by
Hazell Watson & Viney Ltd, Aylesbury, Bucks
Set in Juliana

For Robert Penn Warren

As when the dove
Laments her love,
All on the naked spray,
When he returns
No more she mourns,
But loves the live-long day.
Billing, cooing, panting, wooing!
Melting murmurs! Silver grove!
Melting murmurs! Lasting love!

JOHN GAY
Acis and Galatea

PART ONE

June

1

*Her mother had always dressed June in yellow.
It was a colour the fast American drivers
would find easier to see.*

'Are you sure you're going to be all right?'

June didn't reply. She moved around the room, sipping red wine from her glass, and picking up Christmas cards and staring at them. As each card reached eye-level, the picture on it became blurred, out of focus. She had to hold each card at arm's length in order to read who had sent it. The action of lifting and focusing became automatic.

'I said, "Are you sure you'll be all right?" ' June moved the wine around the inside of her mouth with her tongue, and continued to inspect the cards.

The Heart Foundation. The National Trust. Mentally Handicapped Children. Shelter. Spastics. Autistic Children. The Canine Defence League. Cystic Fibrosis. 'Enter Ye In at the Strait Gate'. Children's Fund, Bromley. The Brain Research Trust – a picture of some Deadly Nightshade. There was even one with a poem by Patience Strong: who the hell was that from? 'And underneath it all, the promise of spring.'

'June, I asked if you . . .' Clive's voice trailed away.

She had opened a card with a picture of a fat partridge on the front, and thought she read, 'This card has helped Doctor Barnardo's to purchase another child.' That couldn't be right.

She had dropped each card after having read it, and found that she had neither the strength nor the inclination to pick them up. Clive spoke louder, determined not to be ignored. Well,

3

she would not, did not ignore him. No sooner had he pronounced the words, 'Are you – ' than June had swung round on him, hurling the two-hundred-year-old rummer through the air, and smashing it into tiny glittering fragments against the chiffonier.

'For Christ's sake, stop it! Stop it! I'll go mad if you don't.'

As always she had aimed just to miss him, and as always he had stood absolutely still, flinching only at the thought of one valuable antique damaging another.

There was a silence, and also a dent in the top drawer of the chiffonier. They both noticed the dent at the same time.

Clive spoke quietly, his voice trailing off into a prolonged sigh. 'Well, that's knocked fifty pounds off the value of that.' June covered her ears, and screamed her Maker's name in the direction of the ceiling. Upstairs Baby John woke, and began to cry. Again Clive spoke quietly, 'Does blasphemy make you feel better?' June glared at him, threatening that if he didn't go, didn't move, didn't leave, didn't get out before saying another word, she would throw something else, but he stood where he was, and said just as softly as before, 'I simply asked if you were sure you'd be all right.'

They moved together, she towards the Elizabeth Frink sculpture, *Harbinger Bird IV*, he with meticulous precision towards the broom cupboard. It was a routine in which he was well practised.

Then he was back, with dustpan and brush, sweeping up the glittering splinters of what had so recently been worth twenty pounds. June sat in an armchair, covered her face with both hands, and listened to the sounds made by brush and splintered glass on bare floorboards – floorboards which she had herself stripped and polished.

He said, 'There's chicory and picking cheese in the fridge. Try not to let it go bad.' Would he never go?

He shook the glittering splinters in the dustpan, looked at them, and sighed. 'There are various tins and things in the pantry. You shouldn't starve. Try to eat something, even if only for Baby John's sake.' Then he stood, leaving the dustpan and brush where they were, and came slowly towards her.

As he drew closer to her, she thought of, and then rejected,

4

the idea of spitting in his face. It would be comic; she was out of practice.

He laid the palm of his right hand on the top of her head, as if he were a priest giving her a blessing, and said, still softly, 'Here, come on, love! It's only for a few days. I'll go up, and quiet him. Will you be all right?'

Then he waited, but, since she did not move, took the hand from her head, and began to turn away. June grabbed the hand, and held it, pressing it tightly between both her own hands, then bringing it up against her face.

Clive sank into a crouching position beside the chair, and used the index finger of his free hand to draw a line down her forehead, over her nose and lips, and round under her chin, where he gently rubbed the backs of his fingers. It was one of his more irritating displays of affection, this tracing of her profile, since he knew, if he stopped to remember, that her profile was the feature of herself which June liked least.

'Why don't you ring someone? Ask them round for a Christmas drink.' June released his hand from hers, and they both remained still and silent, listening to Baby John's crying, each waiting for the other to make the next move.

It was Clive who made it. His calves and thighs had begun to ache; he would have to stand before cramp made standing impossible. He stood. Then he went upstairs.

She sobbed silently and painfully, biting the back of her hand to prevent noise, and listening as Clive paced backwards and forwards above her head, across the new carpet which covered the creaking floorboards, cooing sweet nothings to Baby John whose own tears had now ceased.

Clive struggled to close the front door of their newly acquired house. Her house now. The recent damp spell had caused all the wood to swell. All the doors were difficult to open, and, once opened, almost impossible to close. .The front door was easier to close from the inside, easier to open from the outside. The house, like June, did not like being left.

He did not hear her whisper. He pulled sharply at the knocker, taking the door by surprise. Just so he had surprised June, with

5

his announcement that he intended to spend Christmas with his wife.

The door closed. The consequent sound of the windows shaking in their frames echoed down the street, and Baby John screamed. It was one of his wolf-like gutsy screams. The respectable Jewish neighbour to the left would be lifting the receiver of her telephone to make contact with the respectable Catholic neighbour to the right. The road in which she lived, June thought, might aptly have been named 'Minority Row'.

The Jewish lady on the left had put in an appearance that very morning, picking her way cautiously down the garden path as if it were laid with landmines, holding a piece of old newspaper in hands heavy with rings. What the newspaper contained appeared to be a cross between caviar and the droppings of mice.

'Excuse me. I hope you don't mind. But you've been banging against the wall, haven't you?'

June had wondered if she had overlooked some by-law. If she had, she would soon know it. 'Yes, I was trying to move some old bookshelves.'

'I think you've disturbed some mice. They've been coming through the fireplace.' There was, June knew, a Magi-Coal Electric Fire in that fireplace. Not even mice would have braved real flames. 'I had a man from the Council round, and he asked me to ask you if you'd mind putting this down. Mind you don't touch it. Not with bare flesh. It's terribly poisonous.'

The urge to pick up a handful and place it in her mouth while the woman watched, had lasted only a moment. Instead June had taken the two sides of the newspaper into her own hands, and had thanked the woman for her trouble. Then she had watched her glancing down at the litter in the front garden. Theirs was not a dirty street, but every piece of paper dropped in it seemed to find its way into this garden. This was because the foundations of the garden wall had collapsed, and the wall leaned in towards the house, so that the gate had to be propped permanently open.

Now Clive gave a tug at the permanently open gate, and glanced up at the window behind which Baby John was screaming his wolf-scream.

June remained where she was, watching him unlock the car door. At every step of his progress from the front door to the car, she had said to herself, 'If he goes any further, I will do it. If he moves another inch, it will prove that I must. It will confirm that I'm right.'

He sat in the driver's seat, and turned the key to start the engine, and with it, the car radio. She thought, 'He's doing everything in slow motion to make me squirm.'

What she persisted in calling 'the theme from *Elvira Madigan*' and Clive called the Second Movement of Mozart's Piano Concerto Number – well, what the hell did it matter what Clive called it? – that music floated through the window of the car. It was another sign, another proof. They had driven around Winderton in that car, listening to that music, while she had huddled in the passenger seat, pressing herself against the door in her dirty white mac, feeling like an inmate from the Local Asylum, being taken out for the day. She had sat with her fingers interlocked, the tips of both index fingers touching and pointing like the steeple of a church. *Here's the church; here's the steeple. Look inside, and – look! no people.*

Of course, in *Elvira Madigan*, they had both done it; they had done it together.

The cat's-eyes in the middle of the road had floated towards them, giving the impression that she was being taken somewhere, and the need to keep her own eyes open and her body still had seemed acute. Movement was vulnerability – any movement; it suggested progression. It implied that one was moving through time, not standing still in it. She did not accept the progression. There was none.

Clive's car pulled away from the kerb, and was gone.

In the hall, she moved her hand slowly over the rail of the banister, and felt its roughness. The caustic soda she had used to strip off the old paint had hidden in the joints, only to reappear after she had applied three coats of polyurethane. Its reappearance took the form of little white bubbles, rough to touch, which made the rails look as if old paint had been left on them. Weeks of careful work marred by a poison which hides, only to reappear after everything had been glossed over.

The gas fire hissed in time to the wind outside, and more grit dropped from the ventilator onto the newly painted white hearth. Stupid to paint a hearth white. Defying the laws of nature again.

She turned on the radio to drown out the sound of crying from upstairs. 'This is *Nightline* on M.B.C., and you're talking to Tony Fox. Now let's see who the next caller is going to be, and remember, please remember: first names only, please.'

The wind also slid through the Vent-Axia in the kitchen, and blew out the pilot light of the water heater. North Sea Gas floated around the house, reminding her that it couldn't kill her, but was prepared, unless she turned it off, to make what was left of her life as unpleasant as possible. Therefore June refused to turn it off. Life *should* smell as it was – stale, arid, sickly and expensive.

The North-West Gas Board could whistle for its money. She would not be here to pay for misspent, free-floating, high-speed North Sea Gas. The Board could whistle as its faulty equipment whistled. It could whistle to the moon, if it so wished. June would not be heading in that direction.

She looked at the line of coffee mugs. '*I have measured out my life with coffee spoons.*' She had no favourite among the mugs, but always used the same spoon, a mass-produced Woolworth's apostle-spoon, apt for the measurement of such a useless life.

'*Good morning, madam. I am conducting a Survey on the Meaning of Life. How do you see yourself as using life? How do you occupy its measured hours?*' '*I empty full ashtrays into a pedal-bin.*' June emptied a full ashtray into the pedal-bin in the kitchen, and wondered how it would be to climb inside the black plastic bag which lined her dustbin. Would she be able to manage the operation, while holding a glass of water in one hand and the sixty-nine pills she had saved in the other? Would she then be able to swallow the pills, throw away the glass, and just have time, before blessed unconsciousness supervened, to replace the lid of the dustbin from the inside? Perhaps she might be able to close the plastic bag, by pulling in the top and securing it from below with an elastic band.

By Wednesday she would certainly be ready for collection, more than ready. She tried to imagine the expression which would creep over the black dustman's face, as he watched what he had thrown into the cart making its way between the teeth and rollers of its mechanism.

No flowers by request. Mourners should make their own way to the Municipal Rubbish Dump, Green Lanes, Didsbury. Ashes to ashes, carpet-sweepings to dust, non-returnable bottles to unburnable plastics.

June found the sixty-nine pills she had hidden, and counted them. Once upon a time, she couldn't now remember when, but at some time, Clive had said, 'You can't begrudge her the odd day or two. You really can't, love, be sexually jealous.' And now, time having passed and memory blurred, not thirty minutes ago, in this house, decorated by her, paid for by him, he had said, 'Myra's pregnant. I can't afford to upset her.' They must have been odd days indeed, if Myra had been receiving visits from the Archangel Gabriel.

He had tried his best not to show his pleasure. He had tried to make the pregnancy sound like an irritating mistake, just another vexing trap which life had laid for him, but the tiny horizontal lines at the corners of his eyes had gained small upward-pointing additions, as if he had marked his own handiwork and given himself alpha for effort – the effort he claimed he had never made.

June lifted bastard Baby John from his cot, and placed her cheek against his soft lolling head. She and Clive had invested in an extra-wide double bed, because of the restless nights they would suffer with Baby John. Now she had the restless nights with Baby John, while Clive had them with . . . She imagined Myra sitting up in the centre of the bed, reeking of Johnson's Baby Powder and Boot's Lavender Water. The woman from next door (Number Twenty-Six: June knew the front of the house well) would have been in to do Myra's hair. All over the country, Friday night was a Myra night. In every village, town, and city, in isolated farmhouses, in crofts and bothies, pink brushed-nylon bedjackets were sitting up in bed, squeezing their plump mottled thighs together to hold back a secret, and to keep in the rolled-up Marriage Licences they were using as Tampaxes.

Downstairs on the glass-topped table, among those Christmas cards which were not littering the floor, there were sixty-nine pieces of a jigsaw which needed bringing together. She had hoarded them like a miser. They were of different sizes, different shapes and colours, some tablets, small and white, some capsules, some spansules, green and black, black and red, yellow and black, the colour of hornets, always black somewhere. They were like sweets; she had saved up her sweeties. There were sixty-nine.

Sixty-nine ways out.

She rocked unwanted Baby John in her arms, and began to sing:

> There was a man
> Went round the town,
> To hunt a supper up and dow-how-hown.
> He feels his cash
> To count his pence,
> And all he had was just six cents.
>
> He finds at last
> A right cheap place,
> And stealeth in with bashful fa-hay-hace.
> The bill of fare
> He runneth through
> To see what his six cents would do.
>
> The waiter he
> To him doth call,
> And whispers softly, 'One fish ba-haw-hall.'
> The waiter roars
> It through the hall.
> The guests then start at, 'One fish ball!'
>
> The scantness of
> The fare he sees.
> 'A piece of bread now, if you plea-hee-hease.'

'You get no bread,' she said. 'You get no bread, Baby John, with one fish ball.'

'What's wrong with your marriage, Mrs Jephcott?' The woman

had rested her right elbow on her right knee, and leaned forward, and June had seen her glance at the tiny gold watch on her thin fragile wrist four times in the last five minutes. The wrist carried no scars. Only the mark made by the watch.

'I want to know what you think is wrong with it, not what you say your husband thinks.' God, she was careful! 'What you say your husband thinks'! Why couldn't she admit that she didn't believe a word of it, that she had guessed that June wasn't a 'Mrs' anybody, that June had a husband, it was true, but that he was someone else's husband? What June had was a lover of seven years' standing. At which thought, June had summoned up a picture of Clive, standing to attention like a schoolboy in a corner of the bedroom, and then another of him standing naked with all his bodily parts at attention, and she had smiled at the picture, and then, without thinking, said aloud, 'A seven-year erection,' and had heard her own voice saying it in that quiet dark room, and seen the expression on the face of the woman sitting opposite.

'How many more minutes have I got?'

The woman had then looked at her watch properly for the first time, without any attempt at deceit, and replied, 'Well, I think we could usefully spend the last ten minutes summing up, and work out where we might start from next time.'

June had laughed, and then stood, looking down at the woman. 'There won't be a next time. I'm afraid I'm not very good at sums.'

The woman had shown no surprise. Clearly this had happened to her often. 'That's up to you, of course, but aren't you being a little unfair? I did mention that Marriage Guidance is an ongoing thing, not an instant remedy. We have to end this interview in ten . . . well, in eight minutes now, because someone else is waiting,' but June had reached the door, and turned, and said, 'Please don't concern yourself. I've decided what to do.'

'May I know what it is?'

June had looked at the brown linoleum. 'There isn't the time to tell you.' She had opened the door, and stepped out into the corridor, where there had, indeed, been another woman waiting. The woman had looked up at June, and then at her watch, and

June had said, 'I hope you're good at arithmetic,' and moved on out into the street before the waiting woman could answer.

Baby John had been unable to make his choice known, and so she had chosen for him; she had given birth to him. If she had made the opposite choice, and had aborted him, she would now be free to carry out her plan without having to worry about his safety.

It was Christmas Eve. To do it now would be best. No one would come near for three days, and, since Boxing Day fell on a Sunday, Monday was also a holiday. To do it now would mean that she was as sure as she could be of not being interrupted. Ever.

There was still the problem of Baby John, however. She had no way of knowing how long a two-month-old baby could last without nourishment. It was too late to ring up *The Daily Telegraph* Information Service, and, strangely enough, it was something they had never mentioned at the Dame Alice Harkness School for Girls. Nor could she remember that Doctor Spock had offered the information as part of what every mother should know.

If she attempted to leave him on the doorstep of one of her respectable neighbours, with a note of his feeding times pinned to his bedjacket, she would almost certainly be noted and invited in for tea and ginger-nuts. If not that, then they would come battering at the door when they found him, phone the Police and the Ambulance Service; they were not people who could leave well alone. Nor would simple honesty serve her. She could not say, 'Excuse me, Mrs Goldberg, but since you don't celebrate Christmas, I wondered if you'd mind looking after Baby John until the Festivities are over, after which he will be taken into Care or claimed by his father. I've decided to end it all, but I don't want to take him with me, because he hasn't really had time to find out whether he likes it here or not.'

Baby John was a problem. But all problems have their solutions. She had decided on her own, which was the final one. She should be able first to decide on his.

June walked about the house, touching things – things she had spent so much time and energy on, not to mention money. How could she be absolutely sure that Baby John would be all right? She sat on the stairs, trying to clear her head of every thought except the problem, and feeling with her hands the new thick bitter-chocolate-coloured carpet, and the smoothness of the Brilliant White gloss paint on either side of it, the paint which had taken her so long to apply, because her hand shook and she had been afraid of painting the carpet.

It wasn't wasted, not completely; someone else would probably live here. Clive would probably sell the house fully furnished, and someone, whosoever, would enjoy what she had done.

In the living-room, she stroked her hand up and down the long curtains. She had searched for weeks for material she liked, and then had found this at The Designers' Guild, and then waited more weeks while the friend of a friend made up and lined the curtains, and had then allowed one of her many cats to stain them. But they had been cleaned; she could not see the stain now, only the heavy beige cotton, with wild flowers, mostly bluebells and buttercups, embroidered with brightly coloured wool. She felt the texture of the thick rough embroidered bluebells and buttercups. She liked them, would always like them (for as long as always would now be), liked wild flowers by far the best. She had been born in a house, semi-detached but with a long garden and in a quiet road, and beyond the garden had been a hill which was climbed to reach a wood and bluebells.

She wanted bluebells now, wanted to watch the juice trickle from their stems and see it hang suspended like saliva round a dog's mouth, wanted to be five years old again, and to sit in the sandpit just outside the front gate of that quiet house, watching large lorries full of American soldiers pass by, the quietness disturbed for a few moments while they waved and shouted and threw down chewing-gum to her.

Even the brief glimpses she had caught of those GIs had created in her mind the misconception that American men were more exciting, more physically attractive than other men. She was, it was true, only five years old, and they were, it was true, better nourished than the people of her village. They filled their uniforms, which had been tailored to fit tightly and display the nourishment therein. It had all been propaganda. To a little girl of five, those gum-chewing faces couldn't ever be on the losing side. June had known, long before Churchill or anyone else, that Britain would pull through.

Death had seemed terrible then.

If only her green three-wheeler bicycle could have carried her under one of those large conveyors of confident well-nourished GIs, and if those handsome faces, some white, others black, could have been the last faces at which she'd had to look! She would have lain there, pressed like a buttercup between the pages of a Bible, her green bicycle representing the green twisted stem. Her mother had described it to her like that, the danger, had threatened her with that death, pressed flat by wheels which were at least twice her own size, if ever she were to take her bicycle outside the gates, and had shown her the Bible, with a pressed buttercup covering Matthew, Chapter Five, Verse Four. She had always dressed June in yellow, always yellow. She had explained that it was a colour which the fast American drivers would find it easiest to see.

That was before her mother had lost interest in life.

June pushed the pram containing Baby John into the Casualty Department of the hospital nearest her home, and sat next to a young Irishman, who slept with his arms folded, his head and reddened face lolling forward onto his chest. His cheap pale green lightweight suit was creased from having been slept in, and the lapels were stained with recent vomit. June could smell the exhaled bitter and the remnants of the vomit. Poor old Paddy! Poor Paddy, the Next Best Thing, so far away from home, so lonely and so innocent! When would religion pay back its debt to society?

She counted five other casualties waiting, including a middle-aged couple, both of whom looked so unhappy that she could not tell which was the one in pain.

There seemed to be three very young doctors on duty, one black, one white, and one khaki. All three moved with backs erect and shoulders tight with self-importance, their white coats open and flapping, displaying their suits and ties, the trappings of professional status.

She would tell them that Baby John (who now slept) had coughed up blood. It was difficult to disprove. She would show them his bib with the bloodstains on it. (She had cut her finger, and mixed the blood with some of her own spit, before wiping her fingers on the bib.)

She would be fearful, and would weep, and they would wake Baby John, and most likely be greeted by his wolf-like scream. All three looked to be young, inexperienced, new doctors; they would be worried by the scream, at the sound of which strong men had been known to weep. They would do tests, find nothing wrong, and offer to keep him in overnight.

As far as she could tell, there was no one there, no one at work behind the moveable screen, who knew her, no one to recognize her, no older doctor whose suspicions might be aroused by a middle-class mother with hair which had not been washed for some time, and fingernails which were broken and dirty. The bags under June's eyes were full and violet, but these young boys would put that down to stress over the baby. She was already getting inside her role as a distraught mother, leaning over the sleeping Baby John, and working herself up towards tears. They were young; they wouldn't dare to take risks with a baby, neglect of which might lead to exposure in the Sunday papers. She would tell them that she had heard of babies dying of internal haemorrhages, that she had never before heard Baby John scream like that, and that it was the screaming and the blood coming together which had so frightened her. They would do tests, keep him in overnight, and feed him. Overnight. That was all she needed. Tomorrow, when she didn't turn up to collect him, they would inform the police, but they would probably wait until the evening before doing that. Then the police would have to find her. There would be time.

The sound of an ambulance siren suddenly galvanized the three strutting young doctors and the disinfected nurses into swifter motion. Screens were hurriedly moved, revealing half-dressed patients to those who still waited. These looked round, in some surprise and disarray to find that their semi-nudity now had a larger and unprofessional audience. A thin old man with a bony sunken chest backed, forgetting his ailment, away from these untrained eyes, and collided with a steel trolley loaded with surgical instruments.

White robes and masks were hurriedly donned, and disposable gloves unwrapped. The black, white and khaki doctors moved as if in a speeded-up film. This was drama, the rest, routine. A nurse announced to those waiting, 'I'm very sorry, dears, but we have a real emergency now. An accident. You're going to have to wait.'

The real emergency (as opposed to the unreal ones, who sat around June, sleeping or enduring their pain in silence) was wheeled in on a stretcher, the saline drip already connected, the fight for a life already begun.

June got a brief look at the face on the stretcher before it was pushed hastily into the Intensive Care Unit. It was that of a young man. It wouldn't see the New Year in, not that face. June didn't know how she knew, but she did. She was sure, sure of the waste, sure of her wish to change places, sure that the expression on the young man's face was one of relief.

Without planning, or even thinking about it, she had, after standing to see that face, begun to walk. She kept on walking out into the yard of the hospital, without even looking back, without Baby John and his pram.

He would be all right; he would be safe there. If she hadn't seen that young man's face, she might have weakened, changed her mind as so often before, or simply taken enough booze and pills to knock her out for the two days of the holiday, and then returned for him.

But she had seen the face, and its expression of relief. She was convinced that the expression on the young man's face meant, 'Please don't bother me. I'm all right. Please leave me alone. I'm not going to jump back into life crippled, just to please you.'

She felt a sense of purpose. It gladdened her, and was expressed in her stride. Now she could just go, leave, get out, quit, and Baby John would be taken care of. She had the means, the opportunity, and, most important of all, she had the will. She was determined and committed.

Rather than wake Baby John and a great many neighbours

by tugging and banging it, she had left the front door ajar. It was not a night for burglars, not Christmas Eve. They would all be home, filling their children's stockings. Any chimneys down which they climbed tonight, would be their own.

She took her coat off in the hall, having managed to close and lock the front door quietly. She draped the coat over the banister. It fell to the floor. She stood, looking down at it, unable to decide whether to pick it up. The decision seemed important. She must get everything right this time, and the coat reminded her of the mistakes she had made in the past. So many things could go wrong. She left the coat on the floor, to remind herself how easy it was to fail.

On the glass-topped table, she set out three glass tumblers, and poured what was left of the red wine into them. Then she made herself three mugs of coffee.

The main problem would be to swallow as many of the sixty-nine pills as she could before she became unconscious, and unable to finish the job. With the help of coffee and wine she must fit together inside her stomach the brightly coloured parts of the jigsaw.

Throwing up was another problem. It had happened before. The throat seems to close, rejecting any more, or a capsule breaks in the mouth, leaving an acid taste, and causing nausea.

She went back into the hall, and regarded the coat on the floor. It reminded her of the danger of negative thinking. That had also happened before. One tiny doubt, one hesitation, or just half a second thought, one break in will-power, and the careful acquisition of the means would have been wasted, and the pain endured for nothing.

Back at the glass-topped table, she saw that everything she needed was in front of her. The pills and spansules would be easier to pick up if they were in a bowl or dish than spread out on the table as they were now. Such small details should not be overlooked. She placed the pills in a mixing-bowl, and walked about the room, tidying the Christmas cards. She would not draw the curtains together. If she did, some nosy-parker might notice them closed on Christmas Day, and decide to investigate. But

17

what if the same or a different parker should look in through opened curtains, and see her body on the floor? She would do better to take it all upstairs.

June lifted the glass-topped coffee table carefully, so as to spill neither drink nor pills, and carried it into the hall. Then she saw again her coat lying on the floor.

She didn't like upstairs, didn't like being upstairs alone. And dying in the middle of an extra-wide double bed was so . . . so . . . She couldn't at that particular moment think what it was so, but she knew it wasn't her.

She took the glass-topped table and its contents back to the living-room. She began to tidy up. She was too busy tidying to work out why dying like that wasn't her. She discovered herself to be wiping the stains of red wine from the wall above the chiffonier. She discovered that she was in the kitchen, wiping away the wet rings the coffee mugs had made on the white formica work-surface. Her hands (she discovered) had become damp. She wiped her hands on a tea-towel. They must be steady, her hands, clean and steady.

What she was doing was putting off the moment of starting, and every moment she wasted in putting it off was a moment needed. She needed all the moments she had, to be sure of success.

Sitting on the sofa, with everything laid out in front of her and within reach (she had changed the positions of the red wine and coffee twice), she tried to think of a suitable last thought. A thought for the day, Christmas Day, a thought with which to say, Goodbye. There would be no notes. Notes were not June either. Then she had it. This was her thought: 'Now I lay me down to sleep, I pray the Lord my soul to keep – His hands off.'

The first handful of pills was easy. None got broken; none stuck. There was no retching; there were no half-second-thoughts. Clearly it was wise not to attempt too many at once.

The second handful she swallowed with red wine, and the third with cold coffee. A spansule stuck, and it took a whole mug of coffee to dislodge it. A whole mug of coffee. And time, precious time.

Then there were still at least half the pieces of her jigsaw left on the table, and it was as she reached out for them that the room started to move.

Her arm was heavy, and a little girl's chubby hand came up to meet her lips, crushing brightly coloured flowers between her fingers as saliva dripped from June's mouth.

Then she was pacing about, couldn't stop, backwards and forwards. She knew that something was wrong. Pacing was what kept you alive, if that was what you wanted to be. Did she want to be alive?

The gaps between her teeth became tight. It was as if layers of fine wire had been wound in and out between each tooth, pulling them all together. She put her fingers inside her mouth, and pulled out bunch after bunch of what she knew to be peacock feathers. The feathers were long, meant for display. Each had small silver jointed brackets in the stem.

She smoothed out each feather by pressing it down hard against the glass-topped table with her hand, and left it there to dry.

After a few more tours of the room, the tightness returned, and the process was repeated. More pacing, more feathers. The pacing grew quicker, and the feathers became larger, taller, thicker. Then there was pain.

Her fingernails were scratching at the back of her throat, trying to dislodge something which had stuck there, and was burning, scorching her throat as it melted. She was frightened, terrified, panic-stricken. Her fingernails wouldn't reach.

She was holding her head face upwards under the cold-water tap, her mouth wide open. She felt the full force of the water hit her, hit her, hit her. She swallowed and swallowed, desperately, extravagantly, ravenously, filling herself, feeling her stomach stretch, bloated with water.

The scorching which had started in her gullet was now spreading outwards and downwards inside her chest.

Then she was pulling at all the doors of the house to get out. But the doors were damp and swollen; they kept her in. She was trapped and choking.

Breaking a window with her bare arms, she noticed how dark and ruby-coloured the blood was. She heard her baby cry, heard it scream its wolf-scream. The Social Services had come to take him into Care. They wore a white beard and the red robe of Father Christmas. Beneath the synthetic beard of the Social Services, her baby was fighting for breath and spitting blood.

She was running, falling down and crawling on hands and knees along pavements fouled with dog shit. The stench of it made her vomit, as Paddy the Next Best Thing, the young Irishman in the crumpled green suit, had vomited.

Poor Paddy!

The vomit tasted of acid – anti-depressing, tranquillizing, sleepinducing acid.

She lay on her back, resting for a moment, just a moment. Then she began to move again. Now the dark Christmas morning sky was below her, cutting and nicking her body like sharp new razor-blades as she crawled. Above her back, the dog-stained pavement bore down on her, crushing her. so that she crawled on her belly while the Christmas stars beneath made sharp clean hairline cuts in her knees, belly and elbows, where she had broken the window and pushed herself through it.

Cat's-eyes winked at her, and ran away. Why did sleek black cats have all the luck, and where's the fucking Guiding Star that's supposed to lead me to the child? Which of the bastards is it? She could smell the sodding shepherds and their scabby dogs, but where the hell were the Wise Men. 'Sorry, dear. Wise Men are off. They've all gone. Can't afford them nowadays.' So where was the gold? The frankincense? The baa-lamb?

Then she was up again, and running. Time was important, every moment of it. Turning a corner, she steadied her balance by touching some curved iron railings.

Something, which might have been an electric current, shot up her right arm, and tightened around her chest in stinging bands. Bells were ringing in the roots of her teeth. They were hollow, and they were ringing.

She continued to move forward.

She was there, lying on the steps of the Casualty Department. She had arrived. She was now a real emergency. A real unreal emergency.

The words 'Pheno Barb' were whispered to her with enormous pleasure.

Then the feeling of movement in her stomach. Starting very small, it grew. Eventually the whole Irish Labour Force was inside her, building yet another bloody motorway. If only a betting shop or a pub would open to give her ease.

Poor Paddy!

Above her, the sound of heavy breathing and the smell of stale tobacco. Someone who smoked heavily had just run up several flights of stairs.

'Boring cow!'

They handled her roughly, and asked her why she had never thought of her child.

Never?

Among antiseptic tiles and squeaking highly polished shoes, could be no talk of peacocks' feathers and none of reasons. The grunting cursing Irishmen walked down her throat in heavy boots; she felt the tips of their picks in her pharynx. She groaned, cursing all immigrant labour. This was the fifth scraping and dredging job they had performed on her. Her groans would give pleasure to her rescuers. Pain was a necessary part of the ritual.

They kept her waiting for news of her child. She dared not ask, and the faces which drifted past her bed were tight and dull. The child might be 'as well as can be expected under the circumstances' or 'No change in his condition'. What condition? Had she left the bib, with its prepared bloodstain, in his pram?

No change. That's what it's all about, Baby John, isn't it? No change? After all . . . all *that* . . . here we are again, happy as can be, could be, or ever will be. For ever and ever. No, *please*!

'How do you feel?' The question needed thought. She thought. She answered the questions.

> 'Like a small grey mouse . . .
> in a very large cage . . .
> Running round and round
> and in and out . . .
> through a maze.'

He made a noise of encouragement, a noise that meant, 'Go

on.' She saw no point in going on, but the words would come out anyway. They were the words of her vocation and his trade, of patient and psychiatrist, the dialogue of her life, untidy piles of nouns and pronouns, verbs and adverbs, conjunctions and disjunctions. She saw herself rummaging through the whole world's rubbish-heap of words, looking for those she had lost, the real ones, the important ones, not those she used but those which meant something, the words worth saying.

'Go on.' This time he had used the words themselves instead of the noise which meant the words. But she was still watching herself picking up words which wouldn't do, and casting them aside (so that the rubbish-heap never grew smaller). They wouldn't do; they were overused, they oversimplified what she wished to say.

'Go on.' His words had reached her inner ear, causing her to · feel unbalanced. She reponded automatically, still sifting through the rubbish.

'Go on what?'

'About the maze. You said you felt . . .' He was one of those who left his sentences unfinished.

'Yes. I know what I said.'

He waited. That was his job, most of the time, to wait, and listen, and perhaps to record. Case-notes.

She allowed him to wait. Then she said, 'I told you about the maze?'

He made another noise. This noise meant, 'Yes.'

'Well, the object is to find the exit, right?'

He had nodded when he made the noise, and now nodded again, but without a noise, so that she was reminded of a toy dog looking out of the back window of a Ford Cortina. Then he nodded yet again, and said, 'Yes. If there is an exit. So what's the mouse doing about it?'

'Squeaking blue bloody murder.'

'Instead of?'

'I don't know. You're the expert. You tell me.'

'No one's the expert. There aren't any.'

He paused. June felt tired. Her work on the rubbish-mountain of words had exhausted her. He said, 'So what do you think the mouse should do?'

'Lie down, and go to sleep. Except that it can't sleep. If it tries, it's given a mild electric shock, just enough to make it squirm.'

Both of them waited, each willing the other to speak. Then he gave way. That also was part of his job. 'Let's talk about your depressions. What causes them, do you think?'

He actually had the nerve to ask her what he was being paid by the National Health Service to find out. He waited. She didn't answer.

'The fact that psychiatry has failed to help you in the past needn't preclude your having another go, need it?'

She shrugged her shoulders, thinking, 'Come on! Let's see you earn your money.'

'Despair is fairly common nowadays, particularly in women of your intelligence. Haven't you noticed that?'

'No, I don't find other people's problems very exciting.'

He gestured. He had changed from noises to gestures. What words were represented by the gesture? The only interpretation she felt able to give was that the gesture meant 'San Fairy Ann.' However, words followed it.

'There's no such thing as a totally destructive personality, Mrs Jephcott. I think you're trying to overdramatize your situation by saying that. Wouldn't you agree?' Why not? Yes, of course. Right! Sure! O.K. Fine! Great! Now what? She considered correcting the 'Mrs' to 'Miss', but it was too obvious, and might even be expected. Better to maintain silence.

'There must have been a time when you and Clive were happy together. What caused that happiness? Shall we try to concentrate for a moment on that?'

'Why do you try to justify everything you say by turning it into a question?' No answer. 'Go on, doctor. Make a simple statement, just for the hell of it. I shan't hold you to it; I don't expect you to be God. If you were, you'd have a lot to answer for, and I'd be the first to put the questions.'

He looked at her for what seemed to be a long time. The moment of suspense excited her. Perhaps he would drop her, shrug her off as manipulative and beyond help, pass her on to some poor junior shrink, with ideas and ideals both still bright, who would take one look at her records, and shit himself at the challenge.

He said, 'Have you really set your heart on being the most unhappy person in the world? There are no prizes, you know.'

Now, suddenly she was angry. With the anger, she found energy. 'My heart was "set", as you put it, by someone else. The seed from which it grew was carefully planted in a womb of rotten eggs. The sowing was done between stiffly starched sheets. Unhappily, neither of the parties present on that occasion could have known that, ahead of that tiny bead of spermatozoa, would be thirty-five years of almost total unhappiness. I don't suppose they lay back, panting and thinking to themselves, "Well, there's a right load of misery, to spread gloom and despondency when we've gone. All we have to do now is to make sure it has a really awful childhood, and in no time at all, it'll be wishing you hadn't uncrossed your legs tonight, mother." My mother always had something crossed. Her legs or her fingers. Or her eyes.' She paused. He was watching her show off. She said. 'I don't suppose that conversation really did happen, do you?'

He shook his head. Well, then, he had made her angry. Score for him! Since she had started, she might as well go on, and let the words come whence they might. She leaned back, and looked at the ceiling.

'I was eight when I first wanted to die. Do you know how many times I've tried?'

'Yes, it's all down here.'

'No. Double that figure. At least, double it. I've tried more times than there are days in the month, and I don't mean February. And if I fail until I'm seventy, I shall have tried at least once for every year of my life. I'm committed, you see. Unsuccessful, but committed. For three months after each attempt, I've felt a little better. Told myself it wouldn't happen again. By the fourth month, I'm planning it. I can't see ahead; I can only feel from moment to moment. And what I feel like now is a long continuous weep. The whole of my body is aching from the effort of suppressing waterless tears. You said, "despair". It's like wanting desperately to be sick, and not being able to. It tightens on me like a corset, contracting slowly until it pushes my heart up into

24

my mouth. How can my baby survive having a mother like that?'

He didn't answer the question, but said instead, 'Tell me about when you were seven.'

'I've told you.'

'No. Someone else, perhaps. Not me. I want to know.'

'It'll be in the notes.'

He continued to wait, doing what he was paid to do. Then he said, 'Tell me about the people who adopted you.'

'They were perfectly ordinary middle-class people, who never did a thing wrong in their lives, except in allowing me to grow up.'

'How old were you when they adopted you?'

'Eight.'

'And your real parents?'

'It's in the notes.'

'Yes?'

'I remember her, not him. By the time I was four, he'd gone. I just remember damp soft hands, very soft for a man. That's all. Not much, is it?'

'No.'

'Then there were just the two of us. And she was like me. Couldn't cope. I probably come from a long line of non-copers. Oh, hell!'

He waited. He was paid to wait.

'I suppose it was depression, only they called it Tired Blood in those days, and Iron Tonic was the cure-all. Or Horlicks. No one dished out tranquillizers or anti-depressants where we lived; it was, "Go and get yourself a tonic, girl. You're looking run-down." I remember one or two of them, shouting that to her from the front gate when they saw her in the garden.' She stopped, remembering the Bluebell Wood, the heavy pleasing scent of it, and her own small chubby hand gripping the stems of the flowers so tightly that they wilted before reaching home and water. 'And Wincarnis,' she said.

'Them? Who were "them"?'

'The neighbours. Almost nobody came in through the gate. It was a small village, and I think they sensed that there was more to it than being run-down. Anyway, she wouldn't talk to anybody who did come, so they weren't encouraged to call again.

She didn't even talk to me very much, not my mother. She didn't need anybody, or want anybody. As I grew older, and able to look after myself, she just became less and less . . . less tidy. By the time I was seven, she'd taken to sitting on the doorstep in her nightdress. Day in, day out, she just sat there, resting her chin on her hands, and staring at the lupins. She'd given up Horlicks by that time. The garden was overgrown, but the weeds weren't high enough to stop the neighbours from seeing her over the fence . . . I missed a lot of school. She didn't seem to bother, and you can imagine what it was like with the other children, when your mother's the woman who sits on the doorstep in her nightie. The School Inspectors came round a few times, and had a good look. They couldn't get any sense out of her, and they saw the state of the house, so they sent someone from the Council. She cried, I remember. I didn't. Couldn't. Not then; I've made up for it since. Anyway, I thought it was going to be for a short holiday – that's what they said, "We're taking you off for a short holiday, June, while your mummy has a rest." There were no relatives, it seemed, or anyway, none near enough. I don't think there were any – no aunties, no uncles, no gran. So the holiday was to be with a foster-mother. The adoption came later.'

He was listening, doing his job, the job he was paid to do. Would it be by the hour? For a hospital consultant, perhaps not. At least he hadn't looked at his watch. 'It's all in the notes,' she said. As listeners go, he was fair to average. She had met many listeners, watched them for their reactions as she dug into her dust-mountains of words, picking them out and releasing them like hot-air balloons to be carried who knows where, each one a bubble with the word 'thinks' printed neatly on it in lower-case type.

'Would you like to go back to your mother now?' He was speaking, asking questions, earning his hourly rate. June rubbed her eyes.

'Yes . . . Well . . . That's just what I did, didn't I? Four times. That must be in the notes. I ran away, got a bus back to the village. It was nine or ten miles, must have been; I can't remember; I know it seemed a hell of a long way. They were trying to get her into a hospital – loony-bin, I suppose – shrink-tank. But they couldn't find a place for her right away, so they'd persuaded someone from the village to pop in from time to time to check up on her. The fourth time I went, she wasn't there, and nobody would tell me where she'd gone.'

She stared at the wall in front of her, searching for the words which came next. But she had finished. Surely? 'Finished,' she said, 'It's in the notes.'

But he was waiting, as was his job. So there was more. Something left out. She couldn't have forgotten. He had his living to earn. Something left out. She tried to speak. Perhaps they would come to her, the right words.

'I . . . I . . .' It was then she remembered, and with the memory came anger and tears. The floodgates had opened, and she shouted.

'I . . . I . . . couldn't get her up the bloody stairs; I just couldn't. She wouldn't let me, not until it had gone dark, and then I had to wrap her in a blanket . . . wrap it round her. She was waiting for him, all the time for him. The sodding arsehole of a wet-handed creep! It was for him.' June's face contorted as she tried to control herself. 'We'd have been all right if they'd left us alone.'

She covered her face, and sobbed. He waited. He was paid to wait.

After that the anger was gone, and she was limp, limp and tired, and could speak flatly, factually, pick the words and place them out, flatly, on a board, for his inspection. She had shouted, but there was no justification for such anger after thirty-one years, none whatsoever. To cling so long to anger was obsessive; the past was past.

'The last time I ran away, and went back to her – I mean the last time she was there – the third time, she was . . . she was lying on the bed, wrapped in an old grey blanket, very still. I thought she was dead. And all I could feel was relief that she hadn't . . . that they hadn't taken her away. Then I kissed her, and she moved. She'd no idea who I was. She just stared. I couldn't stand it, couldn't . . . meet her eyes. So I moved round to the other side of her, and lay down on the bed. I was cold.

but I couldn't get under her blanket. I just lay there, shivering, with my arms round her . . . I was eight years old.'

He was crying. Poor sod! She had never made a shrink cry before, except for the one who had wanted to take her to bed. What a way to earn a living!

PART TWO

Walter and June Confined

I

*From the moment the first load of depressed women
arrived, Walter no longer felt brave enough to
inspect his path.*

Walter had spent hours watching the new building rise, brick
by brick. He had seen the ground cleared and levelled, and
trenches dug for sewage pipes and drains, had watched hardcore
brought in lorries, which tipped it into piles for the bulldozer
to spread out evenly, had seen the bricklayers arrive with their
spirit-levels and diamond-shaped trowels, had watched them chip,
and scrape, and pat the bricks into place. And the man who
shovelled sand and cement into the noisy concrete-mixer had
noticed Walter's interest, and had called him over.

The man had lent Walter his shovel, and had told him how
much of each ingredient to throw into the circulating tub. Walter
had made concrete. The man had smoked a cigarette and watched,
as Walter made concrete, and then together Walter and the man
had shovelled Walter's concrete onto the hardcore, and had then
patted it level with the edge of a plank.

It was a path. Walter had made part of a concrete path. The
workman had said, 'That's your stretch of path. You made that.'
And he had smiled at Walter, and Walter had smiled at him;
they had been friendly together. The man had said, 'That'll still
be here when you and I are gone.' Then the man had marked
the stretch of path made by Walter, by painting two thin green
lines on the red brick wall.

After that, he had visited his stretch of path twice a day, just
to look down at it, slide his hand over it, and test its firmness

with his foot, and the painters, carpenters and plumbers had laughed and waved to him, for they all knew it was Walter's piece of path.

Walter had asked members of Staff (more than one, since he wished to be certain) the purpose of this new building, and had been told that it was for mothers with small babies who were depressed and unhappy. At first he had thought that the babies would be depressed and unhappy, but when he had watched the first ambulances of mothers arrive, and had seen their faces and heard some of them crying, he had known that these, the mothers, were the unhappy ones.

What had once been called a Workhouse, and had then become an Asylum, and was now called a Mental Hospital, but which had never changed its outward appearance with all these changes of name, now contained in its grounds a new two-storey building of red brick, with an interior of clean surfaces, many of wood, with furniture of a light appearance and in bright colours, and the name of this building, which was so at odds with the solidly depressing Victorian exterior of the Mental Hospital, was The Mother and Baby Unit. Severe post-natal depression was what had brought most of these mothers with their babies to the Unit. The severity of the depressions endured by these mothers ranged from the extreme depression which had induced them to wish to kill both themselves and their babies to the comparatively modest depression of those who were merely unable to cope with any part of the daily routine of feeding, changing and sterilizing bottles.

From the moment that the first load of depressed women arrived, Walter no longer felt brave enough to go close to the building and inspect his path. He was therefore forced to content himself with admiring it from a distance, and even then only on alternate days when he marched a crocodile of what had been known as 'inmates' when Walter had entered the hospital, but were now called 'patients', past the new Unit and out of the main gate for a walk. Always when passing the Unit, he slowed his pace until he was almost marching on the spot, causing those behind him to run into each other and become momentarily confused. This was not responsible behaviour in Walter, who had been placed in charge of the crocodile because he was a patient of long standing, and trusted by the Staff.

Two months after the first depressed mothers had arrived, and Walter was returning from one such walk, pushing Clifford, his own special charge (who could not speak, could not do anything for himself, for whom everything was done by Walter), he saw someone standing on his path. A woman was standing there. Previously he had seen people walking over it, seen a woman pace up and down over it, covering it several times, had seen a woman pause on it to light a cigarette, but he had never seen anyone remain on it for any length of time. This woman was standing still, doing nothing but stand. Her head faced downwards. She was looking at the path Walter had made.

Walter stopped pushing Clifford. He tried to see what about his path was engaging the attention of the woman, but he was too far away from her to make out such detail. Meanwhile the patients behind Walter, those whom he privately thought of as 'Jesus's mistakes', broke ranks, and began to push at each other, to giggle and to swear, so that Walter felt bound to continue.

Perhaps it had cracked. The workmen had told him that cracking had to be watched for, with paths. 'Too much of one thing, not enough of the other, or a bad frost before she's settled down, and she'll crack before the month's out.' There had been no bad frost. If Walter's path was cracking, it would be because he had put in too much of one thing, or not enough of the other.

That night he lay awake, imagining the cracks in his path getting wider. So deep were they, that people fell through, screaming as they fell, the sound and echo and re-echo of their screams filling the hospital grounds, announcing that it was Walter who was to blame, Walter who had neglected to put in enough of the other, Walter who had doomed them to this long agony of falling. Walter would be called to account, the friendly workman would be sacked, and the husbands of the depressed women who had fallen through the cracks would hang about outside the hospital gates, carrying long knives, athirst for Walter's blood.

The following day was not one on which the crocodile went for its walk, and Walter's duties on the Ward kept him too busy to get out. But if there had been accidents at the Mother and Baby

Unit, the Staff would know, and would speak of it amongst themselves, as Walter listened, and since they did not, the depressed mothers could not yet have been swallowed by cracks.

Next day Walter led his crocodile very slowly past the Unit. The woman was still there, standing on the same spot, still gazing at the path. Walter kept the walk short, and found on his return that the woman was there again, or perhaps had never moved. Yet still that night there was no mention in all the conversation and gossip of the staff of any cracks in the paths which surrounded the Mother and Baby Unit.

Were they keeping it from him?

It was Thursday. No walk to be taken until Friday. But he found five free minutes, and used them to run from his Ward (for Walter had great freedom in the Hospital) to a point from which he could see the new Unit, and his path, and the woman standing on it. But he was still not close enough to see for himself whether there were cracks.

She was still there on Friday when the crocodile went out for its walk, still there when it returned. He was desperate now. He could not wait until the next walk on Monday, and anyway, as long as he was with the crocodile, he still would not be able to get any closer.

But Walter had freedom; he was a trusty; he was trusted. He might go almost anywhere he wished, within the grounds of the Hospital. Outside the Main Gate was another matter, but his path was not outside the Main Gate. On Sunday, he would have some respite from his duties in the Ward; he could find time. He could see for himself on Sunday that all was still right with his path, and he would.

Each day, she had stood as she was standing now, with her back against the wall, her fingers feeling the bricks and the mortar on either side of her, stroking the roughness of the orderly bricks, and running her forefingers along the straight lines of mortar, knowing the lines to be true, but testing them. Whatever the weather or people did, no matter how topsy-turvy, uncertain, illogical or bent her own mind, these truly horizontal lines comforted her.

Well, he had approached, and was standing some four feet away from her. She had noticed him on the very first day she had been allowed out into the air. He had been leading a crocodile of twitching, misshapen, swearing patients from the Hospital. He had led his crocodile out of the gate, and, later, back in again, and both times he had slowed the procession, and had stared at her. He had a beak of a nose in a long face, and wore a flat cap; though he had appeared to be the leader, he must be one of them. After the first time, there had been others, and always he had slowed the crocodile as he came level with her, staring across, and causing his followers to change step or collide.

Yes, he was the leader, no doubt of that. Had he been alone, June felt sure, his arms would have swung in time to *Colonel Bogey*, but in fact they were taken up in pushing a wheelchair containing a man with an enormous head and gaping mouth. Even at that distance, the mouth could be seen to be gaping, the enormous head to be lolling; the man who watched her must care for that gaping mouth and head. He had stared at her. She had grown interested – not that she considered it a possibility that she should have any real interest in another human being, but the pattern of behaviour was interesting; it interested her. She began to time the duration of the crocodile's walk by the clock on the central tower of the Hospital, and noticed that it grew shorter and shorter.

Now it was Sunday. There was no crocodile. He had come alone, and was standing near her. Close as he was, he continued to stare at her, but he did not speak. Therefore June spoke. She said, 'I could stand here all day.'

Though she spoke to him, she did not look directly at him. Nor did the man reply. Since she had not asked a question, perhaps he did not consider a reply to be necessary. She asked a question.

'This patch of concrete we're standing on is level, isn't it?' That was a personal, private question though he could not know it, and it would not be personal to him. But June had made him privy to a private concern of her own that all lines should be straight, all true. all comforting. She had offered him the chance

35

to reassure and comfort her by confirming the straightness of the path. Would he now do so?

Walter looked at the narrow strip of path they were standing on. He had been right; there was something about his path which worried her. He could see no cracks. What had she been looking at?

'They level the ground, and put hardcore down. Then they level the hardcore, and pour on concrete. Then they level that with something, don't they? They level everything.'

Walter had shovelled the concrete on, not poured.

'What's it called, what they use for that, the levelling?' She squinted up at the sky, trying to bring the name to mind. Again she had offered him a question. If he himself had a store of words, different from her own, now was a time for him to use it.

Walter shook his head. The workman had shown him how to smooth the concrete by using the edge of a piece of plank. It had had no special name, and had, earlier on, also been used for scaffolding.

'They pat the concrete with something like the edge of the plank.' June's gaze had dropped a little from the sky to the clock on the central tower. Long ago, when the Hospital had still been a Workhouse, and had grown all its own food on its own farm, tilled by the sweated labour of the unpaid inmates, the tower had been used for water. Now the sometime farm had become Grounds, in which the new Unit stood and mains water had been brought in, so that there was little use for the tower but to hold a clock, reminding the inmates, the patients, those living dead, that there was always time. Time the Healer, Time in which miracles might yet be performed if one waited long enough. The clock was permanently twelve minutes slow. Perhaps Time's first act of healing should be on its own innards. June said, 'The plank makes ripples in the concrete, which flatten out later. Maybe that's all it's called – a plank.' She lowered her glance further, and studied the path. She did not care to look too long at the exterior of the Hospital, which, for some reason, frightened her. 'It's not completely smooth, though, is it?' she said.

Walter drew his right foot across the path, feeling the un-smoothed-out ripples. If this was a fault, it was not his. It was

36

as the workman had told him to do it, and the workman had said it was well done.

'If it were completely smooth, it would get slippery in the rain.'

Walter nodded. The workman had said much the same.

'Hardcore is the most important ingredient, do you agree? Without that, the concrete would sink into the ground, or spread about so thinly that it would crack under pressure. It's very important to have a firm base on which to build one's ...' Her words faded away into thoughts, old, tired, much-used thoughts of knocking everything over, letting it all topple, and starting again.

Frost was what would crack it. The workman had told him.

'Don't you agree?'

She was not looking at him, but at the path. Then she turned her head slowly, and looked directly at him for the first time during this encounter. 'It's not a good day you've chosen for making new acquaintances. Why has it taken you so long to approach me?' She laughed, a short involuntary laugh, which came up suddenly from nowhere, like a burp or a hiccup, so that she excused herself and let go of the wall for a moment to cover her mouth with her hand, before remembering the security of straight lines, and returning her hand quickly to the reassuring mortar.

A silence followed. Walter was used to being silent, and preferred it. In the silence bird-song could be heard, and an aeroplane droning somewhere in the distance. June smiled at him, patted the wall beside her, and said, 'Welcome to my wall.'

It might be her wall, in some way, though Walter knew well enough that she had not made it, having watched those who had. He himself had physically made the patch of path. He wished to tell her so, pointed to the path, and opened his mouth, but no words emerged. He did not know why this should be, and so he turned what should have been a speech into a smile, and leaned against the wall just as she was leaning.

They stood in silence for a long time, both with their backs against the brick wall of the Mother and Baby Unit, to which June had been sent with Baby John from the hospital at which her stomach had been pumped out. She had been told that she would be better here for a while, should not go home, that her baby would be at risk, while here people would help her to care for him, and she herself could be given Tests. What tests? Well, they would try new pills, a different psychiatrist, an altogether new approach. E.C.T.? Well, that was a possibility certainly; that might be something to try. The really important thing was not to give up. All this, June remembered while she stood next to the watching man, her back against the wall, and Walter did not think of anything in particular except that there was, after all, nothing wrong with his path, and that it was pleasant to be in the company of someone who was not Staff, yet who neither twitched, grizzled or dribbled, and who had smiled at him.

This place was to be a halfway house, a stepping-stone, except that no one seemed able or willing to tell her where her feet might land next. Here she was to be under observation; that was all they would say. 'We'd like to try one or two new things, and keep you under observation.' Well, she was certainly being observed, if only by this inmate, who had observed her on the very first day they had allowed her out into the fresh air, and was now leaning on the wall some four feet away.

A man in pyjamas, dressing-gown and bedroom slippers walked past, supported on either side by a nurse. The man's head hung forward, his chin pressing into his Adam's apple, his feet dragging along the ground. A slipper came off his left foot, and was left behind. A few yards further on, the other came off also, and was also left behind. The nurses had noticed the loss of the slippers, but had decided to keep hold of the man and continue walking, thereafter taking a short cut across some gravel, against which the man's bare feet were lightly cut.

Normally Walter would have retrieved the slippers, running after the nurses, and being thanked. But today wasn't a normal day, not for Walter.

June said, 'I'll bet he wishes they'd finish him off.'

This was not a statement fully understood by Walter, but he did not expect all, or even many statements to be fully understandable. Instead he counted the number of bricks between himself and June. Today he had found the courage to approach her, to walk slowly along the narrow concrete path, and then to stop near her, so that now they leaned against the same wall, six bricks apart. She had not screamed, or run away, or even asked him what he wanted. She had not complained about cracks in the path, because there were none. She had remained still, feeling the wall with her hands, and looking at the concrete he himself had made. She had talked to him, and smiled, had patted the wall beside her, inviting him to lean on it. And he had leaned, as she was leaning, and she had talked to him, had asked him why it had taken him so long to come and see her, had known that he had been watching her, and had not minded that.

He could hear the sound of a baby crying. She must have a baby; that would be why she was here. She must be unhappy, must be a mother, must be depressed and unhappy.

It was hard for Walter to believe that anyone who had given birth to a baby could be unhappy. He had seen babies on his walks at the head of his crocodile of Jesus's mistakes. The babies had been in prams, and people had stopped to look at them, and to talk to them in a funny way, with much repetition. The mothers of such babies had seemed proud; they had told their babies' ages, and wiped their mouths, and not appeared at all unhappy. Jesus had made those babies. Jesus had made people, just as he had made pigeons, and both pigeons and people had made more of their kind.

Fifteen years ago, four years after Walter had been taken to the Mental Hospital, but when he was already trusted, and would lead out his crocodile on walks, Walter, thirty-one years old, had returned from one of those walks, on which he had observed prams and the contents of those prams, and the proud mothers who had pushed the prams, and he had said to the Irish Orderly with carrot-red hair, 'I want to make a baby.'

The orderly had looked up from what he was doing, and had seen the seriousness sitting on Walter's face, and had bitten back what would have been a cruel and witty remark, and instead had thought for a while, and then said, 'Well now, Walter! Me, as a man, I understand your feelings, and as a comparatively good Catholic, I should say it's me bounden duty to do likewise. But frankly, Walter, I could not stomach it at all. I have sixty-nine babies to look after in here as it is, you being me only grown-up child, and a blessing you may say on that account. I tell you frankly, Walter, the Blessed Virgin short-changed me in this department, for she gave me the equipment, but forgot to add the desire. Now I have a dog, and if it died or got its poor little self run into, why I'd cry meself out of this Hospital all the way to the Irish Sea, but I wouldn't flutter me eyelids twice to look at a baby in a pram. Think now, Walter. Just think on this for a minute. How many human beings of both the male and female kind are there in this very Hospital – for, sure, I'll not call them men and women, which they are not, Walter, and will never be, saving your own self. Now, will you think how many?' Walter had thought how many. Very many, more than he could count, unless they were all to stand still for a long time. 'And will you think of all the parents of the people in here? Now that must be the real tragedy, mustn't it, to have your beautiful bouncing baby end up in a place like this?'

Walter's expression had been thoughtful. It was true that Jesus's mistakes must begin life in a pram. Perhaps the mothers did not know that Jesus was to get a cross and not a tick for their offspring. The Irish orderly had misread the thoughtfulness, and had added quickly, 'Now, I can say a thing like that to you, Walter, because by rights you shouldn't be in here, and if your parents were still alive, no doubt you wouldn't be. Babies are overrated, Walter. The world's overcrowded as it is, and that's me, a Catholic, speaking. If me life-style doesn't get me Eternal Damnation, to be sure me tongue will.'

He was long gone now from the Hospital, the friendly Irish Orderly with the carrot-red hair. He had been arrested in a Gentlemen's Toilet by an *agent provocateur* in plain clothes, pleaded guilty (on police advice), was sentenced to six months in prison, and lost his job.

Walter had not thought of the Irish orderly for many years. Only the thought of babies had brought back the memory of him. After his disappearance, he had not been much spoken of among the Staff, or not before Walter, who did not know where or why he had gone, but only grieved for him a while, and then forgot. He would like to speak of him to this sad mother – if she was sad; she must be sad, or she would not be here. He would like to speak on many subjects, but it seemed that he could not, since no words emerged when he opened his mouth. In any case, someone had once compared Walter's speech to a fart in a bath of soapy water; it was better that he should not speak. Let her speak, and he would listen.

Two other women came out of the Mother and Baby Unit, carrying their babies and jigging them up and down in their arms as they walked about on the grass. Then a black nurse appeared, and told June that she must go inside; it was time for Baby's feed. The nurse clasped June's arm. Leading her away, and talking to her as if to a child, she said, 'Come on, now, June. Don't you start to be difficult now. Be a good girl.'

Now he knew her name. She had allowed herself to be led away, and had not turned or said, 'Goodbye,' but he knew her name now. Her name was June.

The segregation of the sexes at the Hospital had been discontinued eleven years earlier. The large cast-iron doors dividing one wing from another had been opened. Male patients had, for the first time, been allowed to meet and even to talk to female patients. Female nurses worked on the Men's Wards. Social intercourse was positively encouraged. Every Saturday evening, a Social and Dance would be held in the Main Hall.

A branch of the Gateway Club, which has members in Mental Hospitals all over the country, was started. Walter paid his subscription and received a membership card, which proved that he was a bona fide member and permitted to take part in the Club's Activities.

He had visited every Saturday Night Dance since they began. He had sat and watched male and female patients dancing together, had watched wheelchairs pushed out onto the dance floor, to whirl and spin gravely about in time to the music. But he himself had never attempted to do this with Clifford's chair.

On the stage, a cardboard disc in which were set differently coloured circles of cellophane rotated in front of a spotlight, so that coloured circles of light moved over the walls and ceiling of the Main Hall. Loud music from a record-player with extra large speakers filled the Hall with sound, encouraging the ambulant patients to dance either alone or with a partner.

But Walter never danced. He sat, listening to the music and watching the coloured lights move about. He watched the faces of the dancing patients change colour, from blue to green, from green to pink, from pink to amber, from amber to yellow, and so back to blue.

Every week, he would be approached by female patients, asking him to dance. Usually they came two or three at a time, pushing each other forward, not wishing to be the first to ask. Often the request would be made by a third party, 'Here, will you dance with her?', and the third party would point to 'her', who usually cringed and giggled. Always Walter shook his head. 'How about her, then? Will you dance with her?' Again the shaken head, grave and firm, but not dismissive, since there would be no intention in Walter to give offence. 'Me, then? What about me? Come on! Dance with me.'

Then Walter would say, 'Sorry. I can't dance.'

'What? Can't do *that*?' The spokeswoman for the group would point to the dancers, astonished that Walter should be unable to move clumsily to the music, which was all that she required of him. But Walter was too self-conscious to move in public to music, clumsily or daintily, with or without a partner.

Once he had danced, but that was many years ago, at the Woolworth's Annual Dinner and Dance, held each year in Blackpool. That was when his mother and father were alive, and his father's pigeons lived happily in their Loft in the Yard and mated every spring and throughout the summer, and Walter had worked in the Stock Room at Woolworth's, sweeping up litter, baling paper, and being often praised for the thoroughness of his work. They had gone to Blackpool for the day, all the Staff in a coach, and the dance had been held in the evening. Jean, who looked after the shelves of soap-powders, detergents, pan-scourers, bleach and lavatory cleaners, had pulled him bodily from his place at a table with trainee floorwalkers, who had been trying to get him drunk. Having had some drink herself, she had jumped up and down, holding tightly to Walter's hand, and he had stood, bent forward, with Jean and the Ball Room going round and round him, the red textured wallpaper and the gilt wall-lights turning and spinning, until Jean had realized that he was either going to fall over or to be sick, and perhaps both. So she had taken him away to the table next to her own, away from the trainee floorwalkers, in order to look after him, and she had sat beside him on the coach when they went home, with an arm round his shoulder while he slept.

That was the nearest Walter had ever come to dancing, and the memory of it-made him want to laugh and cry, both at the same time. Jean would be almost sixty by now, and would never know what had happened to him.

'I'll tell you one thing, Pop. We certainly landed in the shit when they brought us here. When I look around, I wonder what I fought and survived two world wars for.'

Walter remembered Pop and his friend Rubber Face, to whom this remark had been made many times more than once, in Walter's hearing. He remembered Rubber Face for his facial contortions, and Dominoes for the blackness of his skin and the whiteness of his round eyes. He remembered Dopey, Sneezy and an Indian patient whom they had christened 'Bombay Curry'. He remembered Ben Gunn, a hairy, thin but strong old man, who had jumped on Walter's bed like a dog, and sexually assaulted him on his first night at the Hospital.

He remembered Maurice and Albert, whom he had washed and dressed every day of the week, right up to and even on the days they had died, Maurice having outlived Albert by three months. He remembered Adrian, who would never allow his body to be clothed, and propelled himself along the floor on knees and elbows, picking up dirt and eating it, and Noddy, who walked round all day in his nightshirt, sucking at a baby's feeding bottle, and Ernest, who drank his own urine, because he liked to make people laugh and hear them call him, 'Dirty bugger!'

He remembered a winter's day in 1960, when all the patients in the ward who could walk were ushered out into the freezing yard, and hosed down with cold water, because one of the nurses had mislaid a pound note. And he remembered Reggie, who had

43

shouted, 'If you can't treat me with kindness, don't treat me at all.'

Walter remembered how the Social Worker, policeman and doctor had dragged him away from the bedside of his dead mother, where he had been waiting for Jesus to decide whether she was to go to Him or not, since if the decision were negative, she might reasonably be expected to return to her own son, who needed her. He remembered the promises they had made to him that they were taking him to a nice place, where he need not stay if he did not like it, and that they had lied. He remembered Bernard, who had once said to him, 'They told me I'd be here for two weeks, just for the rest, and that was forty years ago.' Bernard had been sixty-eight when he had told this to Walter. It was his birthday, and he was crying. He had never had a visitor. He had been sitting beside Walter, sticking labels onto rubber bones for dogs to play with, and the tears had rolled down his sallow wrinkled face, and dropped onto the pile of rubber bones.

And Walter, remembering, was now forty-six. And he had never had a visitor. Nobody had come from Woolworth's to see him, and he had never had any conversation with anyone who was not either Staff or one of Jesus's Mistakes. Until the sad lady in the Mother and Baby Unit had allowed him to approach her, and had spoken to him freely, though he had not been able to reply.

Her name was June.

Bernard had leaned forward over the rubber bones one day in the spring which followed his sixty-eighth birthday, resting his head on the bones, and snoring loudly. The other patients had giggled, and left him alone, thinking that he had fallen asleep, but he had never woken from that sleep, and no one came to claim his body.

Had Bernard been one of Jesus's Mistakes? If so, he had not been a very large Mistake, not one which was immediately clear to see. Walter knew that he himself was not a Mistake at all; in his case, mistakes had been made by others. But perhaps Bernard had thought this also, and perhaps he had been right to think so. During his nineteen years at the Hospital, Walter had been given various tests, but no action seemed to follow them, and whether he was a failure or a success was never divulged to him. They were just 'Tests', part of the Hospital Routine, and he applied himself to them, as to the rest of that routine, as best he could. One test had involved the soldering of four wires of different colours to the correct terminals of an eight-pin television plug, another was the assembly of a bicycle pump, in which nine different operations had to be performed in a certain order, or the pump would not work.

They were just Tests; they were not the same as Work. For much had changed at the Hospital in nineteen years. A swimming pool had been built in what had once been a side-ward, and Walter held a Certificate to prove that he had once swum a width of heavily chlorinated water without his feet ever having touched the bottom. There were, as has been said, social activities. And in the general cause of giving the patients human dignity, there was Work. Walter had stuck purple satin hearts onto Valentine Cards. He had packed dolls' Vanity Sets into boxes. In the Carpentry Shop, he had made bookshelves and boxes for cutlery. On the Hospital Farm, he had dug manure into the ground, and seen the orderly lines of peas and beans he had sown sprout into life and grow. He had learned how to repair boots and shoes.

For Work, Walter was paid; human dignity had to do with money. For a week's work, Walter might be paid – sometimes had been paid – as much as one pound and fifty pence, the money to be spent in the Canteen on sweets or cigarettes (though Walter did not smoke), all his other needs being, of course, provided for. Work was different from Hobbies, which were sometimes called Occupational Therapy, which was not paid. Walter was not good at Hobbies. He had tried to make pottery, and failed; nor could he draw or paint. He was an indifferent performer with a needle, either at embroidery or plain sewing, and all the raffia mats he made had to be unpicked or thrown away. In any case, though time might have to be allowed for Work, and the financial rewards of Work, Walter could not often be spared for Hobbies. Most of his nineteen years at the Hospital continued to be spent in the faded beige overalls he had been given in his first year, and

45

in assisting the Staff to feed, clean, shave, dress and undress the non-ambulant patients. Particularly Clifford.

Once a month, Drama was organized in the Main Hall of the Hospital. The organizer was a large lady with hair of a pepper-and-salt colour, roughly the texture of wire wool, pulled well back and disciplined into a bun at the back. She brought with her five disciples from her Studio in the town, and together they acted out 'situations' with the more tractable ambulant patients.

The situations acted out were simple, even childish to Walter's mind, so that he was unwilling to take part in them, but the large lady regarded them with such seriousness that not to participate would have been impolite, and if what was acted out together rarely had much relevance to life in a Mental Hospital, perhaps it did reflect the reality of life outside the gates.

They had, for instance, to rescue a baby from a tree. In this situation, the five disciples stood in the centre of the Main Hall, holding above their heads a sheet, on which a doll had been placed. The Lady Organizer informed Walter and his colleagues that this doll was her baby, and that the tree had taken it from her. The trees in the Hospital Grounds were common elms and sycamores, which did not go about snatching babies – except that in those days before the building of the Unit, there were no babies inside the Main Gate, so perhaps the trees might have snatched them had there been any to snatch. In any case, Walter and others were enlisted to rescue the doll-baby from the snarling, hissing tree. They were not to go straight in, wasting their lives in a useless unplanned attack. They must first make a plan to cut down the tree, before a strong wind came, and blew the baby out. It seemed to Walter that getting the baby out of the tree was what *he* was being required to do, and if a wind would do it for him, why bother? But the baby, he was told, would break if blown out of the tree by wind, but would be safe if only the tree were chopped down instead by Walter and his companions.

Walter worked away with an imaginary axe, chopping at the kicking legs of the disciples. Other patients mimed sawing the tree down. A patient named Roger, who could read, and did read children's comics (donated and brought round once a week on a trolley), set about planting dynamite in the roots of the tree, and laid a long fuse across the hall to a place of safety from which he could blow the tree, baby and all the rescuers at once to smithereens. The baby had, therefore, to be rescued quickly by non-violent means, which was to charm the tree by the use of music. All the patients present, and the Organizer, *and* her disciples joined together to sing 'Rock-a-Bye, Baby, on the Tree-Top', at which the tree quivered for a while, and then lowered the doll on its sheet gently to the ground, to be reclaimed tearfully by its mother, and the patients thanked. Walter had moved his lips, but did not sing.

Then the Lady Organizer had called for silence. In the general buzz of mutual congratulation, she had to call more than once, but she was a woman of strong personality, and silence was obtained. In that silence, she looked at each patient in turn directly, to compel attention, and then said, very quietly, 'Have you ever thought what would happen to the world, if all the patients all over the country, who are in Mental Hospitals like this one, were suddenly to decide to go on strike, or just walk out?' There was a pause. None of them had ever had that thought. Those who were capable of reason, applied reason to it. The single member of Staff present in case of emergencies, cleared his throat.

The Lady Organizer, who had been sitting cross-legged, still holding the doll, now stood, and gave the doll to a disciple. 'About sixty thousand people live and die in Hospitals like this one,' she said. 'Did you know that?' The disciples began to gather up their props. Drama was over for that month.

Walter remembered the lady's question for a long time, and thought about it often. He knew what a strike was; though he had never taken part in one, strikes had been spoken of when he worked at Woolworth's. But his imagination would not stretch to the concept of sixty thousand people walking out of hospitals all over the country at some prearranged signal. Where would they go, where would they live? He knew well enough that he was not the only patient with no family and no home; most of his fellows in the Hospital were in the same condition, and there were others whose families would not have them at home, because they were too much trouble. The Hospital was their home. Perhaps the Lady Organizer had not thought of that.

Nevertheless the question worried him. It would not have been put if it had not been thought important. Was there, in fact, some provision made for people like Walter, even for Jesus's Mistakes, outside the Hospital, where they could go if they were ever to strike or for any other reason, and was the knowledge of this place being deliberately kept from them?

2

A young man sat cutting his arm with a rusty razor-blade. He said he just wanted to know what it felt like.

In the Mother and Baby Unit, there was a small lounge, with armchairs, a settee, a television set, a radio and a very large supply of back numbers of *Woman* and *Woman's Own*. There was a small kitchen, used mainly by the nurses, and a dining-room with ten chairs set round a central table. Behind each of the ten chairs, pushed against the wall, there was a baby's high chair.

Upstairs there were two bedrooms of three beds, and two of two beds. There were two bathrooms and three W.C.s.

In the corridor between the kitchen and the lounge (where the television set was left on all the time, even when there was only a test card to look at), a tall girl paced backwards and forwards. She was seventeen years old. She was chain-smoking, dragging on each cigarette with exaggerated energy. Every time she reached the door of the lounge, she stopped for a moment, and looked towards her child, who was bouncing up and down in a walking-frame. The child was happy and pretty. Her seventeen-year-old mother had so far made two attempts to kill her.

'Fetch her a nappy.' A young nurse was speaking.

'No. She's all right.' The young mother turned away.

'I said, "Fetch her a nappy." ' The nurse stood, blocking the girl's way.

'I've just changed her.' The young mother dropped her cigarette

49

butt onto the linoleum, and twisted the pad of her carpet-slippered foot on top of it.

'She's damp.'

'So what? She dribbles.' The young mother searched her pocket for matches.

'I'll wait here until you fetch her a clean nappy.'

'You'll wait a fucking long time, then.'

The conversation was about the state of the baby's nappy, but its sub-text was about authority and ownership. Since the young mother's attempts at infanticide, the child had become the property of the State, or rather of the Social Services, whom the nurse was now representing. The baby could be kept if the mother would accept help and treatment, or it could be given away if the mother were, over an acceptable period of trial, to prove to be unfit to keep it. What it could not be was thrown away; what it must not be was abandoned in the Ladies' Waiting-Room of a bus station.

'I left it there because I knew, if I kept it, I'd try to kill it again. I haven't had a moment's happiness since it came. Nobody cares about me any more; it's all her.'

They had made allowances for the mother's youth, and for the fact that the father was already married. No member of the Social Services would easily consent to separating a child from its mother; that was a drastic measure, and should only be undertaken when all else failed. Anyway there is the legal position to consider. Remove a child too readily for fostering and within a month, the mother may demand and receive it back. Time is needed for the mother to consider her position in all its aspects.

While that time is taken, anyone representing the Social Services may expect to have to endure some friction.

Having been unable to find a light for her cigarette, the young mother pushed past the nurse, and went to look for matches. She returned with a box of matches and a clean nappy, and held the nappy out to the nurse. The nurse said, 'You do it.'

'Fuck off, black self-righteous cow ! You're the one who says she's wet. You get paid for this, so you do it; you change her.'

The nappy was thrown at the nurse, who took it, lifted the child from its walking-frame, and talked to it as she changed its nappy.

The young mother watched, drawing even more deeply on her cigarette.

Her name was Kathy. She shared a bedroom with June.

June, watching from the bedroom window, saw Clive's car pull up outside, and watched him as he methodically locked it and went round, checking all the doors. Did he suppose that someone in the Mother and Baby Unit might steal it to make a quick getaway?

She looked beyond the car to the enormous old Mental Hospital, and realized for the first time what they had meant when they had told her that this place was to be a stepping-stone, and why they had avoided saying where next she would go. However, they would not, could not, send Baby John with her to that place. As long as Baby John was with her, she could expect to remain on the stepping-stone.

She debated with herself whether to go down and see her visitor, her very first visitor, her baby's father. But she knew that if she did not go down, the nurses would come upstairs and nag at her until she did. As long as the Victorian hell-hole across the way remained a threat, it would be better to play the nurses' game.

He wanted to kiss her. She turned her face to one side, and allowed him to hug her to him. It would make him feel better, would release some of the emotion he felt and perhaps just a tiny bit of the guilt as well.

She said, 'My hair's falling out. Had you noticed?'

'No.'

'Well, it is.'

The nurses had watched the embrace, and watched while she led him towards the lounge.

'Two handfuls yesterday. I didn't comb it this morning. I think my mind is pushing it out from underneath.'

'Have you been getting headaches?'

'It feels as though it's bursting sometimes. Soon grey jelly will start seeping through my eye-sockets. Not long after, it'll all be over, thank God.'

'I'm afraid I didn't bring anything. Grapes or anything.' The only other occupant of the lounge was Kathy's little girl in her walking-frame.

51

'I don't know what's going on. There is something going on. Something strange, but I can't describe it.' They were still standing. 'Do you want to sit down? Take your coat off? How long can you stay?'

He took off his coat, and sat down, but avoided answering her third question, knowing that whatever he said would not please her.

She sat beside him. She had become thoughtful and serious. Now there would be no playing games with herself and him; he knew them all. To her own surprise, she realized that she wanted him to like her. But that was too much to expect, after seven misspent years.

'I'm the only one who knows what goes on inside my head, and I can't describe it to them, so how can they make me better?'

Kathy's baby girl pointed her chubby fingers at Clive, and made gurgling noises.

'All the others know why they're here. Andrea wants to give her baby away. Kathy thinks she may kill hers. Janice's mother wouldn't stop touching her baby, so Janice screamed until someone took notice, and brought her here. Rita has the mind of a seven-year-old, and was raped in the back of a car. All the others have simple post-natal depression, cured by the passing of time, and simple doses of pills. I'm the only one they can't help, because I can't explain. They think I'm not trying.' She was twisting a strand of Rita's knitting wool round and round her right index finger, pulling it tight to make the finger change colour.

'God's the only other person who knows what's going on inside my head. Why does He let people go insane? Why does He allow places like this?'

Clive didn't know. He shook his head.

'The vicar was here. He doesn't count as a visitor. He comes to see us all. I asked him. I said, 'Why does God allow it?''

'What did he answer?'

'I can't remember.'

'It couldn't have been very enlightening.' He was not used to her new-found interest in religion. 'Anyway, I thought you didn't believe in God.'

She frowned. Either she had not heard him, or had not under-

52

stood. She said, 'I don't see why people shouldn't be allowed just to be put to sleep, do you? What's the point of Mental Hospitals?'

'Some people get well.' There was no conviction in his voice.

She thought he looked fatter. He looked well. Myra must be looking after him. He must be sleeping, living a restful uneventful unhysterical quiet life.

It was time. While with her, he had lost weight, developed bags under his eyes from lack of sleep, had always looked shell-shocked, always waiting for the next attack, mental or physical. He had never hit back. Never. Not even once. With her, he had been perpetually off balance, from dodging the missiles she threw. The screaming! crying! sulking! She remembered her own guilt, and the aftertaste of pointlessness, and the numbing calm before the next attack. One psychiatrist had called it 'psychic numbing'. So much of psychiatry seemed to her to be more to do with the giving of names than of curing.

Yes, he looked well. She had spoiled and wasted seven years of his life. She owed him an explanation.

'I never knew, you see. I never realized that people could know they were going mad, and not be able to do anything about it. I'd always thought it just happened, without one's knowing, that one went on believing that one was just the same and it was the others who'd changed. Everyone out of step but me. Do you understand what I mean?'

He nodded.

'It's cruel, isn't it? When you know it's happening?' Again he nodded. 'How can they help me, if I can't tell them what's wrong?' She saw that he was wary, unsure as to whether she were playing one of her little games with him. He wasn't used to her being serious, not about something as important as this. But she was sure, as sure as she could ever be about anything. She was sure. She was serious.

His bewildered expression told her that he couldn't help. He looked well and prosperous, he had put on weight, but he couldn't help.

'The other day was good. I knew that the voices on the radio were real, and that the lawn outside was real; I walked on it. I have been outside; I am allowed. We could go for a walk now if we wanted.'

He held her look for a moment. It was a moment that seemed to contain all those other moments when they had been physically close, and she almost cried out for the comfort in those moments. Then he looked down at his wrist, and June noticed his watch, and realized that the comfort of those physically close moments was all in the past.

She had cried 'Wolf!' too often. It was unfair even to consider that he might help her. She would let him off the hook gently. She owed him that, at least.

'But then that meant that up until that time, I couldn't have known that the voices on the radio and the lawn outside were real.'

There, she had done it, had admitted that she was not well, suffered hallucinations, could be considered mad. Therefore he had been right to leave her; he was not a psychiatrist, and could not have helped. She watched the muscles in his face relax. He was no longer responsible for her.

A thought: 'June needs help' does not mean, 'June requires support and assistance from those who love her,' but, 'June has no right to expect anything, even love, from those who say they love her, but must seek assistance from the place authorized to give it, which is the Bin.'

Kathy's little girl had managed to move the walking-frame, and was standing close to Clive, with a sticky hand held out, patting his knee. The child's face looked up at him, bright and alive with hope. Kathy paced the corridor, and stopped each time at the door to look at her child, as if she were trying to come to a decision.

Clive touched the fine blonde hair of Kathy's little girl. He said, 'Who are you, then? Who do you belong to?' The baby made gurgling noises of laughter, and patted harder at this unfamiliar knee covered with fawn cavalry twill.

June said, 'Do you want to see Baby John?'

'Yes, of course. Where is he?'

'Sleeping. I'll get him in a moment.' He reached for her hand, and took it inside his. 'Now he feels secure,' she thought. 'He knows there isn't going to be a scene. No demands, no threats. Poor love! he's so transparent.'

Her hand was cold and dry, and the skin hard. Difficult to believe it could ever had been sensitive to touch. The knuckles were hard, like knots in oak. He didn't remember her hands like this. These were the hands of a stranger, not the hands which once had been able to arouse him. These were dead hands. Perhaps that was where death started, at the extremities. It couldn't be far away from her; he had seen it in her face. She had often said that death was what she had always wanted. But what would happen to the child – his child?

'Today isn't a normal day.'

'Why not?'

'It just isn't.'

'Is it better or worse?'

'Both.' Kathy had stopped pacing, and stood just outside the door, looking at her child, and scowling. Clive moved his hand away from the child's head.

'I'd give anything not to be here. I made a pact with God. He can have all my hair and teeth if He'll give me my mind back.'

'I thought it was your mind you were trying to get away from.' She thought, 'If only he wouldn't preface every remark by saying "I thought" in that way ! Doesn't he know how it provokes me?' There was nothing for him here. Why bother to come? She was not his wife. They had pretended; that was all. Myra had the ring. the licence, and now what went with them, her husband. He was back. He had just been away for a rather long holiday, a seven-year sabbatical. Soon Myra would be presenting him with a legitimate baby. Why had he come?

'Why did you come?'

'To see you.'

'Why?'

'You've no one else.'

'Is that a good enough reason?'

'I think so.'

'Does Myra know?'

'Yes, of course she does.'

He was lying. Childishly he had allowed himself to be led into a trap. He had given himself away, and the likelihood was that, when he got home to Myra, she would also know that he was lying about where he'd been. The idea almost made June laugh, but she forbore. Instead she thought, 'If I feel nothing, then death is not taking place.'

A young man had arrived to see one of the other women. The two of them sat holding hands in the opposite corner of the lounge, and talked in whispers. She was called Enid. She was about to be sent home.

'Are you sure you want to see Baby John? You don't have to, just to be polite.'

'I want to see him.'

She released her dead hand from his, and stood up. 'I'll see if he's awake.'

She did not come back, and, after waiting fifteen minutes, Clive asked one of the nurses to make sure that June was all right. The nurse returned to tell Clive that June was in the bath. And so he left.

The sun shone directly through the window. She lay in the bath, hands on either side of her nose, eyes not quite fully closed, and felt the ache of disappointment well up from the base of her stomach.

What she saw were the translucent gossamer wings of butterflies, made in collaboration by the strong sun and her lowered eyelashes. What she felt was disappointment enough to make her cry, to break her heart, all that. (Her heart, she decided. was pumping a little faster than usual.) It was the injustice of her disappointment which was unbearable, like heartburn which never went away, and could not be alleviated by Bisodol. Had anyone died of a continuous heartburn?

She looked down at her body. It was hers, but she did not wish to have it.

'It's yourself you're trying to punish, not me. Your anger's directed towards you really, not me. It's you whom you wish to harm, not me. Why?'

She didn't know why. Of all the people she had ever known, only Clive used the word 'whom'. And she used it sometimes.

'That's why you had asthma as a child.' Was that Clive? No, it was the therapist. Therefore, recast the phrasing. Therapists ask

56

questions; they rarely make statements. 'Was that why you had asthma as a child?' Better. 'Self-inflicted hysteria, do you think? Isn't your anger really fear? So where does that leave us?'

Surely he meant, where did it leave her? She had thought about the question, stretching her mind to pull it free from the numbing effects of Valium and anti-depressants, and had spoken slowly, hearing her words slur. 'I'm angry with myself, and the anger is really fear?' The shrink had nodded, pleased that she had it right. It had seemed to June that she was like Frankenstein's Monster, slowly repeating well-rehearsed sentences to prove it was human. 'You're saying that I'm frightened of myself, and not of life?'

A pause. Then, 'What do you think?'

She thought. 'I think you're sitting in the wrong chair, doctor.'

Puzzled. 'What makes you say that?'

'Nothing makes me; I just chose to. I'd disproved all that Freudian "self-fear" crap before I was twenty. Where have you been, doctor?'

He had swallowed. Score! She had thrown him. Then, 'I'm quite aware of your intellectual – '

'Then, don't insult it, for Christ's sake.'

Blinked. Reached for a prop to occupy his hands. It had been a gold propelling-pencil. 'Why do you write something off, just because it seems simplistic?' Still strong with the questions.

She had brought his face into as sharp a focus as the drugs would allow, and studied it. Did he really believe what he had said, or was he just treading water while he sought for something more convincing?

She had tried to help him. 'Couldn't we at least start from the point where I blame myself for what happened to my mother, so it's not just myself that I'm angry at stroke frightened of; it's my performance. Or to put it more simply, doctor, it's what I do that makes me angry and frightened, not what I am. I know how an intelligent woman ought to behave, but I don't wish to "behave"; it bores me. And boredom frightens me. The blank pointlessness of one day following another without change. The daily routine, that's what sends me flying to the aspirin bottle.' He had continued to watch her, his fingers twisting the propelling-pencil. 'I once tried one of those Therapeutic Communities; you know the sort of

57

thing – "Growth through shared living"; we were going to discuss and question some common assumptions. Sounded like an excuse for several days of free groping and a bit of tripping the light fan-ego – "Ego-trips round the lighthouse, and home for a Cream Tea." Well, it was a mess, of course, but not in the way I'd expected. Most of that happy group were so bored that they couldn't even bear being awake. One young man sat cutting his arm with a rusty razor-blade; he said he just wanted to know what it felt like. Well, that's me, doctor; I'm him. Except that I'm a physical coward.'

He had not reacted, and his expression had been similar to expressions June had very often seen before, and which had usually meant, 'Don't ring us. We'll ring you.'

The bath water was cold, and a nurse was banging at the door. There were no locks on the door, for obvious reasons. The nurse came in.

'Get out of that bath, you selfish person. We only got two baths up here, and you lie there for over an hour like Lady Muck. Three more minutes, then I pull you out by the hair myself, OK?'

June leaned forward, and pulled the plug out. Stepping-stone or no, she did not have to step, and would not, not to there, not to that piece of Victorian ugliness, not to any Mental Hospital. The black, brown, Irish, Scottish, Welsh and yellow sods in white coats who had fucked up her plans, and forced her to live, taken away her positive wish to die and left only a hole where once it was, could go and screw themselves.

Next time she would make sure, do it quickly, use a bread knife. Surely it was only like cutting a finger, over in a minute, and no comeback. She certainly wouldn't use pills again. Most of them were bloody placebos anyway. And gas had lost its lethal effectiveness. Thanks to the bloody North Sea, one could no longer either commit suicide or simmer a stew; everything burned on North Sea Gas except the human soul. A double-barrelled shotgun up through the mouth would be quick, providing one's arms were long enough to reach the trigger. Perhaps she should fall onto a bread knife, as people in Shakespeare fell on their swords. *Hold here this bread knife, Rufio, while I run upon it.*

Slit wrists in a warm bath might be colourful and noble, but some sod would be bound to want to borrow a cup of sugar, or sell you an Encyclopedia before the water had time to cool.

The water in her own bath had meanwhile run away, down the plughole.

some pretended, not nobody. In anyone's eyes. Walter saw only his self reflected unflatteringly. He could see no further than the skin he was in, and no better than anyone's own reflection.

3

If she were to compete, she knew, she would lose him completely.

They met every day, leaned against the same bricks in the same wall, and looked down at Walter's stretch of concrete. He would have told her that it was he who had made what they were standing on, and that it was level and safe, without cracks, but he dared not speak. She talked; he listened. Sometimes he would nod, sometimes shake his head, but he never spoke, for he remembered, 'Your voice sounds like a fart in a bath of soapy water.'

The second time they had met, she had asked him what his name was, and he had produced a pencil from his pocket, and printed 'WALTER' on one of the new red bricks. Then she had said his name, and told him hers was June (which he knew), printing it on the brick next to the one he had used. Then she had asked him why he never spoke, and he had not answered. She had waited, and then asked gently if it was because he couldn't speak. He had looked at the ground, unable to lie and unable to tell the truth. She had nodded slowly, and touched his hand, and Walter guessed that she had taken his lack of a reply to mean that he wasn't able. She had said, 'What can't speak, can't lie. What isn't a lie must be true, Walter. True; straight; level, like this wall. You must have your own built-in spirit-level, set into your head.'

He had nothing set into his head, though one of the inmates of his Ward had a metal plate, the result of an attack by boys while he was still Outside. But he would not contradict her.

June thought it ironic that truth should be found here, not locked in, but confined, all the same, by ignorance, that she should bump up against truth by accident in a Mental Home, where more lies are told by the minute than in any other human institution, save perhaps the House of Commons.

Time passed, and nothing changed but the cloud formations, and they changed slowly. She did not talk all the time, nor did he listen. She was thirty-eight years old, with a wealth of experience (most of which she would have been happier without) and he was forty-six with very little experience of the world outside those large wrought-iron gates, towards which she would often look. When this happened, Walter felt cold, shut out, empty, as he had on the day his father died. He wanted to say something to distract her attention from the gates, but dared not speak now, or she would be angry with him for deceiving her.

He was aware that, since he had begun to come and stand here beside her, his mind had slowly changed, and that he now believed that the real world began outside the Hospital gates, not inside. His world inside the gates was real too, but it was different, a different world for people who were different, who were too sad, too odd, too old, too handicapped to look after themselves, or for violent people who might harm others and themselves. June was not part of this world. Neither was he. If June was sad, that was something which passed. (For Walter, sadness was something which always passed.) He and June were not there because they were mistakes made by Jesus. They were there because of mistakes made by people outside the main gates.

She was looking outside. He scraped the side of his shoe across the ripples in the concrete to distract her, and she turned, and looked at him. She said, 'What are you thinking?'

He tried to smile without showing his teeth. She would not be pleased by their colour.

'Did you never learn Sign Language?' He shook his head.

'Not that it would help us, unless I learned it too.'

He wanted to know why she was here, why she was unhappy; he wanted to see her baby. He took out his pencil, and printed 'BOY OR GRIL?' on one of the bricks. Then he pointed to the door of the Mother and Baby Unit.

'It's a boy. Baby John. Don't ask me why I call him "Baby"; I don't know. Except perhaps to remind myself that he *is* a baby, and helpless.' She had never thought of it until now.

'Babies survive, though, most of them at least. There are a lot of people looking after their interests. It's the grown-up babies like me who need help. My baby eats, sleeps, cries, breaks wind, and smiles. They tell me the first three months is the most important time for him. If I give him enough affection, and make him feel secure, he'll grow into a healthy normal upright boring citizen, and resent visiting me at Christmas. But how do you give affection if fear is a regular part of your day, and you can't even fight it, because you don't know where it's come from, or why it's there?'

She had lost him. He was looking at the Main Gate. Their relationship was based on simple thoughts, simply transmitted, and received in a simple way. It was one-sided, since she spoke and he wrote misspelled words on bricks or made primitive signs, but she welcomed it, and found it relaxing. No performance, no games, no need to compete or to pretend. If she did, she was sure she would lose him completely, scare him away, and she needed him, needed his truth, needed someone who couldn't, wouldn't judge her. He stood there, with his flat cap above his beak of a nose, and received all she said without evaluation. She had arrived in Hell, and found a soulmate.

'Will you hold my hand?' She held a hand out towards Walter, and he looked down at it. Slowly he lifted his own arm, and took her small fingers into his.

'Thank you. It's more reassuring than holding the wall.' Her fingers tightened their grasp on his. The dry hardness of her hand surprised him.

Four days later, he brought her a present.

He had made a small box out of cardboard and Sellotape. He had stolen a piece of purple satin, used in the making of Valentines. He had placed the piece of satin (which had the words 'My Valentine' printed on it in gold) inside the box, and placed on top of it his mother's diamanté ear-rings. Of the objects which he had brought with him to the Hospital, they were the only ones still in his possession.

Bright red tissue paper, left over from the previous Christmas, had been used to wrap the box, and silver tinsel tied in a bow which it had taken him thirty minutes to perfect.

Then he had carried the beautifully wrapped present around in his pocket for six days, unable to find the right moment to give it to her.

Now he held out the present. She took it from his outstretched hand, and began slowly to unwrap it, frequently pausing to look up at him and show her pleasure.

'You've wrapped it beautifully. It must have taken hours.' She removed the lid of the home-made box.

'Ear-rings! They're lovely.' She held them up to the sun, and they glittered. 'It's the Eiffel Tower, isn't it?' Walter nodded.

'But where did you get them?' Walter printed 'M.U.M.' on one of the bricks. Soon they would have to leave his patch of concrete path in order to reach clean bricks on which to write. Nothing was ever rubbed out or written over.

'Are you sure you really want me to have them?' Walter nodded vigorously.

'I need my hair done properly now, to show them off.' Walter smiled, hiding his teeth. It had been all right. She had not laughed at him.

By now Walter had begun to neglect the jobs he did for the Staff on the wards. From some he excused himself, some he delegated to other patients, and some he did at twice his normal speed. Fortunately, the job which, up to five years ago, had taken most of his time, was now automated. No longer had he to marshal his charges outside the Wash Room for shaving, run in to soap six chins, run out again to reorganize those waiting, while an orderly scraped at chins on which the soap was already drying with a blunt Seven O'Clock blade. There were two electric shavers fastened to the wall in each of the wards for men, and Walter lined up those to be shaved in short lines, as far as the flex would reach, allowing them to lean against the wall like puppets some of whose strings have been cut, and when they were shaved it was without cuts or irritating rashes.

Members of Staff, nurses in white coats, orderlies in brown, noticed Walter's new neglect of his duties, and resented it. He was a trusty; they trusted him. Once he had lied for them – or had, at least, not told the truth – had covered up neglect, the murder of one patient by another in the Wash Room, but few of those members of Staff whom he had protected now remained; the episode was forgotten, except by Walter. What members of Staff knew now was that someone who had felt pleasure and pride in being at their beck and call, now spent all the time he could make in leaning against the wall of the Mother and Baby Unit, holding the hand of a female patient. They became jocular with him. 'Here's our Casanova. Here's our sexy Walter. Got the ring yet, Walter? Has she proposed to you yet? Going steady? Got a ready-made family there, Walter. Has she given you your oats yet? Shown you how it's done? Have to keep your pencil sharp, Walter.'

Just so, long ago, before he ever entered the bounds of the Hospital, mock had been made of Walter by the bus-conductor and his friendly passengers, and by the trainee floorwalkers of Woolworth's. *I laugh. He laughs. They laugh.*

'How old are you, Walter?'

Walter scribbled on a brick, first the number four, then the number six. He did not feel forty-six, or even twenty-six, had no real notion of age, which was to do with birthdays which were not celebrated in the Hospital. Nineteen years he had been here. Nineteen years spent, quite gone; they would not be given back to him for good service. He couldn't even begin to add up the number of mornings he had woken up in the same bed, or the number of meals he had fed to Clifford, or the number of faces on which he had spread shaving-soap.

Ben Gunn had died long ago, eleven years. He would not have been allowed into Paradise. Jesus would not have wished Ben Gunn to live with Him for ever. Even a short visit was unlikely. The Devil would have taken Benn Gunn in. Perhaps Ben Gunn had known this, and his behaviour in the Ward had merely been practice for Hell.

Clifford remained. Walter tried to imagine Clifford wearing long white flowing robes. He would stain them, and if he continued to stink as he stank now, Paradise would cease to be paradisal. Yet, as far as anyone was able to tell, Clifford was good, not evil. Speechless and confined, as he was, in a wheelchair, his opportunities for evil-doing were not many. Also, as far as could be guessed, he suffered, and it was only fair that he should at last experience bliss.

As Walter watched the clouds moving slowly, he thought of meeting his parents again in Paradise, of being above those slow-moving clouds. Would there be pigeons? His father, he knew, would wish them. The Russian High-Fliers which had been kept in the Loft at the end of the yard had, even in this life, often ventured above the clouds, and had to be brought down again by the shaking of a food tin or the sending out of Freda, the dove, best-loved, as a decoy.

He was alone, and no thinking of a Paradise full of pigeons and of parents (though his mother had never liked them) could make him less so. Only holding June's hand, and listening to her talk, made him less alone. But now, although he was with her, she was leaning back against the wall, with her head turned towards the Main Gate, and his sense of aloneness was as complete as it had ever been.

His mother had told him that Jesus had given him his body to look after. It was his, but only on loan until he died, and he had a duty to keep it well, and clean at all times, ready for Judgement Day, when Jesus was to decide who should live with Him and who must go elsewhere. And yet his mother herself had gone to Jesus with pigeon droppings in her hair, and He had not sent her back to brush them out.

He had more than his own body to look after now. Maurice and Albert, he had cared for them more intimately than his own mother had cared for him, touching and cleaning parts his mother would not touch. Clifford ... it was a long losing battle he had with Clifford's body, perpetually renewed; it would never end. What would happen to Clifford – her head was still turned towards the Main Gate – what would happen to Clifford if Walter were ever to leave the Hospital?

June had not slept, had lain awake all night wondering which of her memories the current of electricity would blot out, had made a list in her head of priorities, which should go first, had contemplated the uniqueness of human memory, no two minds recalling the same incident in the same way, had forgotten totally the many times she had wished to be without those memories which were now in danger and which she had now begun to cherish.

She had laughed when they had said to her, 'It leaves no lasting deficit,' which made it sound like an overdraft at the Midland Bank. She had laughed, imagining old Thanatos, the death-wish, in unarmed combat with tiddly little Eros, the libido, the life-wish. 'Watch out, Eros. Your loincloth's slipping.'

Now she was watching the light grow through the gap in the curtains. It must be six o'clock, or maybe seven. She never wore a watch.

At ten thirty, they were coming to collect her, and take her over to the 'treatment' room.

The Sister had said, 'There's nothing whatsoever to be frightened of,' and June had replied, 'I give you full permission to finish me off. I'll put it in writing if you like. I'm not afraid of death, only pain.' The Sister had made a sound with her tongue and teeth, signifying that she had lost all patience.

Oh, Sister, you have lost all patients. That would be the day.

June lay on her bed, on top of the covers, staring at the lamp-shade, patterned with flowers. There were no bluebells, no snow-drops, no wild flowers. The flowers were not identifiable at all; they were an unimaginative designer's impression of flowers, simple lines and unnatural colours, confected to be mass-produced, as untruthful as people. Except, of course, for Walter.

What was she doing, still in this world, filling up space and breathing air, both of which might be put to a more productive use?

At ten twenty-four, two nurses came for her. They were the same two who had walked the man over the gravel in his bare feet. They smiled, and nodded towards her, and said, 'How are we this morning?' without desiring a reply, but she had had her answer ready, 'Ready to lose our head.' Then they had both laughed, without conviction, and one of them had said, 'Your boyfriend's outside. You'd better comb your hair.'

It was true; Walter was outside, leaning against the wall. He had been there since nine o'clock. When the nurses appeared, holding June by the arms, he stood almost to attention, and gave a half-hearted wave.

June didn't see the wave. She was concentrating on what her feet were doing. She did not wish to lose her slippers. One of the nurses shouted to Walter, 'She'll be all right tomorrow. Come and see her then.' Walter's mouth opened, and he was about to shout his thanks, but he remembered in time that he was dumb, closed his mouth again, and put his hand over it to keep it shut.

'You're early. I haven't done this one yet.' A man in a white coat spoke to the two nurses.

'We'll wait.' Along the wall was a line of chairs, and the two nurses sat down, leaving a chair between them on which June was to sit. June sat.

'This one' was a woman in her fifties, who lay on a high bed. She was quite conscious, and she turned her head towards June, opening her toothless mouth, and saying, 'You'll not want to watch this, love. Get them to walk you outside for a bit.' June noticed that the woman's false teeth and brooch were on top of the cabinet next to the high bed.

The man in the white coat, who now held a syringe, said, 'You stop being bossy, Mary, or I'll change this sharp needle for a blunt one.'

'Well, look at 'um. Lazy so-and-so's!' She referred to the two nurses.

After the injection, the man cleaned Mary's hair with spirit, and applied a white lotion to her forehead. The nurses made no move to take June away. One of them had picked up a magazine, and was reading how to mask unsightly spots or acne. The man looked at the nurses from time to time, and clearly would have preferred June not to watch, but only when he was standing with the E.C.T. machine switched on, and the headphone-like contraption in his hands did he say, 'Well, if you're not going to take her away, you'd better bring the screens.' The nurse who was not reading sighed noisily as she crossed the room and brought one hospital screen of tubular frame and green cloth, which she placed in front of June instead of around the woman in bed. The other nurse stopped reading in order to laugh.

'I don't know why you're so sensitive about her feelings. You should see her card. This one's tried to kill herself more times than you've had hot dinners.'

June could see almost as much through the gap between the steel frame and the green cloth as she could before the screen had been placed round her. It was almost as if the nurses wanted her to see what was going to happen to her.

The man placed the headphones on the front of Mary's head, each round piece covering a temple, and Mary's body went into convulsions, her legs kicking out wildly and her arms swinging and thumping the bed. The limbs came down so hard that June felt sure one of them would break. Then white foam appeared at the corner of the woman's mouth; she looked like a dog in the throes of distemper. Mickey had looked like that.

June closed her eyes, and thought of the memories she might lose, thought of her list of priorities, of her mother sitting on the door-step in her nightdress, her mother lying on the bed looking up at her without seeing her, of the grey blanket she couldn't get under, of walking and running miles back to see her, of her not being there, and of crying for days thereafter without stopping. She thought of the children's shrink who had told her, told a child who could not have been capable of understanding such a thought, that her tears were a protest, and that after them would come mourning, mourning for the lost object, and then – had he predicted Thanatos, the death wish? No, he could not have done that, would never have made such a prediction to a child, would have told her (had he?) that after a proper period of mourning the 'process of healing' could begin. But it had not begun, because all too soon came Mickey, and the woman's flying limbs now brought back the feeling and smell of Mickey so strongly that June leaned back and banged her head against the wall to stop the flow of moving pictures in her mind.

Mickey had looked like that, just like that, the last time she had seen him. They had shared a bedroom. Both were foster-children, fostered by a woman they had called 'Auntie Eva.' Mickey was a year and three months younger than June, and, as well as a room, they had shared a feeling of separateness, both being in mourning for the loss of their love. They shared each other's secrets and brushed each other's hair, whenever either of them felt the need for tears, since they had forbidden themselves tears.

Someone was holding June's head, to prevent her banging it

against the wall. The teeth of the two nurses were clenched with the effort of keeping June's head still.

Mickey had clenched his teeth; he had looked like these two faces, one on each side of her. He had galloped along the path through the field in front of her, pretending to be a horse, and she had galloped behind, holding on to the end of his school tie, pretending to be his charioteer. Then he had fallen in front of her, and she had stumbled over him, laughing, believing that he had fallen on purpose in order to wrestle with her on the ground. He had done that before.

Only, this time he didn't laugh with her, or lunge at her, rolling with her over and over in the grass. This time he shook, his limbs jerking and thumping the ground, as if he were a shot rabbit, except that a shot rabbit squeals, and Mickey made no sound at all but the sound of his limbs thrashing the ground. He had looked at her, and she had seen from his face that he was terrified, and noticed for the first time how green his eyes were, pale green like the colour of unripe apples.

Froth had come from Mickey's mouth, just as it came now from the mouth of the woman on the high bed. And June had run home, screaming – no, not home; she had never called it that – had run to Auntie Eva's house, screaming and crying and trying to get the words out to tell what had happened. They had run back together to where Mickey lay, but he had stopped struggling and kicking by the time they reached him, and lay still, with his school tie draped across his chalk-white face and covering his left eye.

She had watched Auntie Eva undo Mickey's tie and some of his shirt buttons, and lift him in her arms, pressing him against her purple cardigan, and talk to him as if he were still alive. 'Come on home, Mickey darling. Come on home for your tea. What did you do today? Did you eat your dinner? Were you a good boy?'

Auntie Eva had carried Mickey home in her arms, and June had remained where she was, looking down at the trodden grass.

She had never seen him again. She had never asked about him, and his name was never mentioned again in Aunt Eva's house. She was now Auntie Eva's only child – her only foster-child. She and Uncle Phil never asked for another.

Four weeks later at school, another boy had told her that he knew where Mickey the Mouse was buried. He said he had seen men digging a new hole, a small one, and had later watched them filling the hole in again, after people in their best clothes had walked away from it. The boy had asked her whether she had seen Mickey die, and what a dead person looked like. She had told the boy that it was just as if they'd gone to sleep, and the boy had said he did not believe her.

But Mickey had looked like that. In the end.

Her eyes opened, and she tried to focus them. She saw a lampshade, with artificial flowers painted on it. She had been asleep, but for how long? She could tell by the amount of light coming through the gap in the curtains that it must be either early evening or early morning. But which? And at what time of year?

She lifted her head from the pillow, and a sharp pain shot through her left temple. She felt heavy, too heavy to lift herself up onto an elbow. Her head ached.

There was another bed in the room, unmade. June smiled. Mickey had never made his bed. Why did she feel so heavy, so large? Was this the day she had planned to go home? Had they guessed that she intended to run away again, and had given her something to make her heavy so that she could not run?

Someone was arguing downstairs. Shouting. She could not make out the words. A woman's voice was screaming hysterically. Was it her mother? Had her mother come to take her home? Auntie Eva never shouted like that. She must get up quickly, go downstairs, see her mother, persuade her mother to take her away from here. That was why they had given her something to make her sleep.

June rolled onto her side, and reached for the floor with her left hand. The pain in her head grew worse. Someone was tugging her hair out by the roots. With her hand on the floor, she lowered her left leg to the ground, then her right hand, and finally her right leg. She was out of bed, but could not truthfully be called 'up'. Why did every action take so long?

She crawled on hands and knees towards the door. The carpet was new. There had been no carpet before; she remembered boards, dark oak-stained floorboards surrounding a square of blue lino.

There were toys too on the floor. She could not recognize them. They were not hers or Mickey's; they were for a baby.

At the door, she reached up for the handle, and used it to pull herself to her feet, but her legs buckled, and she slid to the floor again.

If only she could get downstairs where they were arguing! Even if it wasn't her mother's voice she could hear, but the voice of a stranger, she would still be able to sneak out by the back way, and run to the railway line. Then all she would have to do would be to follow it. She had not been that way before. They would not think of it. Why did her head hurt so much?

'You stupid fucking cow, I'll knock your teeth out if you don't shut up. You put her down.' Kathy was pacing the Television Lounge, the veins in her neck standing out, as she screamed at the woman who sat holding her little girl. The other woman tried to ignore Kathy, and to watch the television.

'Put her down. She's sodding well mine.'

The woman holding Kathy's little girl remained absolutely still, her right hand pressing the child's head against her chest.

'Please do as she says. Put her baby down.' A nurse, who had up until now watched in silence, was speaking.

'Not until she finds the manners to say "Please". She's not fit to have a lovely little baby like you, is she, my love?'

Kathy darted across the room, pulled the baby from the woman's arms, and flung it to the floor. It screamed, and the nurse rushed forwards. As the woman started to rise, Kathy grabbed her hair, and smashed her head against the television screen. The whole of one side of the woman's face oozed blood, where it had been torn by the jagged glass of the screen.

June had managed to get the bedroom door open and had slithered downstairs in a sitting position. She had almost reached the bottom when she heard more screams, as women ran out of the Television Lounge.

'Fucking stupid silly cow! Wouldn't listen. I warned her.' Two nurses were struggling to hold Kathy's arms. Nobody would spare time and effort to attend to the woman with the cut face. Kathy

71

broke free of the nurses, caught her little girl up in her arms, and ran past June and up the stairs.

June, who could make out only that a woman carrying something was rushing past her, shouted, 'Where are you going, Mummy? I'm here. Don't go. What are you carrying? I don't want another doll. *Please! Take me home!*' Up above, a bedroom door could be heard to slam.

When June reached the door of the Television Lounge, she saw two nurses leaning over a woman in a purple cardigan, whose face was covered in blood. The nurses were picking pieces of broken glass out of the face, and the woman sobbed as they did so. This woman was Kathy's mother.

June said, 'Why does she never talk about Mickey? Can you tell me?'

*Let's go over to the dead elm, and watch its
nerve-ends drop to the ground.*

'A blow-fly's brain weighs only point eight four milligrams. Yet its
behaviour may be richly complex.' She waited for a response. The
day was cold.

'What do you think about that?' Since, even if he had been
capable of any positive response, it could hardly have been written
on a brick, Walter shrugged his shoulders, and smiled.

'It was in *The Reader's Digest*. All human life is there.' Walter
frowned. Her voice sounded different. Louder. Sharper. She was
leaning against the wall as usual, but rubbing her knuckles over
the bricks, and bruising them. He held out his hand, and she took
it. 'Yes, hold my hand. I was so frightened yesterday. I almost came
to look for you.' He placed both his hands round her bruised hand,
and held it tight.

'Why do you never talk to me? Why won't you? Why do I
have to talk for both of us?'

Walter looked at her, puzzled and wary. She knew he could
talk. How? He took the pencil from his pocket, and searched for
a clean brick on which to write, but she took hold of the hand
which held the pencil, and said, 'No, don't do that. Please! Say
anything, anything at all. I know you can speak. You have a past;
tell me about that. What happened to your parents?'

She knew he could speak. Consequently he was not able to speak.

Slowly he returned the pencil to his pocket. She watched. She
was upsetting him, making him anxious; he might walk away, and
leave her on her own. She must be careful.

'Please, Walter.' It was unfair that he should not speak, when she had told him she knew he could. She wished to be diverted from her own life, did not wish to talk or even think about that; she had spoken to him at length about her own life, her fears, her hates, her desire for death, and now she required diversion, and his life would do. He owed her that. He had deceived her, had allowed her to believe him dumb, allowed her to say silly things while he had listened. At least, she supposed he had listened; he had usually responded in some way – a smile, a frown, a shake or a nod of the head, a word on a brick.

They had shared an unspoken understanding, unspoken because he never spoke. But if he could speak, did that not destroy the understanding? He had visited her every day, and lately they had held hands, and he had looked at her. The penetration of his stare had at first unnerved her, but now she welcomed it, needed it, needed his listening since no one else seemed to listen to her any more, needed his truth.

But if he was deceiving her, where was the truth?

Even now, he did not speak. Why not?

Other people, when she spoke, wore a mask of interest, but behind it would be busy with thoughts of their own. Even when they made notes of what she said, their attention would be given more to the making of notes than to her, than to June.

'What are you thinking about?'

Walter shrugged.

'Until the year 1770, long before you and I were born, visitors were allowed to enter a Loony Bin called Bethel for a penny a time, just to watch the antics of the lunatics. I doubt if they'd pay anything just to watch you and me standing here.'

Walter had never had a visitor, of a paying or any other sort. Why did she want him to talk?

From where they stood, they could see the bare branches of a tree. It was an elm; it was dying of Dutch Elm Disease, dead twigs still clinging to a branch, the trunk held still by its roots. Perhaps even the roots, deep underground, were decaying, but the fine delicate twigs still moved in the wind, brushed against each other, touched and momentarily held, waiting for leaves, waiting for life, which would never return to them.

'I'm a tree with Dutch Elm Disease. My nerve-ends are like twigs.

They protrude in delicate bunches, and if a strong wind comes along, they'll snap off. Meanwhile I wait.' She sighed. 'I'm thinking aloud, and expecting you to listen. It's better that you don't understand what I say. They don't in there, so why should you? The rooms inside there are too small, and the world outside here is too big. Have you noticed how I cling to this wall? Or to you?' He nodded. 'I never cross a room now; I walk round it, holding on to the furniture. I have to hold onto something, or I notice myself shaking, and that frightens me. I never used to be like that; it must be the drugs. And now there's the E.C.T.' She attempted a smile, and Walter, relieved that she seemed no longer to desire any other response, squeezed the hand he was holding.

Again she fell silent, and watched the comings and goings of nurses and patients. The nurses walked decisively, the patients less so. She watched the decisive nurses, and reminded herself that what she stood on was a stepping-stone. Soon she would be forced to take the next step. Kathy had given her little girl away for adoption, and agreed to be sterilized. This done, they had sent her home. More women had arrived, and left, and the rumour was of a shortage of beds in the Mother and Baby Unit. June now shared a bedroom with Rita, physically thirty-one, mentally and emotionally a child, who had nightmares, and kept June awake. Also the room seemed to be full of dolls and the prams of dolls and scrapbooks containing coloured pictures of the Royal Family and a general abundance of toys.

Walter was looking beyond her, wondering what, if she should insist on his speaking, he would find to say. He could see trees behind her, and grass, and a sky of blue-grey, and then a bird. It was a pigeon.

'What are you looking at?'

He pointed. 'Oh, a bird.' He was still holding her hand. 'Let's go over to the dead elm, and watch its nerve-ends drop to the ground.' Walter was uncertain. 'It's all right; I'm allowed out as far as that. I just need something to hold onto.'

Still holding her hand, he walked with her. She was a woman. He was holding her hand, and walking with her, across grass. His knowledge of women was small. He remembered the pictures of naked ladies he had been shown at Woolworth's. Those pictures had been mucky, he knew, because the word had been used to describe them, but in some way desirable. A flash of memory brought back to him what had been (though he had not known then that it was) his only sexual experience, when his willy had been stroked by a girl with whom he had been playing hide-and-seek, and he had ... it had ... he shivered. That had been on grass behind a bush. He was walking across the grass, holding June's hand. He remembered one of the trainee floorwalkers at Woolworth's, rogering his young lady against the wall of the yard, while Walter swept up litter. He was forty-six years old, and for the last ten weeks his private thoughts had been of June, with whom, hand in hand, he now walked across grass towards a dead elm.

'*I can read you like a book, my lad. Nothing you think is hidden from me.*'

That was his mother. She had always been right. In every way.

They reached the dead tree, and walked round its thick trunk so that they were hidden from the Hospital. June loosed his hand, and leaned against the tree, looking out first across the open country, then above her at the dead branches. She smiled, and said, 'Are you happy, Walter?'

Was she teasing him? Had she read his thoughts?

'You're not mad, are you?'

He shook his head.

'But is it O.K., being you?'

He thought for a while, then nodded.

'Don't you ever have complicated thoughts, or are they all simple unworried ones?'

Again he frowned, trying to guess what the right answer was, the answer which would please her. Though if he should find it, how could he utter it?

'I know you can talk. I've asked my nurses, and they've spoken to your nurses.'

There! It was out! She did know. He had not told a lie. He had never said he couldn't talk. But he had allowed her to think so.

'Most of the time you look happy – for someone in here, anyway. At least not tormented.' She was tormenting him now, and his face showed the strain of it.

She could not know about the goldfish which were darting about inside Walter's head, all the questions without answers, the thoughts interrupted by other thoughts, none of them finished, none giving him a clue as to what she wanted him to say. There was always a right answer to every question, hidden behind all the wrong answers. There was always one right answer; his mother had taught him that. All you had to do was look for it. But how could he even begin to look when his thoughts would not keep still, but flickered like fishes in a glass bowl?

'Why don't you speak to me, now that we both know you can? Is it because I'm bonkers, and you're not?'

He smiled, couldn't help doing so; for a moment the fish were still. 'Bonkers'. He liked the word. It rhymed with 'conkers'. Which were the colour of her eyes.

It was cold. The cold wind crept its way into her open-knit cardigan. She had been pulling it round herself, but now she let it go, and began instead slowly to undo the top button of her blouse. Walter's eyes moved away from her to the dead twigs of the elm beneath their feet, but he knew what she was doing.

'Give me your hand.' She took his hand, and slid it between the opening of her blouse and the inside of her bra. His hand had been inside his trouser pocket, and was warm, rough, and very large. He discovered that his hand was cupping her left breast, supporting it from beneath, while his forefinger found the nipple, and moved it from side to side.

'Don't be surprised if it leaks on you a bit. Baby John rejected his mother this morning in preference for a bottle. Sometimes they hurt when they get so full.'

June closed her eyes, and leaned back against the tree again. As she moved, Walter attempted to withdraw his hand, but she gripped his wrist, and placed the hand back where it had been. Walter glanced about him, worried that someone might see them. June said, 'Please don't look so worried. This is doing us both some good. Only a baby has been near that for many a long day. They're not the best pair of knockers in the world, but considering their neglected state, they're not too bad. What do you say?'

Walter opened his mouth, formed the words 'Thank you,' and withdrew his hand slowly.

He had spoken.

'I'm sorry if I've shocked you.'

'You were warm.'

'Inside. Yes.' A silence followed. His eyes were turned towards the ground, hers on him, watching and willing him to look at her. And when he did, she smiled, and said, 'Hello, Walter.'

'Hello ... June.'

She had not laughed at the sound his voice made.

Another silence, broken when June said, 'Now you've made *me* silent. Some would call that a miracle. It's up to you to talk now.'

'Your ...' He could not bring himself to say the word, but gestured towards the blouse.

'Breasts?'

'Like pigeons. Doves. Touching ... your ... Like smoothness. They ...' He tapped his fingers against his heart to illustrate his meaning. 'Heart ... beat.' If you wished to lift a pigeon, the left hand must be placed in the air some way above its head to attract its attention, while the right was slid underneath, touching the warm softness of the pigeon's breast. And at those moments you could feel its heart. All this, Walter knew, but his attempt to put it into words succeeded only partially.

'Thank you, Walter.'

She was serious. What he had said had pleased her. She leaned back against the trunk of the tree, her head tilted up to study the sky. It was cold, but it was clear. There was silence in her head. All those prompting, clever, destructive voices which roamed the caverns and corridors of her mind had been struck dumb by one small compliment. No witty venomous toads dropped from her tongue. It was peaceful; she enjoyed the peace, which must, of course, soon end, since it was not in the nature of peace to persist.

'Do you know about doves?'

He did; that knowledge had not gone away, during the long years at the Mental Hospital. There by the tree, grass and dead twigs below their feet, bare branches above, he told her of his father's pigeons, in all their several kinds, the White-Lace Fantails, the Russian High-Fliers, the Long-Faced English Tumblers and the Turbits, of Freda, the dropper, sent up as a decoy to bring the Russians down, who had won a prize, and of the death of Freda, her face turned to the wall and her feathers fluffed out. As they walked back across the grass to the Mother and Baby Unit, holding hands again, he looking down at her, her face turned up to his, he told her of being taken by his father to the Harrogate Show, when Amy, the Tumbler, had come third in her class, of how a small boy had tried to run away with a Black-Lace Fantail, knocked over a whole row of cages, and sent a flight of Antwerp Smerles to roost in the rafters. He told her how, after his father had been taken to Jesus, he himself had looked after the pigeons, fed them, and controlled their breeding by taking their eggs, how then Jesus had taken his mother also, and while Walter had waited to see whether Jesus would keep her or send her back, he had only been able to look after the pigeons by moving them into his mother's bedroom, where Linda and Enid, Fantails, had done battle with their own reflections in the dressing-room mirror, Norman, a Russian, had occupied the pink basketwork chair, Edna and William, Turbits, had used the lampshade as a swing, Marge and Lionel, Tumblers, had copulated on the full-length mirror, and all had shat profusely on his mother's hair.

He had brushed his mother's hair, and tried to keep it free of pigeon droppings, and she had lain for days beneath a purple counterpane on which had been embroidered a gold dragon breathing out green and scarlet flames, and in the end Jesus had made no decision at all, or at least none which he had communicated to Walter, but a Social Worker, a doctor and a policeman had come, and taken Walter away from his mother and from the pigeons, so that he had not seen any of them again since, but assumed that his mother must, after all, be with Jesus, since otherwise she would not have left him in this place.

He talked, and she listened. They walked round the Mother and Baby Unit five times. Words spilled out of Walter's mouth, one memory following another, as if they had been locked up for too long. Then Walter noticed the clock on the central tower, and said that he would be late; he had to help with the handing out of tea. And June said, 'Will you come and see me again?' knowing that he would, and Walter asked whether it was all right for him to come at the same time tomorrow, knowing that it was, and June smiled and nodded, and Walter ran off across the grass, leaving her standing on the concrete he had laid, one hand against the line of

79

bricks in the wall behind her, the other touching the buttons of her blouse.

His voice, if she allowed herself to think of it, was rather like a fart in a bath of soapy water, but there was a comfort in him. He brought peace.

5

A man in a white car stopped and asked me if I knew the way to Oldham

'Will you come with me? Tonight?' She had turned her head to face him, and he could see his own reflection in each of the dark shiny brown conkers which were her eyes.

They were going to move her into the main building. The Mother and Baby Unit was not intended to deal with the problems of long-stay patients. Most of its mothers, if not positively elated, at least less depressed than when they came, were returned to what was called 'the home environment', to be visited by Social Workers; they became out-patients, and attended an Out-Patients' Clinic. Some few, who did not respond to treatment at the Mother and Baby Unit, would require to be separated for a while, for just a while, from the babies with which they could not cope, and would receive more intensive treatment in a hospital environment. This would be for their own good and for their babies' good. The babies would be well looked after while the mothers were receiving this more intensive treatment, and in the end, when the mothers were well again, they would be reunited.

June was, of course, quite free to refuse this treatment. She was not free to remain forever at the Mother and Baby Unit, to break its rules and become its first long-stay patient, but she was free to leave it and to return home. She was free to go wherever she wished, but not (again each freedom brings its own curtailment), not to take Baby John with her. They were sure at the Mother and Baby Unit that June, as an intelligent and responsible woman, would agree that she could not be allowed to take Baby John with her, since, in her present disturbed and depressed state, she might harm him. She had abandoned him once, and attempted suicide. They must assume that, lacking the benefits of more intensive treatment, she would be likely to do so again.

So?

So, if she were to refuse the more intensive treatment and discharge herself, she would not be allowed to keep the baby. The Social Services would apply for a Court Order, to take Baby John into care.

'Will you come with me? I can't do it on my own. I need you to help me.'

She was not stupid; she knew a trick worth two of theirs. They might apply for a Court Order, but if she did not appear, the case could not come to Court; it must be adjourned. Adjourned and adjourned. No magistrate would take a child from its mother without at least hearing what its mother had to say. The Social Services would have the care of Baby John while she was gone; that could not be avoided, whichever choice she made, but it would not be official, it would not be Care, not the subject of a Court Order; they could not, as they had done to June herself, place him with foster-parents or into a Home; he would still be hers.

Only she could not do it alone. She must have help. Walter must help her.

'I've got to get away. Will you come with me? I can't do it on my own.'

Minutes passed. He wanted to tell her that the forbidding Victorian building in which he himself had lived for nineteen years wasn't as frightening as she thought, but though the regime had changed much since he had entered it nineteen years ago, though one grew used to it, she was no more one of Jesus's Mistakes than he was; he knew that; it would not do for her.

He wanted to help her. They had talked together, as he had talked to nobody else. They had held hands, and were holding hands now. His hand had held her breast. But he had responsibilities. Also, during all his time there, he had never broken one of the Hospital's rules, and did not know what would happen if he did. He was a trusty. They trusted him.

82

Her neck was so fine, like a female dove's. He could have made her a necklace of his thumbs and forefingers.

'I . . . can't. Sorry.'

Her lips were dark and dry from the cold, and puckered where the mouth-drying properties of anti-depressant drugs had caused them to split and then heal. She held his hand against her skirt, so that his warm palm was against her body, and the tips of his fingers just touched the mount of Venus. He closed his eyes, and attempted to stop the goldfish darting about inside his head. Mixed with the flashing gold were the coloured lights which moved over the faces of the jigging patients and over the face of Clifford, turning his large open mouth, with its thick lips and suspended saliva, purple. And overlapping with Clifford and the lights and the goldfish there was Mike, the trainee floorwalker, moving his hand up and down inside the knickers of the girlfriend whom he pressed against the wall of Woolworth's yard, while Walter swept up toffee papers and empty cigarette packets and dirt.

'I've got to look after Clifford.'

Beyond the wrought-iron spears of the Main Gate was the road, which led to the world he only saw during walks. In that world there were buses, cars, lorries, people who ate with knives and forks instead of spoons, and wore trousers with buttons and flies for which they were themselves responsible. People in that world slept alone or in pairs, as his parents had done, in small rooms which didn't stink of piss and shit. People in that world made babies as freely as pigeons did, instead of exciting themselves into handkerchiefs or toilet paper and hiding the evidence in their pockets to be flushed down the W.C. later, flushing away what had been given by Jesus to make babies.

'They'll find someone else to look after Clifford.'

'And the others. I help them.'

'They'll find someone else to look after the others. You've done your share. What if Clifford died soon? You'd have wasted your life for nothing. What would your mother say if she knew you'd wasted your life?'

His mother could see him now. She would be looking down at him, with Jesus. She knew what he did with the body he was supposed to be keeping clean for Judgement Day.

He moved his hand slowly away from her stomach. He wanted above all else to help her. If they ran away, they would be caught, he supposed, and punished. He could not bear that she should be punished alone.

'Please help me.'

'I . . . can't.'

He knew he would have to help her. And she knew he would.

Since it was Saturday evening, Walter washed, and put on his best clothes to go to the dance in the Main Hall as usual. He had been lucky enough to have found two plastic carrier bags in Sister's office, and had filled them with his belongings. He had tied the bags to the underside of Clifford's wheelchair, and draped a blanket over the chair while he had bathed and dressed Clifford ready for the dance. Clifford's eyes had followed Walter's, as Walter had applied Brylcreem to Clifford's hair, and experimented with five different partings. While Walter cut Clifford's fingernails, Clifford watched. On most days, Clifford seemed uninterested in what was done to him for his own cleanliness and comfort. On most days, his eyes only made contact with Walter's at the moment of waking, when it seemed that he required reassurance that Walter was still there. Once, when Walter had been placed in another ward because of flu, tales of Clifford's misdeeds and lack of cooperation had filtered through to Walter, and Walter had been pleased.

Walter had become expert at interpreting the tiny changes of expression which flickered across Clifford's face. He knew what he could expect to see if he were about to lead some of the other patients out on a walk, and leave Clifford behind. He knew the expression in Clifford's eyes when Clifford wished to thank him.

Most of the time, what Walter did for Clifford was taken for granted, since he did so much. What Clifford most liked was physical contact, his hands rubbed, or, as Walter always did when drying them, his feet gently stroked. He liked toffees or chocolates, but took them as part of his rations, without thanks or acknowledgement. He liked food and sleep. Many people might be able to recognize pleasure or displeasure in Clifford, but only Walter was able to mark degrees of feeling, and where others might see only physical expressions having to do with the breaking of wind or with the motor reaction to a scratch, itch or tickle, only Walter knew that such physical expressions also contained – and even communicated to those who could read the code – thoughts. Walter knew that Clifford was capable of something else besides thought, and if he had known its name might have called it by that name, 'intuition'. It was because of this something else that he was unable to make contact with Clifford's eyes this Saturday evening; he was afraid of what might be communicated by that contact. If Clifford were to sense what was going to happen, he might start to play up, make noises, stamp his feet on the footrest of the chair, and so draw attention to them both. Partly for this reason, and partly in order to clear his own thoughts, Walter did what he had often done when alone with Clifford. He spoke his thought aloud.

'I don't have to. I can always change my mind. I don't have to do what she said.' He knew, even as he said it, that he was not convincing himself, but hoped that it would convince Clifford and forestall tantrums.

At the door of the Main Hall, he showed his and Clifford's membership cards, took five pence out of his own pocket and five pence out of Clifford's hand, and gave it to the man on the door. Even though they had been coming here for many years, it was important to show their cards and do things right. This was the only Club of which he and Clifford were members. Outside the Hospital gates, he would not be a member of anything.

He wheeled Clifford over to their usual place, and sat down. They were early, as always; the music had not begun, and some of the abler patients played skittles in the centre of the hall. Clifford's eyes still watched him. He forced himself to look into those eyes and to speak to Clifford. He touched Clifford's hand, and, smiling, said, 'Are you all right?' The eyes stared back. 'We've come to the Dance, see?' He gestured perfunctorily towards some of the other club members, and Clifford's eyelids flickered for a moment, but he did not look away from Walter.

When all membership cards had been examined, and sufficient time allowed for the accommodation of latecomers, the man on the door would leave his post, and would join in the dancing. Then the members would be allowed to come and go as they wished. Some might even leave as couples, to hide in dark corners of the hospital, and kiss. Walter had never done so, but he knew that it was done.

From the beginning of that period of freedom to the ending of the Dance, when freedom would also end, and the members return to being patients, there was a time during which he must act. It would be dark outside. He would be able to push Clifford in his wheelchair over the neatly trimmed grass to the Special Activities Unit, where there was a room with a mattress laid out on the floor, kept for violent or self-mutilating patients who required calming music and observation. The spare key for the Special Activities Unit was kept hidden behind a loose brick; this practice had obtained ever since three members of staff had left the hospital, all forgetting to hand in their keys to the Unit, which had resulted in the Unit's being locked, with no key available to release a trainee therapist and four large and disturbed patients. Walter knew the hiding-place because he was a trusty, and one of his many duties was to escort difficult patients from their wards to the Special Activities Unit.

Here he was a trusty. Outside he would not be anything. This was not a thought to be spoken aloud.

Clifford would be safe in the Special Activities Unit. He would sleep on a mattress, and be discovered in the morning. He would miss breakfast, but it would be made up to him.

Walter would allow half an hour after the main lights of the Hall had been turned off, and only the circles of coloured lights illuminated the dancers' faces. There would be less chance then of anyone's seeing them leave. Also he wanted to watch for the last time the faces changing from pink to amber to green and back to blue.

He listened to the loud music. His thoughts danced, not confusingly, but in alarming order. What was the real nature of the world outside the gates? Here he was liked, had a place, and was given privileges. Outside he would have nothing except what was in the two plastic carrier bags tied to the underside of Clifford's wheelchair.

For nineteen years he had concentrated on doing well whatever he had been asked to do, first in the hope that they would realize their mistake, and let him go, and later because it had become a habit. Out there, what would they ask him to do, and how well would he be able to do it?

June had asked him to help her get away. She could not manage without his help.

The time for leaving was growing nearer. He would allow ten more minutes, just to be sure. He was afraid.

June paced the room she shared with Rita. Both babies, her own Baby John and Rita's Robin Christopher, were asleep. Her suitcase had been packed all day. She had explained four times to Rita that she was to be transferred to another part of the hospital. It had to work.

Rita sat on her bed, cutting pictures of animals out of women's magazines and sticking them into a scrapbook with flour-and-water paste. Since she had lost the brush, she applied the paste with two fingers, wiping them clean on her Winceyette nightdress. Although she was thirty years old, Rita still wore white ankle-socks and a hair-slide in the shape of a butterfly.

Downstairs, at a desk near the door, reading the latest Denise Robins, there was a Staff Nurse. To use the fire-escape, one had to break a glass panel and pull a handle which caused alarm bells to sound all over the building. No way out there.

June could hear dance music. Of course – it was Saturday night. Would Walter have gone to the Dance? She opened her suitcase, and stared down at her trousseau for this elopement. What was there was all she owned now.

'Do you like ducks?'

'Yes, with orange sauce.'

Rita made a noise and also a face, both intended to signify repulsion of eating meat and fruit at the same time. Rita's mother had kept her in the clothes she had been wearing as a girl of sixteen, simply letting them out with patches of different materials as Rita grew larger. Since she was a skilful sempstress, these patches had always seemed somehow to be part of the dress, but Rita's pregnancy (which she would in any case not accept as a fact) defeated her, so that she had simply let in a large piece of scarlet taffeta to the front of all Rita's still wearable dresses, so that now Rita seemed always to be wearing a bloodstained apron over the offending spot.

87

It was dark outside. June rested the side of her face against the cold window, and looked towards the lights of the Main Hall. Surely he would have left by now.

'What are you looking at?'

'Fairies at the bottom of the garden.'

'Are they dancing in a ring?'

'No, they're drinking Guinness, and telling dirty stories.'

'When Mummy worked at the Mill, the old lady next door let me do this every day.'

'What?'

'Cut out pictures, and paint.' Rita watched the white sticky paste roll from her fingertips to her wrist, and recited, 'Pretty girl. Box of paints. Sucked her brush. Joined the saints.' The point of her tongue jabbed tentatively at the white gook. Noticing the expression on June's face, she said, 'It's only flour and water. I like it.'

Rita had a mental age of seven and a half. Since her father's death, when she was six, she had lived with her mother in a cottage between Rawtenstall and Birtle. Rita's mother had worked on the same six old-fashioned looms for twenty-five years until the introduction of automatic looms had led to early retirement. Her belief was that the decline of the Lancashire cotton industry was directly due to automation. Her life with Rita had been one of peace and routine. Neither she nor Rita would accept the fact that physically Rita had grown into womanhood.

When would the dratted girl stop cutting, sticking and sucking, and go to sleep? The other women in the Unit had already begun to complain about the holes in *Woman* and *Woman's Own*.

'Do you want to know how I came to get Robin Christopher?'

'No. Go to sleep.' She wished she could be certain Walter would come.

Clifford's wheelchair had started to squeak, and Walter was conscious that the wheels and his own best shoes were leaving marks on the trim lawn. He wished he could be certain that what he was doing was right.

The key was where he had expected to find it, and the door opened without too much noise. But what should he do about the light? If he switched it on, it might be noticed. If he left it off, Clifford might become alarmed at being undressed in the dark.

Walter stood in the darkness, his hands on Clifford's shoulders, and tried to remember the lay-out of the Special Activities Unit. When his eyes had adjusted to the darkness, he pushed the wheel-chair towards the corner where screens surrounded the mattresses on the floor.

He found a mattress by feeling for it, and began to remove first Clifford's jacket, then his tie and shirt. Clifford mustn't be allowed to sleep in his best suit.

There was just enough light for Walter to see Clifford's eyes, still watching him in everything he did. He had forgotten to bring pyjamas, and in the nineteen years he had dressed and undressed Clifford he had not known him to possess underclothes. The room was warm enough, but the feel of woollen blankets next to his skin would be yet another strange experience for Clifford, and might induce perturbation.

Shoes and socks off. Walter lifted Clifford's upper body from the wheelchair, and supported it with one shoulder while he undid the loose-fitting trousers and manoeuvred them to the floor. This was the moment Clifford chose (if choice came into it) to urinate. The warm piss splashed down onto Walter's hands and the sleeves of his jacket, onto the trousers round Clifford's feet, the cheap hair-cord carpet and the edge of the mattress on which Walter was about to place him. Walter withdrew his hands quickly, and placed them on Clifford's hips above the line of fire.

Like two Saturday night drunks, the two men leaned against each other, as they waited for Clifford's bladder to empty. How could he have forgotten? Clifford was always taken to the lavatory before being put to bed.

Walter lowered his right hand, and shook out the last few drops as instinctively and habitually as he would shake his own penis so as to avoid stains on his underpants. It was just one of the many physical actions he performed for Clifford without thinking about them. Only now he was thinking about them, because today wasn't like the other six thousand, nine hundred and thirty-five days he had held Clifford's 'private thing' in his hand.

Why, after all those hundreds of times, should he feel strange now about touching Clifford? Clifford wasn't watching him any longer, couldn't see Walter's face; he was leaning over, waiting for the pyjamas which Walter had forgotten to bring to be placed upon him. He was staring through the darkness to the mattress, and adding saliva to the already wet trousers around his feet.

Walter's feelings were too complicated to be sorted out. He did not wish to remember that this would be the last time he would see Clifford. He must not allow himself to become sad. He had made a promise to June; it must be kept. His mother and Jesus would be watching to make sure he kept it.

The thought which pushed him into further action was that Clifford might assume that Walter was waiting for him to relieve himself more fully, and might, if he were not laid quickly down upon the mattress, present him with a going-away present he did not wish.

Clifford lay on his side on the sheetless mattress, and allowed Walter to place two blankets over him, tucking them under the mattress for warmth. He was again watching, but showed no other sign that matters were not as they had always been.

Walter fussed around the mattress on his knees, unable to accept that all he had to do here was now done. His next task, which was to locate a ladder, would be more difficult.

He looked into the watching eyes, and sighing said, 'I've got to go.' And then, knowing that what he hoped was impossible, waited for Clifford by some miracle to reply, to tell him that what he was doing was right, perhaps even to smile. He wondered if he should find Clifford's hand under the blanket, and shake it, or touch his face. He waited, unable to decide, feeling the sadness he had promised himself not to feel until slowly, more slowly than Walter had ever seen him do so before, Clifford closed his eyes and their glimmer of white could no longer be seen in the dark.

Walter stood, and walked out of the Special Activities Unit.

'A man in a white car stopped, and asked me if I knew the way to Oldham. I said I didn't. I was picking flowers. It was very hot. I remember that.'

If Walter came while Rita was still awake, they would have to bind and gag her.

'What are you listening for?'

'Nothing. Go to sleep.' June continued to walk, and to touch the wall.

'He bought me some cashew nuts and brown ale. I never had beer before. It's very nice, isn't it?'

She had pointed out the window. She had said slowly, spelling it out, 'Third window from the left.' She had not asked whether he knew left from right, but he couldn't have climbed up to the wrong one; she'd been watching.

'He said he'd drive me home. Then he stopped. He said it was hot. He took off his jacket. It wasn't a proper road he stopped on. It was a track.'

He had promised. Given his word. He had said, 'I promise,' and his voice had sounded like a fart in a bath of soapy water.

'He started tickling me. I'm very ticklish. We were giggling, and tickling each other all over.'

He had given her his dead mother's diamanté ear-rings, vulgar replicas of the Eiffel Tower.

'The door was locked. I tried to climb over the back seat to get away from him. He was being naughty. It hurt. Like what dogs do to lady dogs. He had his hands up here, squeezing my chest. I had to cry. Then suddenly he made ever such a funny grunting noise, and just stopped.'

His oily hair stank of lavender brilliantine. She had no idea men still used it.

'Then we listened to music on the car radio. The second time, it didn't hurt at all.'

Even if she could climb from the window without a ladder, she was frightened of the fields.

'But that was outside on the grass. We'd gone outside because it was hot. We laid on the grass, and he stroked me all over, and put his hand between my legs.'

'You really must go to sleep, Rita. Think of what your Mummy will say if I tell her you stayed awake all night telling me about the travelling salesman who fucked you in so many different positions until you were sore.'

91

'That's a rude word. Only nasty people say it.'

'Well, I am nasty. Nasty and desperate, so go to sleep.' He wouldn't come at all now. She'd been wrong. He would be too frightened of the world outside, too scared of what he believed 'they' might do to him if he were caught.

Perhaps he had been unable to find a ladder.

'Tell me a story.'

'No. Go to sleep.'

'How did you get Baby John?'

'I advertised in *Exchange and Mart*.'

'Read to me.'

'No, it's too late.'

'Shall we play Snakes and Ladders? Just one game.' June beat her clenched fist against her thigh, and let out a gasp of frustration.

'Mummy said I should have taken down his car number. The police would have beaten him up.'

Then she heard it. Just a noise. Her heart skipped a beat. Suddenly she was scared, scared and excited. The noise happened again. It was, it must be, the sound of a ladder being rested on a window-ledge.

'What's that?'

'What?'

'Noise.' Rita was pointing to the window.

'It's nothing.' Rita was getting out of bed. June grabbed her. 'Yes, well, it is something actually.' She was thinking fast, holding onto Rita with one hand and reaching for a pillow from her own bed with the other. 'It's a game.' She hoped she was sounding joky and relaxed; she certainly didn't feel so. 'A surprise for you, Rita.' Rita's expression was more of suspicion than of surprise. 'A secret game I'm going to teach you.'

Rita was backing away as far as the length of June's arm would allow. 'You're hurting my arm.'

'I'll bet you've never heard of this game, have you?'

Rita moved her head very slowly from side to side. June had released her arm, and was ripping the pillowcase down its seams. There were more noises from outside. Walter was climbing the ladder, which had squeaky rungs. The two women watched each other. June knew that Rita might scream at any minute, and would certainly do so if she saw Walter's face pressed against the other side of the window.

Holding the pieces of pillowcase, June advanced slowly on Rita. As she advanced, she smiled in what she hoped was a reassuring manner.

'What's that noise?'

'That's a friend, come to collect me.'

'Why?'

'I'm doing what all those girls do in the school stories. I'm running away.' June was close now. She had twisted one piece of the pillowcase to make a gag.

'I can't read long story books, only comics.'

At this moment, Walter's face appeared at the window. Rita's pointing finger shot out, and her mouth dropped open to form a scream. June pounced. The piece of pillowcase was stuffed into the middle of that mouth, and Rita's head forced down, so that the ends of the cloth could be tied at the back of her neck. Rita was a well-developed thirty-year-old, and sticky with paste. June was reminded of women wrestling in mud, and wondered how the travelling salesman in the white car had got away with his balls still hanging where they should.

She had left the window slightly open. She dared not release Rita, but signalled to Walter to come in. Together they tied Rita's hands with the rest of the pillowcase, then her legs with the cord of her dressing-gown, and strapped a leather belt round her knees. Though Walter could not understand why all this was being done, he was much more adept at doing it, having had plenty of experience in the restraint of agitated patients.

Rita would be found in time. She would not choke, or if she did, that could not be helped. A moment's hesitation. Would she, in fact, choke? No, she would not; she was a survivor. June picked up her case. Walter preceded her down the ladder. She switched the light out. The elopement had begun.

When they were both on the ground, she helped him lift the ladder away from the wall and lay it on the grass where it would be less conspicuous. He was no more burdened by worldly goods than she. Less so; all he had was in two carrier bags. She took his hand in hers, and said, 'I was beginning to get worried, but you kept your promise. I shan't forget.'

They staggered hand in hand over the clayey wet furrows of a field, she carrying her suitcase, he his carrier bags. When they reached the other side, they stood for a moment by the hedge, trying to get breath back and to decide which way would lead them to a gap or gate. Walter took June's suitcase, realizing that he should have offered to carry it from the beginning, for she was clearly exhausted, bent double taking in deep gasps of air, and holding onto his arm for support.

'I'm sorry.'

'What for?'

'Not carrying your suitcase. It's heavy.'

June stretched herself up on her toes, and kissed the side of his face. 'It's all I've got in the world now.' She could just make out the outline of his beaky nose and the long jaw and the flat cap he always wore. 'It's all I have in the world now, except you.' She stroked the cheek she had just kissed, using the back of her mud-covered fingers, and was sure it was wet. His cheeks were wet. He was crying. Walter was crying.

For once in her life, she had made someone happy. Usually she had the opposite effect on people. (It never occurred to her that these might not be tears of joy.) They started walking again, he with the suitcases now balancing the carrier bags. They had chosen to walk to the right out of instinct.

Walter was now hers, and she was his, a heavy responsibility for them both.

PART THREE

Walter and June Liberated

1

Whatever happened from now on, as long as he could be with her, he would remain happy

It was September. They would go south with the migrating birds. To the north there was nothing except rough country, depressed towns and Scotland. Scotland wouldn't welcome them.

To the west there was very little land before one reached the coast. Fleetwood, Southport and Morecambe would all be counting the season's takings, covering the turnstiles, pulling down the shutters on the Bingo stalls, and sweeping up the last few grains of sand from the floors of Guest House bedrooms. Only Blackpool, with its flickering illuminations, would be making a last attempt to squeeze a few more pence from the weekend motorists and cut-rate coach-trippers, jammed together and overheating, on the Golden Mile to see the Lights. Blackpool wouldn't welcome them.

South. It would be easy to navigate. June looked at the sky, and made arbitrary identifications of the Pole Star, the Plough and the Bear. They would turn left at the next crossroads.

They walked, counting the telegraph poles. At every tenth pole, they rested for the time it took June to count a hundred. They turned and turned again, lost the telegraph poles, and counted cat's-eyes, resting after each hundred pairs. Then, finding a road too narrow for cat's-eyes, counted strides, resting after each hundred and fifty. Since June's strides were shorter than Walter's, he had to skip from time to time so as to match her.

The moon raced along, always keeping just ahead of them, as if it were their own very personal usherette's torch, leading them closer and closer to the large Cinemascope screen, before which they would sit, heads back, necks aching, holding hands and

97

watching the garishly coloured world in which no one was ever really hurt, and the failures always came out on top. Meanwhile, in order to continue to hold June's hand as he walked, Walter was forced to cross behind her every time he needed to change her heavy suitcase from one hand to the other. June carried his two plastic bags, which were considerably lighter.

June felt high, light-headed, enjoying her new-found freedom. She had brought no tranquillizers. Who needed them? She knew from experience that anti-depressants took nine or ten days before they began to make any effect. Logically, therefore, they should be effective for nine or ten days after she had ceased to take them. Anyway, to be walking along a road under a sky full of stars, with any and every possibility open to her, was too pleasant, too exciting to be spoiled by caution or logic. 'Logic!' she shouted towards the sky. 'Logic is what you make it.' Walter, who was embarrassed by this loud shouting, and fearful that it might attract attention and pursuit, ran quickly behind her, changing the suitcase to his other hand and using his free hand to hold as still as he could at least one of the two hands with which she was swinging the plastic bags which contained all his worldly goods.

'Logic is for fools who need their foolishness explained to them.' The carrier bags were safe now, but June's voice remained loud and shrill. This was not an aspect of her personality which she had previously shown to Walter, and he was worried by it.

'Logic could never begin to explain why I feel like bursting with happiness, because my feet are blistered, and I'm cold and wet, nor why I'm here on this particular bit of road with you to hold onto.' Happiness filled her to overflowing, and she skipped along the road for a hundred yards, leaving Walter behind to pick up the knife, fork, spoon and shoe-cleaning brush which fell from the carrier bags as she twirled them.

Then she was standing still in the middle of the road, head back, watching the wisps of grey cloud rush past, between her and the moon. Her voice was soft and gentle, as if singing to a sleeping child.

> 'There was a man
> Went round the town,
> To hunt a supper up and down.

98

> *The bill of fare*
> *He runneth through*
> *To see what his six cents would do.'*

Walter reached her. He stood beside her, with one arm around her shoulder. She turned her face to him, and he saw that her face was wet. 'Why did you come with me? Why did you lumber yourself with a stretcher-case like me?' No answer. Walter pressed his lips against her forehead. 'It's all illogical. Logic has been ill for some time, requiring rest and quiet and no questions asked of it.'

They began to walk on again slowly, Walter's arm still around her shoulder. 'I love the night-time, as long as I'm not alone. I love the thought that all these fields and bushes are teeming with night-life, just like the West End of London. Foxes, stoats and weasels, preening themselves to go out and dazzle the punters. Badgers trying desperately to remember their kerb-drill, as they dodge the hooting taxis in the Charing Cross Road. You've never been to our lovely old capital, have you?' Walter shook his head. 'We'll go. That's where we're going. I haven't seen much of it either, not since I was a student. We'll see it properly – not one of your quick dashes round the Tate, and being groped front and rear by Persian teenagers in Madame Tussaud's. No rush for us. No expensive tourists' rip-offs. We'll sit and stare. Ships, towers, domes, theatres and temples lie, open unto the fields and to the sky; all bright and glittering in the smokeless air.'

Then it hit them. The heavens opened, and heavy raindrops almost the size of hailstones struck the tops of their heads with such force that for a few seconds they were stunned. Then they began to run, not knowing where they were running to. 'Sodding Wordsworth !' June shouted. 'He's watering his sodding daffodils. Sod doesn't realize it's the wrong time of year.'

Twenty minutes later, they were running breathlessly between the gravestones of a churchyard. June twisted and pushed at the heavy iron ring which opened the grey weathered oak door. It opened, and they were out of the drenching rain. 'God !' June wrang out the edge of her coat, and watched the rainwater pour from it onto the stone floor.

'Pity it's not a Catholic church. We could light all the candles, and get some warmth.' The echo of their footfalls on the stone floor and the sound of June's voice ringing round the church brought into Walter's mind his first day at the Hospital, and his walk with the Social Worker down the half mile of corridor, in which old men and some less old stood at corners, waiting, hugging themselves and talking to themselves. Waiting, all waiting. Much later, when Walter had thought it all over, he had realized that the only possible eventuality for which the men could be waiting must be death. Churches reminded Walter of death. His mother had said, 'They're the nearest we can get to Jesus while we're on this earth.'

He watched June slip off both her wet shoes and hang them on two posts at the end of a pew. She was thirsty. She went to look at the font, but all it contained was dust and fallen plaster.

'They haven't christened anyone here for years. Either they're all barren or on the pill.' Walter was sure they would be heard. At any moment, a door would open, and they would be told to leave. The flowers on the altar table were fresh; the large brass eagle which supported the lectern shone like gold. Certainly it had been polished this week. Walter knew about brass and the polishing of it.

'Don't suppose they keep the sacramental wine on the premises.' Walter's clothes and boots had formed a puddle on the short stretch of threadbare carpet between the pews. 'No? Ah, well, thanks a lot. Big G. I'll do the same for you some day.'

When June stopped shouting, it was not a silence which followed, but the quietness in which the ticking of a clock seemed exaggeratedly loud. 'Did I do that. Did I start the clock?' She pointed at a bright red fire extinguisher hanging on the wall. 'Hey ! What do they want with a fire extinguisher? Maybe they think Satan will drop in to sign the Visitors' Book.' She laid her wet coat flat, supported by the backs of three pews.

Walter knew that his mother would have said that the loud ticking of the clock was to remind the congregation that their days were numbered. He wished to unlace his boots, which had walked and run a long way, but instead he stared upwards towards the dark rafters. At any moment, Jesus and his mother would see them. They would have heard June shouting in God's House. There would need to be a great many trumpets in Heaven to drown out June's voice.

June had taken off some of her wet clothing, and was pacing about, trying to find something with which to dry herself. Walter waited. His feet were wet. He and June had run through deep puddles without noticing them, while rain had run down their backs, beneath their collars. He had never been out in rain so heavy, and now he stood in a church, soaked and waiting to know what he should do. In the Hospital, he had known what to do; the range of permissible activities was not large, was easily learned, and did not change. Here, in the real world, things happened so much more quickly and could not be predicted. He was forty-six. How much time would it take him to learn how to be like the people of the real world? Would he always be waiting, forever waiting for someone to tell him what to do? He would stand out, look odd. It was a mistake. He had made it. A mistake.

June had found a long red velvet curtain hanging near the organ, and was busy unhooking the brass curtain rings.

It would not be as simple as leading a crocodile of Jesus's Mistakes through the town, and remembering where it was safe to take them. Now there would be hundreds of decisions to make every day. He had not been away from the Hospital more than three hours, and already he was frightened, cold, shivering and wet. His boots might just as well have been made from cheap cardboard for all the protection they had given to his feet. And they were muddy, soiling the floor of God's House.

June now had the curtain down from its rail, and was using it as a beach-robe. She undressed beneath it, removing all her wet clothes, and hanging them to dry where the curtain had been.

Walter's boots looked like two large dollops of over-broiled pig's liver, and as he moved his feet inside them, water squelched through the seams. It was no good; he had made a mistake, and would have to go back. He had let Clifford and the rest down for nothing. In the real world, he couldn't take care of himself.

'Hey! Come on, love. Get out of that wet suit.' June stood before him, naked beneath the red velvet curtain, which trailed on the floor behind her. She lifted her arms to rub Walter's hair, releasing the scent of lavender brilliantine like incense into the air of the holy place. Walter kept his eyes focused on a piece of the floor.

'What's made you so sad?' She waited, wiping his face, neck and ears dry. 'Come on. Tell me.' She wiped, and waited. 'Is it me? Have I upset you? I'm overexcited and happy. I don't mean to be silly. Is it that?'

Walter kept his eyes down, and shook his head.

'Well, what is it, then?' She undid his tie, and top button of his shirt. 'Give me your jacket.' She slid the lapels of his jacket back over his shoulders, and undid the three buttons. Then she moved behind him to pull at the sleeves until it was off, and she draped it over the back of a pew.

'Do you know much of the Bible, Walter?' It seemed easier to shake his head. 'There's a bit that says, "In my Father's house are many mansions. There have I prepared a place for you". I think he knew we were coming, don't you?' No reply. 'Might have turned the heating on, though.'

Walter stood like a dray horse, pawing the ground while its owner removes harness, bridle and reins. He allowed June to unlace each of his boots, and lifted each foot in turn while she pulled the boots off. 'Aren't you going to tell me what's wrong?' His shirt and vest were now off, and she wiped his torso and arms slowly with the velvet curtain, so that Walter must have seen her nakedness if his eyes had not been tightly shut.

She placed her hand on the buckle of his belt, the backs of her fingers against the skin of his stomach. Walter did not move. She shivered, then stood on her toes, pressing her dry chapped lips first against his forehead, then against his left ear, into which she whispered, 'Please put your arms around me. We're both cold.'

Walter did as he was asked, sliding his arms slowly beneath the velvet curtain and under June's arms to touch her naked back. His eyes remained closed.

'May I take these off?' She waited, and after a moment, he nodded slowly. She undid the buckle of the belt and the top button of his trousers, and slowly lowered the zip, placing her hand inside.

At the moment June touched what his mother would never touch, almost the whole of Walter's weight came forward onto her, and sinking his face against her right shoulder, he sobbed and blubbered, making sounds she had never heard before, and amongst all those gasps and groans and cries and wails which seemed to come from low down in his chest, she understood three words, 'Don't . . . know . . . how.'

He had only ever seen pigeons making love, and his mother had said it would never happen to him. The pigeons had billed, the female putting her beak into the male's mouth, their heads moving from side to side, rocking each other in a shared pleasure. Perhaps tongues were to be used as beaks. He had never seen pigeons do what Mike at Woolworth's had done.

Now he felt warm breath against his mouth, and small dry lips were pressed against his own lips, and cold fingers moved the hair on the back of his neck up and down and round, twisting it into little curls. His neck tingled, and his spine shivered.

'I'll show you.' She reached for his hands, and drew him down onto the stone floor beside her.

Parted from the rocking kiss, the female bird crouched low, tapping one of her wings rhythmically, while the male circled and strutted, with his chest out and his tail lowered, scraping the ground, then stopping to preen the crouching female's neck feathers, ruffling them gently with his beak as the crouching bird's eyelids moved upwards, covering her eyes from below, signifying an extreme enjoyment.

June moved the tips of her fingers over Walter's face, lifting his chin. His eyes were still closed. June said, 'Look at me, Walter. Don't pretend it's not happening.'

He looked into her eyes. They were dark like conkers. He saw himself reflected in them, saw his own face, his own ugliness, saw what had caused children and adults to laugh. But June had never laughed at his face, never stifled her giggles with one hand over her mouth, while she pointed at him with the other. Now her hands were moving over his face, neck and ears, exciting him.

The male bird had strutted round its mate yet again, drawing out his anticipation of what was to come, before carefully standing on the crouching bird's back, flapping his wings, partly to balance himself and partly to make himself lighter.

June was pulling Walter on top of her, lifting and spreading

103

her legs. She was small, and he was heavy, and had no wings to lighten him. He would crush her.

Walter placed his hands on the cold stone floor of the church, supporting most of his own weight, while June held his private thing in her bony fingers, feeling the size and weight of it, then slithered towards it, lifting her hips to meet it.

She gasped, and bit her lower lip, as the knob of it entered her, digging her fingernails into the sides of his buttocks to stop him going any deeper. She slowed down her breathing in order to relax her body, then, after a few such breaths, leaned her head back, smiled to reassure him, and whispered the word, 'Gently.'

Supporting himself with one arm, he placed his right hand over the breast she had made him touch as they had stood beneath the dead elm. Now he could see as well as feel it, and he repeated what he had done before, cupping his hand underneath it, as he would if it were really a dove. So he felt the heart-beat, the life-pulse, faint but there. She was so small, so delicate; he must take care.

By now she had relaxed, and pulled him further inside her. Her insides had closed around his private thing. They were wet now, opening and closing, pulling and sucking at him, exciting him to go further, inciting him to go harder, higher and deeper.

There was no care now for him to take. Walter was lost; there was no Walter to care, no witless Walter with beak nose and flat cap and stained protruding teeth. There was only pleasure, so complete that it blotted out both past and future. There was only this moment of pleasure, then the next of more pleasure, pleasure building with each moment and each movement, each total within itself as he, Walter, was totally inside her. And she was holding him there, grasping at him to pull him deeper into her, then releasing him to make a sound of pleasure. *Her* pleasure. *He* made it. She was holding his buttocks and pulling him higher, then pushing him back, then squirming, whispering his name, and pulling him forward again. *His* name. Walter.

Then there was a moment more complete than all before it, and for the seconds (minutes? hours?) that it lasted, Walter moved even further away from himself and from any idea he had ever held of himself. He was not Walter; he was not anybody; he was a sensation. It was not his seed that left him. Nothing left him. He himself, the sensation, expanded to fill June and the world.

He had seen pigeons transfer their sperm in but the blinking of an eye, and both birds, satisfied that the job was well done, had strutted and circled each other, with chests out and tails down, before suddenly taking off into a flight of triumph, making wide circles in the sky together, dropping and climbing, playing tricks on each other, diving, sometimes tumbling, threatening to leave with a sudden extra burst of speed, then slowing down to be caught. Then they would return, staidly, keeping each other's pace and height, showing the world that they were married, paired for life.

Walter imagined himself up there in the sky on a clear day, diving, swooping, climbing over the house tops. From that height, he looked down on the church. The wind changed as he rose even higher. He planed on the air-currents, June beside him, as they glided together on the friendly wind, with no fear of falling. They had fed extensively on hemp, rape, tares, niger, maize, linseed and maple peas. They could fly for ever.

'You're heavy, Walter.' June used her elbows to draw herself backwards so that she and Walter were face to face. He was crying silently, tears of happiness and gratitude, of pleasure and achievement. She wiped the tears away with the tips of her fingers, and, between silent sobs, Walter said, 'I did it,' and June replied, 'Yes, you did it very well.'

Walter opened his eyes, and saw patches of coloured light projected on to a whitewashed wall. These would be the rotating coloured lights of the dance in the Main Hall. He must have dozed off. He reached out a hand, expecting to make contact with Clifford, but the lights were not rotating, and outside he could hear bird-song, and there was a body beside him which was not Clifford. The body had a name. Its name was June.

The coloured light on the wall was the morning, filtered through stained glass. Walter turned his head to look at the window. In the centre pane, Jesus stood with his right arm raised, pointing to his halo. The woman who knelt at his feet was clearly being reminded who the boss was. Walter's own mother was close to

Jesus at this very moment, but he did not think she would be kneeling at his feet.

June was still asleep. Her hair had dried during the night, and had become wavy; feather-like wisps framed the sides of her face. The skin on her face was pale, almost white, her eyelashes dark, almost black. A nerve or small vein at the outside corner of her left eye beat out its pulse just under the surface of smooth skin.

Walter watched the jumping pulse, and wondered if June were dreaming, and if so, of what. After they had made love, he had watched her dress, taking dry clothes from the heavy suitcase. She had laughed, and said she had nothing that would fit him. He had held the red velvet curtain around himself, still in a maze at what had happened, moony with it.

The pew benches had not been wide enough for two bodies to lie side by side, so they had collected ten hassocks and placed them side by side in the narrow aisle between the pews, covering them with narrow strips of threadbare blue carpet taken from the pew seats. Walter had lain down on the hassock-bed, waiting for her, and she had laughed and said, 'I'm coming inside that curtain too,' and as he had opened the curtain, exposing himself, she had thrown some silk underwear, two sweaters and a tweed skirt on top of him for extra warmth.

Then they had both laughed, and she had lain down beside him, and he had wrapped the red velvet curtain round them both.

They had lain close together, keeping each other warm. She had taken both his arms, and wrapped them around her. His hands had hung limply behind her back, and although he felt awkward, he had waited. She was so close to him that he could both hear and feel her breath on his face, and he had waited, happy, afraid to make any move that might spoil his happiness, hearing and feeling her breath and trying to match his breathing to hers, until at last he had fallen asleep.

By now they would have found Clifford, lying on a mattress in the Special Activities Unit, and the woman in June's bedroom, bound and gagged. By now the Night Duty Staff would have noticed that two of the beds in Ward 3 C were unoccupied, and would have begun a search. By now they would have called the police. Every policeman in the district would have been supplied with June's description and his own, and men and dogs would be walking in lines across muddy fields. (Walter did not know that both he and June might have left the Hospital at any time they had positively announced a wish to do so.)

The decision as to whether he should wake June in case the policemen and dogs were already near the village was too difficult for him to make. She needed sleep. They had walked a long way. She might be angry with him if he woke her, and he knew that he would not be able to bear her anger, to see her now sleeping face screwed up as it had been when she had shouted at him for not talking to her.

And at that moment, when he knew how he would feel to see her unhappy, that was the moment at which he realized that the feeling he had for her, this woman sleeping so close to him, was stronger than any feeling he had felt for anyone and that it made him happier than he could ever remember being. Whatever happened hereafter, as long as he could be with June, he would remain happy. Even if they had to walk all the way to London.

At seven forty-six by the clock with the loud tick, Walter heard a woman's voice singing and the iron ring on the church door being turned and pushed. Pulling as much of the red velvet curtain as he could retrieve from June around his nakedness, he watched the door open inwards, and a huge bunch of chrysanthemums and a pair of female legs appear. 'Jesus wants me for a sunbeam, to shine for him each day.' The woman's contralto voice was a little impaired by her absence of teeth.

'In every way to please him – ' Walter ducked his head, and tried not to move, hoping that June would not move either. Almost at once, the back of his throat tickled, and a wish to cough had to be suppressed. The chrysanthemum legs announced that they wished to please Jesus at home, at school and at play. June rolled over onto her back, and pulled at the red velvet curtain. Parts of Walter were revealed which he did not wish even chrysanthemums to observe. Moreover June seemed to be about to wake. He placed a hand over her mouth, and her eyes opened.

'A sunbeam ! A sunbeam ! Good morning, Sir.' The woman had

stopped singing, and an arm, only just visible behind the flowers, was waving towards the altar.

To whom could she be speaking?

'And a beautiful morning it is, Sir, after all that rain You showered down on us last night. Another drop, and we'd all have been lost at sea.'

One of June's shoes was perched on the knob at the end of the choir stall, and the woman's waving hand touched it. 'Whose is this?' She lowered the flowers, so that her face could now be seen. She was looking towards the altar, and her manner suggested that she expected an answer, that she was, indeed, in the habit of getting replies to her questions straight from the Almighty. June lifted Walter's hand away from her mouth.

'It's a woman's.' Suddenly the woman let out a loud asthmatic cackle of a laugh, and rocked backwards and forwards on her heels, the large bunch of chrysanthemums rocking backwards and forwards with her.

'Have you been having a fancy woman in here, Sir? Have you?' The cackle turned into a bronchitic cough, and the woman thumped herself pleasantly on the chest.

Walter's efforts to breathe normally in spite of the tickle in his throat had caused his eyes to water.

'If you've been seeing other women, I'll not stand for it.' The woman's gaze roamed round the church. Walter covered his head with the red velvet curtain. Perhaps, if he could not see the woman, she would not be able to see him. Perhaps she would mistake him for a pile of rags.

'You emptied your bath-water, and then got your young lady drenched in it. You don't deserve fresh flowers. I'm in a good mind to take them home. Randy old Goat!'

Walter could hardly believe his ears. He remembered that his mother had told him to say his prayers to Jesus as if he were talking to a friend, and not to reel them off as if they were multiplication tables, but there was a difference between respectful friendship and gross familiarity. This woman talked to Jesus as if she were His wife.

Walter and June peeped over the top of the pew, and watched the woman's back moving, as she pulled old flowers from the vase before the altar, and replaced them with her chrysanthemums. Her hands worked away, breaking stalks and arranging blooms, while she continued laughing and talking.

'Come out, come out, whoever you are!' She must know they were still in the church. She lifted her head towards the cross above the altar. 'Don't you complain! These are all I've got left in the garden.' The flowers were white, red, yellow and bronze. 'If you don't like the colours, you know what you can do, don't you? You can do the other. Like as not, you were doing a bit of the other in here last night. And don't you forget, I want a nice sunny day from you, a week tomorrow, for Gladys Earnshaw's wedding. I booked you for it two weeks ago, but you've a head like a sieve . . . You owe it to her. She's been unlucky in love more than enough times, and never laid eyes on a good whist-hand.'

The woman had finished her arrangement, and, using the altar rail to get to her feet, she groaned, 'One of these days, I want a few quiet words with you about my knees. It's no joke having knees like these two. A bee wouldn't be seen dead with them.' The church was filled again with the sound of her wheezing laughter, as she climbed up onto the organ seat. When the laughter and its echo had both ended, she said, 'And those not a million miles away from this organ who've made off with my red velvet curtain can put it back from whence it came.' And again laughed. Walter looked at June, and June at Walter, and Walter cleared his throat.

The woman's hands were poised over the keys of the organ, and she once again addressed the cross above the altar, but this time in a serious voice. 'Are you ready, Lord?' She paused for the length of time it would take Him to answer. 'This is the nearest to a service this village can give you, sharing our vicar with so many other parishes, but at least we have two more in the congregation than usual. I hope they'll stay to the end.'

At first the sound which came out of the organ was not unlike the woman's own wheezing breath, but when the pipes had cleared themselves of the week's dust, the music swelled nobly out. Walter and June sat still and listened. What was being played was not a Sunday School hymn, but a prelude and fugue by J. S. Bach, and it was played delicately and surely and with such controlled emotion that no one could have left before the end.

Walter was reminded of the School Band which came to the Hospital every year just before Christmas to play carols to the patients, and of the nineteen times he had sat next to Clifford, holding Clifford's hand and gripping it hard every time one of the tunes made him feel both full and empty, reminding him of his mother's voice, singing to him. It was at those times he had felt most secure. And June was reminded of some time, not to be fixed in her memory, when she had heard a young boy with a clear unbroken voice, singing his well-rehearsed solo for the Nativity. That high pure voice, giving its witness to the joy of living, had tricked her for a few moments into a sense of belonging to something, perhaps even to someone. But it had been only a trick then, was only a trick now. There were far too many shopping days left before Christmas.

The music stopped. The woman removed her fingers from the keyboard, and lowered her head as the vibration died away. Then she turned to face them.

'Thank you for staying. I played as well as I can today. I'm pleased you heard it.'

June said, 'It was beautiful. I'm sorry about the curtain. We got rather wet.'

'There's a man with you, isn't there?'

June said, 'Yes, this is Walter. I'm June.' And as she spoke, she realized that the woman's eyes were opaque, and that she wasn't looking at them after all, because she couldn't.

2

Haven't you noticed how many of the pigeons have deformed feet

It was the hub of Empire. June had told him so. 'Hub' was the centre, the dead centre of the British Empire. They were sitting together at the hub of Empire in Jubilee Year, resting their feet.

'This is where it's all happening. Look.' Walter looked. He had done little else over the past four days. He had walked and looked. He had waited by the roadside for lifts from lorry drivers, and looked. He had looked at the stained-glass windows of churches, at the Shopping Centres of provincial towns (all of which looked very much like one another), at the formica-topped tables of Transport Cafes; he had sat down by the bank of a canal, and looked at the water. June had said, 'I'll show you the Thames. It moves like oil at night.'

They had eaten seldom and badly. Walter's stomach, which was used to three meals a day of starch and calories, had started and was continuing to complain. He said nothing of this to June, for he knew that they had only thirty-two pence left between them. His amazement at what things cost in the real world had still not left him.

It was the hub of Empire. Eros pointed his arrow towards a large poster close to the Clydesdale Bank, which depicted an enormous naked girl, whose name was Emmanuelle. The naked girl smiled back at Eros. One hand, in obedience to the 1973 Obscenity Act, modestly covered a mount of Venus only slightly smaller than Ben Nevis. The poster was in two parts. One part announced that *Emmanuelle Discovers America*, the other that *Emmanuelle Goes Kinky*. 'She certainly gets around,' said June.

'Look.' Walter had looked. He continued to look. June had read to him the legend inscribed on the statue of Eros, from which it appeared that the boy with the arrow was also a certain Anthony Ashley Cooper, who was to be ever remembered for the strong sympathies of his heart and the great power of his mind, and who had (June said) taken children from the coal mines, in which they were being worked to death by their starving parents.

There were children all about them at the hub of Empire, sitting with them, resting their feet. Well, perhaps not children, though some were young, some not so young, all distinguished by chalk-white faces and long unkempt hair. Some sat on the island on which Eros stood, surrounded by traffic; others seemed to wish to get closer to Boot's, the all-night chemists, so that they should be first in the queue at midnight when their prescriptions became valid. The Right Honourable Anthony Ashley Cooper had alleviated the plight of boy chimney-sweeps, and ensured that children under the age of eleven should not be employed in the textile industry. Drug abuse in his day, June told Walter, had been strictly the prerogative of the rich.

They were at the hub of Empire. They had passed a shop named Cuddly Dudley's, in which customers could see themselves on closed-circuit television, and buy T-shirts on which by some magic photographs of those very faces, frozen by the television camera, had been printed. 'Everybody wants to be famous and remembered, 'cept thee and me.' June prodded at Walter's ribs, which had already become sore from such prodding. Her Lancashire accent had broadened from the moment they had approached Watford.

Walter watched the water which spurted from the mouths of the intertwined fish and the cherubs which surrounded Eros, and which made pools on the pavement and steps before running away down the nearest gutter. It was beginning to grow dark. Three black youths rollerskated through the pools of water, making damp wheelmarks on the pavement. It seemed to him that he had begun to be surrounded by coloured lights, and since he knew that this could not be so, and that hunger and weakness must have carried his mind back to the dances at the Main Hall of the Hospital, he concentrated harder on simply watching the damp wheelmarks fade from the pavement, and hoped that this attack would go away, and that he would not faint, and disgrace June at the hub of Empire. It did not go away. The coloured lights persisted and were joined by a high squeaking noise, as if millions of rubber soles were skipping over highly polished linoleum. The goldfish which had once inhabited his head, in order to confuse him by their darting about, had now been replaced by flickering Christmas Lights, and thousands of tiny children Country Dancing in black plimsolls. He closed his eyes. If he could sleep, even for a little while, they would go away.

'Look, Walter!'

Walter opened his eyes, and looked. The lights and noises were not inside his head; they were outside and all around him. Strips of light in every colour flickered on and off, some forming words, others shapes or pictures. The lights moved, danced, cascaded into patterns, and then were gone, only to begin the dance again the moment after. And the noise came from starlings, thousands of them, drowning out the traffic, as they swarmed on all the ledges of all the buildings, from Swan and Edgar's to Lillywhites, from the Piccadilly Theatre (where the lights advertised a production of *Wild Oats* by the Royal Shakespeare Company) to the Criterion Theatre, outside which there was a picture of the actor Leslie Phillips, holding up a pair of knickers. It was the hub of Empire.

Starlings covered the ledges, the windows, the columns, the arches, even the supports of the very coloured lights which seemed to be the cause of their chatter. They lined up like disorderly soldiers, forever fighting amongst themselves, breaking ranks and reforming. Suddenly a whole kit (larger, so much larger than any kit of pigeons) would take off together, swerving and swooping over tourists and traffic, before fighting for places on a building very similar to the one they had just left. Only the London Pavilion remained untouched. It had been newly painted, and Walter thought it a delicacy in the starlings to avoid a building which was still clean and refurbished.

'They paint the building with something which burns the birds' feet. Haven't you noticed how many pigeons have deformed feet?' Walter had noticed, and had wondered why.

It was the hub of Empire, but the great wheel of that Empire was much diminished now. The wheel would no longer turn.

Enormous sections of it had fallen away, and the hub was all barnacled over with Sex Shops and Souvenir Shops, amusement arcades at which the youth of Empire gambled away its pennies while waiting to be accosted by punters, and cinemas showing X-certificate films.

The Souvenir Shops sold patriotic dolls in Welsh, Scottish or Irish national costume and Fun Dolls in busby hats. They sold keyrings, Jubilee mugs, teacloths, back-scratchers and egg-warmers, cowboy boots and hats, fringed shirts of leatherette, multi-pocketed jackets and jeans, jeans and still more jeans. They sold pub mirrors, on which had been superimposed the faces of Marilyn Monroe, Starsky and Hutch, Elvis Presley, Humphrey Bogart, James Dean and Laurel and Hardy, plastic belts advertising Coca-Cola, Kit-Kat or Cinzano, belts which were also tape-measures and hessian shopping bags advertising Guinness or the Sex Pistols.

The Sex Shops sold, not sex itself, but Aids to Sex. Some of these aids were magazines and books, neatly covered in transparent plastic so as to avoid their being marked by the sweaty hands of punters. Some were mechanical (The Non-Doctor Vibrator), some medicinal (Libido Tablets and Orgasm Cream). One frivolous Sex Shop sold Jubilee Knickers with a Union Jack. Another sold the Oriental Duotonal Balls. June had left Walter standing outside the shop while she went in to inquire what was the function of these balls. At first the assistant had refused to believe that she did not already know, and guessed from her accent that she was one of a coach-party of ladies from the north and had been sent in by the other ladies to embarrass him. But since there were no other ladies, but only Walter, outside the window of the shop looking in, he relented and explained that the Duotonal Balls were not intended as replacements to be used by men who had carelessly mislaid their own, but were for the pleasuring of lonely or at least unsatisfied ladies. Placed in the vagina, the Duotonal Balls aroused excitement, and the string which connected them was not merely a useful device to allow them to be recovered; of itself, it massaged the clitoris. The housewife without a man, or whose husband was much away during the daytime and overtired at night, might, by the simple insertion of Duotonal Balls, obtain sexual relief, while doing the housework, and actually achieve an orgasm while Hoovering under the bed.

June had left the shop without buying a pair of Oriental Duotonal Balls. She had not liked to tell the assistant that she and Walter had only thirty-two pence between them.

'Are you hungry?' Walter nodded. 'You should tell me.'

They should both go down below Eros to the Piccadilly Underground Station, where there were toilets. June would visit the Ladies, Walter the Gents, and they would both wash their faces and comb their hair, because they were about to eat in a restaurant, where people notice such things. 'Come back, and wait for me here when you're ready,' June said, and she picked up her suitcase, and moved away from him. 'I won't be long. Yours is over there, down those steps.'

Walter looked where she pointed, and, when he turned back, discovered that he had already lost sight of her in the crowd of people on the other side of the road.

Since leaving the Hospital, the only times they had been separated were when Nature called, and even then, since Nature had seemed to call most often when they were in the countryside, only by a bush or a hedge; they had still been within shouting distance. Here shouts would not be heard. There were no bushes, hedges or even trees, save those they had passed in Leicester Square, which had electric cables nailed to their trunks and floodlights secured to their branches. Even dogs were forbidden by a public notice from answering a call of Nature against those trees.

Walter waited for the lights to change so that he could cross the four lanes of traffic which separated him from the stairs to which June had pointed. He wondered how, with only thirty-two pence, they were to eat in a restaurant where people would notice whether he had combed his hair. They had started with six pounds and thirty-two, of which sixty pence had been his. He had been unable to draw out the twenty-five pounds and eleven pence he had saved at the Hospital, because there had not been time to do so, and in any case Walter was known not to take money out, but to put it in, and taking it out would have aroused suspicion. Walter had never been able to understand why he had saved, except that clearly it was an activity his mother would have approved, and there was very little on which to spend the one pound fifty which might be the reward of a week's digging. He had never needed to buy food (except for sweets) or clothes. His mother had done that for him until she had gone to stay with Jesus, and then the Hospital had done it.

He stood pissing into the urinal, and wondered why the Gents here was so crowded, and why everyone seemed to be looking (or avoiding looking) at everybody else. It was the hub of Empire, but that was hardly an explanation. Three men, who had finished at the urinal, stood combing their hair; this grooming seemed to take them some considerable time. Another rubbed his hands in a current of warm air, and every time the current appeared to be about to stop, he pressed a button, and started it again. Another leaned against the white-tiled wall beneath a notice which read, 'No loitering', and blew smoke rings from his cigarette. Others stood at the urinals, not pissing at all, but shaking and rubbing their private things, their heads turning from left to right, as though looking for someone or expecting to meet a friend. Walter became convinced that he had found his way into a place where criminals collected. He had heard that London was full of crooks, and they must meet somewhere.

It cost Walter five pence to wash his face and hands, and even in the Wash Room, men looked at each other's faces reflected in the mirrors. He stood at the washbasin, supporting his two plastic carrier bags between his legs for fear that one of the crooks should make a grab for them.

He shaved, using the cheap safety razor and blades June had purchased for him on their second day of freedom. The soap he had brought with him from the Hospital would have to last a long time, so he used the soap provided by the Wash Room. After all, he had paid for it.

Then he removed his cap, and tried to comb his hair. It was matted, and there were knots; it needed washing. He had forgotten to bring any lavender brilliantine, so his hair stuck up where he had lain on it, and would not lie down. He would be bound to have to remove his cap in a restaurant in which appearances were noticed. He had better wash his hair.

He refilled the basin with warm water, and dipped his head in it, pressing the carrier bags between his legs in a vice-like grip. Someone tapped at his right shoulder. This sudden contact so surprised Walter that he straightened his back, and turned round so quickly that water from his hair sprayed round the room, and particularly across the face of the man who had done the tapping.

Walter drew back the wet hair from his eyes, and blinked in order to focus on his assailant. It was the Wash Room attendant, who now stood in front of him, and with deliberate slowness removed a spotlessly clean handkerchief from his trouser pocket, raising it to dry his closed eyes and dripping chin.

'Don't do that.' The attendant's eyes were still closed.

'Sorry.' Walter bent down quickly to retrieve the pullover and stained underpants which had fallen from one of the carrier bags. The attendant explained that the nearest Public Baths were in Marshall Street. These basins were for the washing of faces and hands, but not hair. Hair clogged the pipes and plughole. There are men who lose hair during the washing of it. Anyone who has experienced the removal of large quantities of hair of various colours, textures and shapes from plugholes already in receipt of the natural oils and greases of the body, to say nothing of the soap-scum caused by the hard water of London, does not wish to repeat the experience.

The Wash Room attendant had started by simply addressing his remarks to Walter, but as his recollections grew and his anger with them at the injustice of fate which had brought him to this profession and his revulsion at handling the world's redundant hair, he addressed his remarks to a wider audience, spreading them around the Wash Room and out into the room in which men both old and young stood at urinals pretending to piss.

Walter listened. Water ran from his hair into his eyes. It dripped onto the collar and lapels of his jacket. As it ran between the soaking collar of his none-too-clean shirt and made its way from vertebra to vertebra, it cooled. After some time, the attendant discovered that he had expressed his anger and frustration as fully as he had the energy to do, and ceased. The silent disassociation by the men young and old, waiting about in the underground toilet, of themselves from the attendant's unhappiness could almost be felt. Only Walter gave attention, and that attention, hang-dog,

117

pathetic, gaping, was entire. 'Better rinse out the soap now you've started,' the attendant said, and Walter, who knew well that no soap had yet been added to his hair or the water, let the discoloured water out, and seeing that the attendant had been right, and that three long hairs had indeed come out of his head, removed them from the plughole, and refilled the basin with clean water.

'I'll get you a towel.' Walter took the towel, and rubbed at his head, thinking it better not to mention his own towel, which was in one of the carrier bags. 'Where have you come from?' Walter considered, and decided that it was safe to answer, 'Hospital.' The attendant nodded wisely. 'And I don't suppose you've got another five pence for the use of the towel?' Walter stopped rubbing his head, and shook it. The attendant, wishing no longer to be reminded of his excess of emotion, said, 'All right, we'll pretend you didn't use it. Now off you go.'

Since even Walter could see that the towel was now dirty as well as extremely wet, he did not think that anyone would accept it as an unused towel. 'Now off you go' had been intended as friendly appeasement by the attendant, but Walter interpreted it as an order, and left the Wash Room at once, as he was, his hair still damp and frizzy from the rubbing, his cap and carrier bags in his hands, backing away before anything else went wrong, or the gang of crooks for whom all the other men were clearly waiting, turned up, and shot up the joint.

'I would like a Dover Sole with French-fried potatoes and peas, and my companion will have the Jumbo Mixed Grill, with rump steak, chips, etc. We'll both have Mixed Salads, followed by Vanilla Ice Cream with Hot Chocolate Sauce, two large white coffees, and a bottle of Tavel as soon as you can, please, since I see by your Wine List that you don't have Cendré.'

They were sitting in Hennekey's Grill and Griddle. Their table was near the door.

'Are these your bags, madam?' The waiter looked timidly at the now muddy suitcase and plastic carrier-bags.

'Yes. Why. Are they in the way?'

'No, madam, but we have to be careful of bombs.'

'Yes, one would have to be careful of those, but not in my

luggage. As you can see from its rather muddy state, a porter dropped it in a puddle, but I was the only thing to explode.'

'Very good, madam.' The waiter left them, and June turned to Walter, who sat opposite her, and smiled. She had changed her clothes, and now wore make-up. Not as much as Mrs Silver, who had supervised the Cosmetics Counter at Woolworth's, but enough to fascinate Walter. He had never seen her looking so much like a film star and so happy.

'Feeling better?' Walter smiled and nodded. She had been waiting for him, as anxious as a parent who has lost its child or a child who has lost its parent. She almost cried with relief when she had seen him approaching, his hair all damp and frizzy. She had hugged him to her, smelling of make-up and perfume. He had tried to tell her why he had taken so long, and they had sat together on the steps below Eros, while she had combed his hair gently, unravelling the knots, and used the same comb to clean his fingernails.

Then they had walked arm in arm across the street, and now here they were in an expensive restaurant where appearances were noticed. He had not changed his shirt, which was still wet and dirty, but the lights were set against the wall, and covered with dark-red shades which matched the textured wallpaper. There was not enough light in this restaurant where appearances were noticed for anyone to see the dirt on his shirt-collar. It was warm here. His hair would dry flat, as June had combed it. Perhaps steam would be rising from it even now. He touched his head, feeling and flattening his hair.

June reached across the table for his hand, and he gave it to her.

'Don't be nervous.' Somehow she must have found some money to pay for the meal.

'When we've finished the wine and the coffee, all you have to do is what I tell you. All right?' Walter nodded.

The bill amounted to nine pounds forty, including service, and arrived with the coffee. June made a point of adding it up, and searching her pockets for her purse. She placed the closed purse on the plate next to the bill, and told Walter to take his time drinking his coffee. There was no need to rush.

Their next project, June said, involved another long walk.

When she and Walter had both finished their second cups of coffee, June spoke to Walter in a quiet voice, her lips hidden by the now empty coffee cup.

'I'm going to take the bill and my purse, and stand up. When I've done this, you pick up the suitcase and the bags, and get out of that door. Don't rush, and don't stop or look back. Just keep walking. Turn right outside the door, and keep walking. I'll meet you by the City Guide in Leicester Square – you remember that large map we stopped and looked at? Just keep walking in a straight line, and you'll come to it. All right?' Walter nodded.

'Here goes.' June stood, and moved slowly towards the back of the restaurant, peering closely at the bill as if she were short-sighted. Walter also stood, and picked up the luggage as he had been told. Luckily, customers about to enter the restaurant held the door wide open for him, so that he was soon out in the street and heading towards Leicester Square.

The waiter approached June. He smiled over her shoulder at the incoming customers. 'A table for four? Certainly, sir. I'll be with you in a moment.' He said to June, 'Is there some trouble, madam?' and she squinted at the bill, holding it even closer to her eyes, and said, 'Yes, I don't seem to be able to bring it into focus.'

Then suddenly, with an expression which any drama students would be delighted to have in their repertoires, she clutched at her chest, and bent double. This was followed by noisy and hysterical inhalations of breath and by wild gestures towards the door. The waiter backed away a little, and the customers at the nearest table pretended to be blind and deaf. More gulps of air, and between each gulp, painful words. 'Pills . . . he . . . he's got . . . pills . . . heart . . . heart pills . . . must . . .' June turned, and began an unsteady walk towards the door. The turn concealed from the waiter her next action, which was to push one finger of the hand already covering her mouth well down into her throat, touching the back. June retched convincingly. More customers had entered, and, in some concern for themselves and their clothes, leaned backwards over the already seated diners, so that the way to the door was clear and any pursuit impeded.

Once outside the door, June continued her performance for only a short time, not wishing to attract too much attention. Then she began to run.

Walter waited as he had been told, and June appeared, skipping over the flagstones.

'Old gags are best.' She placed her warm and somewhat sweaty hand into Walter's, picked up both plastic carrier bags with the other, and began to walk. Walter, as usual, carried the suitcase, which never seemed to get lighter. He wondered why he had been sent on ahead and where she had found money to pay the bill. He stroked the palm of her clammy hand with his thumb. Her hands had never been like this before. He said, 'You were frightened.'

June stopped and looked at him, surprised by his intuition. Then she said, 'Yes. That's half the fun.' She smiled, lifted his hand to her mouth, and kissed the back of it. 'Anyway, it's a very long time since I did anything like that. Clive would never let me.' Her smile turned into a giggle. 'He was always afraid there might be someone in the restaurant who knew him.' She began to walk again, and Walter concentrated on keeping up, and hoped he would not soon have to change hands. 'Since he always cheated the Income Tax, by claiming every meal out as a business expense, he said it wasn't worth the risks. Clive took more foreigners out to meals than the American Ambassador, and most of them were really me, and most of the time I didn't really enjoy it.'

She paused again to study the bust of Shakespeare, which stood on a pedestal roughly in the middle of Leicester Square. In the four corners were busts of Joshua Reynolds, Isaac Newton, William Hogarth and John Hunter, and since it was Jubilee Year, each of these famous men had recently been cleaned, and the cleaner had placed a transparent plastic bag over each of the famous heads. The London pigeons had ignored the plastic bags; there was clearly no pleasure to be found in shitting on plastic. Consequently Shakespeare, who had not yet been cleaned and had no bag, had received more than his fair share of their attention. Walter was reminded of his dead mother's hair, all matted with pigeon droppings.

They were so close still, Walter and June, to the hub of Empire. Someone had discarded a large fish-head, together with some of the fish's skin, and near it a Japanese boy sat, reading a tiny book held very close to his face. His spectacles reflected the floodlights set in the trees of the Square. Next to him was a fat man with a shaven head and dirty overcoat. As Walter watched, the fat man rose from the bench and felt in all his pockets several times over for a key which, in fact, was dangling from his thick belt on a long chain, striking against the paving stones each time the fat man moved his hands from one pocket to another.

No one was in a hurry. If the people in the Square had places to go, they also had the time to get there.

An elderly man in a greasy raincoat rose from another of the benches, and, with the aid of his steel elbow-crutch, made three strides before the crutch slipped, and the man fell backwards, his legs and arms in the air, and lay there like a dog which is hoping for its stomach to be rubbed.

June and Walter moved to help, but were beaten to it by two younger men.

'Look at the poor fucker. He's pissed itself.'

'Got a bottle in his pocket. Lucky you didn't break your bottle, mate, as well as your water.'

They had lifted the man to his feet, and he stood there, looking down in disbelief at the front of his wet trousers. The two young men moved on, laughing.

The elderly man's eyes focused on no one in particular, and his remarks were addressed generally to his surroundings. 'Crutch slipped,' he said, his eyes opaque and blinking like a bird's. 'Didn't you see it? Crutch slipped.' He looked again at his stained trousers. 'Surprised me. I was going . . .' he gestured vaguely towards the Gentlemen's Toilet which is at one corner of the Square. 'I was on my way.' His small features crumpled, and his eyes shed water, and his lips were trembling. 'What's the point?'

June ceased altogether to feel gay. Her high spirits were replaced by a generalized sadness, which caused her to cry both with and for the elderly man, who never saw her tears, but walked away, wiping his face with the back of his free hand, walking unsteadily, his trousers wet, his pride injured.

'If a child in Tasmania itches, I scratch. If the man in the moon pricks his finger, I feel the pain, and self-pity leaks from me at every pore.' June drew in a deep breath. 'Waterloo, Walter; that's where we're bound. You'll see the river at night, the bridges lighted up and the water moving like oil to ease the hinges of this once-great city.' Her mascara was running, and the make-up on her face felt thick and heavy. She would wash it off.

Her hand touched the handle of the drinking fountain, but it was out of order. No water spurted up to cool and cleanse her face. 'Nothing works for long, does it?' She looked up at Walter, who was watching the two black lines run down her cheeks. She said, 'Wrap yourself around me for a minute, and tell me I'll be all right.'

Walter stood with his arms around June, the right side of his face resting on the top of her head, and wondered where and when they were going to sleep. But all he said was, 'You'll be all right, June. We'll both be all right.'

He wanted to add that he loved her, which was what people in films said to each other. Laurel and Hardy did not say it, but it was said by some, particularly those in the position in which he now found himself, holding each other, standing up, perhaps in some public place. But Walter could not say it, couldn't form the words. Instead he said, 'Will you show me the river now, please?'

3

*She wondered if there were a rule in the Police
Manual that they should continue to give the
kiss of life until the ambulance arrived.*

The river at night moved like oil, just as June had promised. If
Walter concentrated on a small area, it almost comforted him.
There were even ducks swimming around the SS *Hispaniola*, which
was now a floating restaurant. They waited for bread.

But it was hard to narrow his concentration down to the comforting ducks. The width of the river, the length of the bridge, the
towering buildings on each side, some illuminated, some in darkness, with only the thousands of windows reflecting the lights of
the river and the streets, these were altogether outside his range
of comprehension. The Royal Festival Hall, the Shell Building, the
National Film Theatre threatened him from across the water,
and the enormous concrete slabs of the National Theatre looked
like a crouched and frozen animal. On his own side, Cleopatra's
Needle and the distant floodlit dome of St Paul's, set among the
tower blocks of the Barbican, said to him, 'There is no home for
you here, Walter. You are too small; you are nothing.' To be alone
here, to be lost, would be terrifying.

Walter was not lost, was not alone. June was with him.

The people here moved fast, looking down or straight ahead.
They moved past Walter like buses one has just missed. Even if
he were brave enough to shout after them, they would not turn
round; he would have to wait for the next. The people who lived
in London must all be like Mike, the Trainee Floorwalker in the
Stock Room at Woolworth's, intelligent, quick-talking, moving,

always moving, on the move, on the way to somewhere. 'Come on, Walter, move your arse!' If you didn't, you'd soon get knocked over, trodden on, lying there under the feet of the quick-talking, fast-moving people. It would be hard to be old here. No wonder there were benches in Leicester Square.

The coloured lights of the SS *Hispaniola*, reflected in the thick black oil of the Thames, reminded him of a taffeta dress his mother had once worn. He allowed his mind to be drawn into them, pulled down into warm sleep (for oil was always warm). He could forget his cold feet and face, forget the rubbish and beer cans floating in the river, forget that they only had thirty-two pence and nowhere to sleep. He closed his eyes, and imagined that he was being rocked, wrapped in warm taffeta, in time to the soft rhythmical tapping of the river against the wall. Soon June would want to move on.

But June began to hum. She would not take him away yet. She was humming to herself, and he knew the song, could remember some of the words, sung so often by his mother in the days before the Hospital. Walter lowered his head onto the backs of his hands, saying the words silently inside his head.

> 'We shall gather at the river,
> The beautiful, beautiful river,
> Gather with the Saints by the river
> That flows by the hand of God.'

It was cold, very cold. They had reached the Arches, close to what the student June had once known as Charing Cross Underground Station, but had now been renamed Embankment.

It was 1977, the year of the Queen's Jubilee, and fifty-seven bodies were lying on the pavement under the arches down by the river. The bodies were pressed together for warmth, and because there were more bodies than space.

It was Jubilee Year. During the nineteen thirties at a time of unemployment, hunger marches and strikes, when George Orwell was living down and out, there were seldom more than two hundred people living rough in London. In 1947, the L.C.C. (as it then was) had abandoned its count, having found only six. But there had been progress, prosperity and achievement since then, twenty-five years of the New Elizabethan Age (1952-1977), and when, in 1973, the journalists of *The Sunday Times* had gone out to do a head count of those sleeping rough in London, they had found one thousand, four hundred and fifteen, not counting those sleeping in derelict buildings which had been reckoned too dangerous for the journalists of *The Sunday Times* to enter.

Her Majesty had gone walkabout all over her domain, walking through lines of prosperous and progressive citizens of the New Elizabethan Age, waving Union Jacks. Walter and June stood looking down at the lines of horizontal bodies under the Arches, fifty-seven of them with another four (June had done her own head count) sleeping on the steps of a building appropriately announcing itself as the 'B.B.C. Layhouse'. One of the bodies on the Layhouse steps was that of a woman who had crammed herself into a blue plastic milk-crate for warmth.

The bodies lay on flattened cardboard boxes, some with newspaper wrapped and tied around their legs, others with a covering of black polythene. One man had made a tube of cardboard boxes like a coffin and wrapped polythene round it; only the top of his head was visible. Some had their feet inside boxes; most had piled rags on top of them and wore several layers of clothing. Above them could be seen an official notice: 'THE DEPARTMENT OF PUBLIC HEALTH. ACTION WILL BE TAKEN WITHOUT PRIOR NOTICE AGAINST ANY UNAUTHORIZED PERSON PARKING, TRESPASSING OR DUMPING RUBBISH ON THESE PREMISES.'

It was 1977, Her Majesty's Jubilee Year, less than a mile from the Hub of Empire. Walter picked up a bottle which had once contained Mellow Brown Full Sweet South African Sherry, and now lay in the gutter, where it would break and puncture the wheels of passing cars. In a corner nearby were at least a dozen similar bottles, which had severally contained Dulcet Cream, Full Rich Tarragona from Yates's Wine Lodge and Maryland Sweet White. He placed the bottle from the gutter with these others, and hoped it would stay.

It was so very cold. He grasped June's hand. Surely this couldn't be where she had intended them to stay the night? Yet she stood, gripping his hand tightly, and staring down at the bodies huddled together.

He had learned much about June since they had met, some of it contradictory. He knew that it would not be beyond her to lie down with these people, simply in order to add her own body-warmth to theirs.

Walter tugged at June's hand. She pulled him closer to her. 'It's all right. We'll go soon. Never let me get as cold as they must be.' And then, after a moment, 'There isn't a God. There can't be.'

The homeless heads, sixty-one of them, counted by June, slept in snatches. There was always noise, always coughing. The sleepless listened to the coughing, wondering whether each cough would be the cougher's last. Even dead, the cougher could not be colder. *The Sunday Times* had quoted Colonel McAllister of the Salvation Army, who had attributed the enormous increase in the number of those sleeping rough to the Mental Health Act of 1960, which had allowed Mental Hospitals to release long-stay patients back into the Community – 'the Community', that is, the Arches at Charing Cross, the B.B.C. Layhouse steps, the Bull-Ring in Birmingham, St Peter's Square in Manchester, Leeds Railway Station, various spikes (but never enough) in Peckham and points north; that is the Community. And since a newspaper must be fair, and seen to be so, *The Sunday Times* had also quoted a consultant psychiatrist (anonymous, because the medical profession must not advertise) who had defended the Mental Health Act, 1960, which had freed the Hospitals from acting as mere Asylums and protecting totally useless people who cannot and will not learn, and who only want to be kept, although they are not mentally ill.

Two policemen were sitting in the front of a dark-blue van waiting for trouble. They told each other jokes, and chuckled. One of them looked down the long line of cardboard, polythene and rags. The street lamps were reflected in his rimless spectacles, as he watched urine trickling from the bodies of the counted heads, and running along the pavement to join and mix with the other rubbish in the gutter.

Would he move from the warmth of his cab to pull the body of a counted head to its feet? Would he order it into the back of the van? Would he tell it to move on? If he did, where would it go?

No. Not tonight. Not on such a cold night of Her Majesty's Jubilee Year. The dark-blue van began very slowly to back away from the lines of bodies, crunching plastic cups beneath its wheels.

On the other side of the road, another van had stopped. This was a much older van, containing not policemen, but young people, four of them, who jumped briskly from it. Two of them lifted out a large container of stainless steel. It was a quarter to midnight. The soup had arrived.

Only three of the sixty-one heads looked out from under their coverings. None moved quickly. The three lookers became three standers, and arranged their paper and polythene to indicate that they would be coming back.

One of the four young people sported an Afro haircut. He carried round a large pan of soup, pouring it into plastic cups for those who did not wish to unwrap themselves from their coverings.

A woman sitting upright beside a pram loaded with carrier bags and cases was muttering something, some complaint which, since her voice was hoarse, did not carry to the young people. She wore a child's blue gabardine macintosh and lace-up boots. What she was saying was, 'Tell him to come over here. Tell him to bring some here.' A strip of once white net had been tucked under her headscarf. This was a veil. It hung over her forehead, and shielded her eyes from the street lamps. No one was allowed to see her eyes.

One of the young people noticed that her lips were moving, and went over to see what she wanted. The veiled woman waved her arms angrily at the girl, and mouthed complaints. Why couldn't she ask politely? Why did she snarl?

Now she was asking for more bread, and sliding what she had already been given beneath the lapels of her threadbare gabardine mac.

Two of the young people carried walkie-talkie radios. They held them to an ear to listen, to a mouth to speak. They were reporting back to headquarters, letting it be known where they were, in case they should be somewhere else. If medical help were needed – an ambulance, perhaps a coffin – here under the Arches, they would be able to say so to headquarters, and headquarters would dispatch it. These walkie-talkie radios had been bought with money subscribed by the public.

Twenty-five years of progress and achievement in the New Elizabethan Age. Mount Everest had been climbed, the first Morris Mini launched and the first hovercraft. Roger Bannister had run a mile in four minutes; the first steerable radio-telescope had been installed at Jodrell Bank; Sir Francis Chichester had sailed a thirty-foot ketch around the world, and Concorde had made a flight faster than sound. The youth with the Afro hairstyle held a pocket mirror to the mouths of those counted heads which had not moved.

'ANGELA RICHARDS WON'T DROP HER STANDARS FOR ANYONE.' A weakness in the neon sign had dimmed the important 'D'. London Transport and British Rail maintain a careful, almost puritanical censorship over the advertising material they are prepared to display to their customers and employees, but had not yet been able to have the sign repaired. Below Angela's un-droppable standars another advertisement asked, 'Is This the Right Time to Invest in Gold?' Neither June or Walter felt disposed to give an answer. They were sitting on a bench on Waterloo Station, waiting for time to pass, sharing tea from a plastic cup, sipping it slowly in turns, trying to make it last. It had cost them ten pence.

'No, I wouldn't tell you a lie; don't believe in it. I'm an Alk . . . Alk . . . an Alko Holic. Can't even say it.' Michael smiles, and takes another sip from his quarter bottle of Teacher's. He is in his mid-thirties, clean-shaven, Irish. He is sitting on the same bench as Walter and June, watching the late-night travellers arrive and depart.

'I drink, but I work for it.' He takes another sip. At the Destination Board in front of them, names revolve and are replaced by other names: it happens of itself, to Walter's puzzlement. 'Andover. Salisbury. Winchester. Southampton. Weymouth.' He cannot read these names, and would not know where the places are, but he knows they are different from the names which they have replaced.

'What at? I suppose you'll ask.' They have not asked. Michael taps the side of his nose with a finger. 'Ah, well, I know that. Would you like some of this in your tea?'

June shakes her head. There has been music from hidden loud-speakers, but it has stopped. Walter has turned his attention to a man with bandaged feet, who has placed his two walking sticks against a bench, and is resting his feet by leaning on the bench and lifting one foot at a time. This man is a Regular at Waterloo Station, there being nowhere else in particular for him to go and nothing else in particular for him to do. He can hardly walk, yet if he were to sit, he would be unable to get up again, and the police have moved him once already tonight.

'No, I never lie. Where do I work, then? Ah, well, I'm a landscape gardener. Would you like one of these?' Michael has taken a handful of pills from his inside pocket and holds them out towards June.

'What are they?'

'Mog. Modger. Mon.'

'Mogadon?'

'That's the one. You know them?' June nods. 'Will you have one with me?' June smiles, but shakes her head.

June says, 'You don't have any Valium, I suppose?'

This time, Michael shakes his head. 'Slow you down, them things. Stop you thinking.'

'That's what I need.'

Michael considers this, then leans closer to June, staring into her eyes. 'You're needing them now?' June nods. The top of the whisky bottle is found and replaced. Michael stands unsteadily, shoves the bottle into the pocket of his jacket, says, 'Wait there.'

June watches, as he weaves his way to another bench, and whispers to three of its occupants. They turn to look at her, and shake their heads. One of them, a woman, points to the other end of the Concourse. Michael gives June the thumbs-up sign, and tries to walk in a straight line to where the woman has pointed.

Two more men have joined the man with bandaged feet, one leaning on the other for support. The supporting man asks Walter for a cigarette in a thick Glaswegian accent, which Walter doesn't understand, so he smiles and shakes his head. The man with bandaged feet is complaining to the others that the police have warned him off sleeping on the trains, and have told the porters to prevent him, should he try to pass through the barrier. He tells them that he is convinced that he will die tonight because of the cold. It is a simple statement, simply stated, and he adds another, that he hopes it will happen quickly, so that he will no longer have to wait about on this fucking station.

'George is bringing you some.' Michael has returned.

'Thank you. That's very kind.' The euphoria achieved with Mogadon and whisky causes Michael to sway and grin.

'Don't you know George? He has the pills. All sorts. Where did you sleep last night?' Michael does not require an answer to any of his questions. 'Didn't you see me go through that gate over there? You have to get on the right train; you have to know how to do it. They don't move Number Six till nine in the morning. The police never move me on, hardly at all. You have to look smart, though. Does he want a shave?'

Michael is pointing at Walter, who, feeling threatened, has passed June what is left of the tea, and taken hold of her free hand.

'He had one earlier.'

Michael is disappointed. His help in this respect has been refused. His loneliness returns, breaking through the comfort of whisky and Mogadon. He sways, and looks round the Station Concourse like a child on its first day at school.

June pats the bench beside her. 'Come and sit down.'

'George is coming.' This statement is more to reassure himself than her. 'Florrie!' He waves to a woman on another bench, and beckons to her to come over, before carefully sitting down again next to June.

'He can have a shave, if he wants one. Here.' Michael brings from his pocket a sponge-bag, and shows its contents to June – a razor, a bar of Knight's Castile soap, a toothbrush and toothpaste containing fluoride for the protection of both teeth and gums, even a pocket-sized deodorant spray. 'Here! Smell this.' Michael takes June's fingers gently in his, and squirts deodorant onto the back of her hand, the two hands, his and hers, touching each other, then shaking her hand and sniffing it before releasing it, as if sampling expensive perfume.

'Good, isn't it?'

June agrees, and Michael is happy again. 'Did I tell you I worked?'

Time passes.

131

It is twelve forty-five, and an Indian porter is giving a display of his ability to control an electric cleaner, steering it round and round in ever decreasing circles with one hand, then revving up and speeding towards the Bookstall, only to swerve aside at the last moment and skim past a notice warning passengers not to feed the pigeons, the large rotating brush at the front of the vehicle sweeping plastic cups, empty crisp bags and cigarette ends under the wheels to be sucked up inside.

Pigeons. They would be asleep.

'Eee! I've got more scarves than money.' This is Florrie, the lady who came over from the other bench, and now sits between June and Michael, whom she insists on calling 'Paddy'. Michael greeted Florrie like a long-lost relation, with a kiss and a hug, but in fact, as it seems, they have only met twice before.

Florrie twists and untwists her headscarf. 'No, don't grease me coat, Paddy. Tell me without touching me. Get your fingers off; they're covered with soup or something. I've got to make this coat last. He gets silly when he's drunk. Only time these blokes can talk is when they've had too much. I was sixty last week. I want to see George mesel; I've gorra toothache.'

In fact, Florrie is toothless, except for one tiny monument which stands, misshapen but defiant, like a relic of Stonehenge, guarding her lower jaw from any further attack by National Health dentistry.

'Anybody got a smoke?' Michael obliges with a small Silk Cut cigarette.

'He works, does this one. In the Parks for the Corporation. Hey! You haven't bought me for a cigarette, you know. I don't go behind the wall for a low-tar fag.' Florrie opens her mouth wide to laugh and let the smoke out. Her face is pinched and drawn, but her eyes are lively, missing nothing. As she speaks, she looks about her with quick jerks of her head, and at roughly three-minute intervals she ties and unties her brown chiffon headscarf. It is now one fifteen a.m.

'Ahm back up north after Christmas to live wi' me son. He said I could, now ahm over sixty. He's asked Council, and they've said it's all right, as long as ahm sixty. That's nice, intit? I don't like London, do you? Haven't I seen you down the Webber Street

Mission?' June shakes her head. 'I've been in every hostel in London. Some of them are all right. He doesn't know I come here, you know, me son. He thinks I'm booked in to a hostel. Well, I will be tomorrow – or Tuesday. If it gets any colder. Have you seen Kathy? You must know her. She comes on the trains here. Big tall woman, wi' one eye, just the one. She's sixty-two, and still works, has done all her life. She cleans down the Blackfriars Road.'

Michael's head is resting on her shoulder. 'When's George coming, eh, Paddy?'

'Don't call me "Paddy". Here, give us a kiss.'

'Hey up! I don't think I can be bothered. They don't bother me, you know, men. I can talk to them all right – be civil – but I've been on me own twenty years now. I don't need a man. Stop leaning over me like that, Paddy. If they see you like that, they'll not let you through barrier. They don't want sick all over their trains. Cleaners don't like it.'

Time passes. Long lines of trolleys, piled high with mailbags and thick wedges of the day's newsprint, begin to twist and curl around the Concourse like snakes.

It is almost one forty-five a.m. 'God, I feel awful. Thought I was going to die.' George has arrived. George is having a coughing fit. Slumped down next to Walter, his head lowered between his knees, he almost chokes on the phlegm he coughs up. He grips Walter's arm tightly, gasps for breath, and tries to speak.

'Sitting ... in the ... lavatory, I was. Come on all ... of a sudden. Feel like ripping me chest open ... Getting better ... Some bloke asked if ... wanted a hand ... get up the stairs ... Couldn't answer ... Making it worse.'

The others wait for George to recover. The fit subsides. George looks round to make sure that he is not being watched. 'Now, who needs the neurotic little comforters?' His dirty fingers delve in and out of the many patchwork pockets that he has sewn on the inside of his torn and threadbare overcoat. Seven different containers of various types of pills are brought out and held very close to his eyes for him to read the labels.

'Some of these dates are difficult to make out. Don't want to give you heap bad medicine.'

And then the eighth container. 'Valium. Five milligrams. One to be taken three times a day. Mrs Eastwood. Fourth of the third, seventy-six. Last year's. A good year for Happies. Had them before?'

June nods. 'I've nothing to give you for them.'

'Did I ask?' June shakes her head. 'My life! She thinks I'm a pusher.' George looks at the others, and laughs, and the laughter starts him coughing again.

'No, sweetheart. Here, take them in health! Oh, hell! Don't make me laugh.'

The last of the tea in the plastic cup has gone long ago, and June sucks at the inside of her mouth to fill it with saliva with which to swallow one of the pills.

'Have you nothing for your chest?' Florrie has brought herself to George's attention. Soon she will speak of her toothache.

'Lost ... prescription. Five ... five weeks ago. Ooooh, Jesus! Can't find ... another bronchitic to rob.' George laughs and coughs, holding his chest and spitting at Walter's feet.

'You sound dreadful. I'd go to the hospital.'

'What can they do? ... They're not miracle workers ... Least ... least that's what they tell you. Prison ... best place for medical treatment ... Look after you there ... Three months for shoplifting ... Recommend it for anyone with an ailment.'

'Are they any good with teeth?'

'Only if you want your gold fillings removed in a hurry.' George seems to be able to laugh now without coughing.

'I've got a toothache. Right at the back.' Florrie has opened her mouth wide, and is pointing an index finger down her throat. George leans across Walter to peer into Florrie's mouth.

'Shut it quickly, woman, before they start posting letters.' He hands her something from one of his inside pockets.

'What are they?'

'Aspirin. I've run out of general anaesthetics. Here! Your mouth just reminded me; I was told a joke. There was this chap nearly drowned himself off Brighton beach, and when they got him out, a crowd gathered, and two men took it in turns to administer the Kiss of Life up his arse. Then the ambulance arrived, all flashing lights and smelling of Dettol, and the doctor came rushing over, and shouted, "Hey! What are you doing?" "Giving him the Kiss of Life," they said. "You don't give it there." "We know," they said, "but have you smelt his breath?" '

Time passes. At two fifteen, Florrie wakes Michael up, and says she is getting on a train. She has been watching the movements of the porters for some time, and has seen her opportunity. The regular porters are no danger; they know what goes on. But if Florrie were spotted by a new porter, or by the police, she would be turned away, and would have to spend the rest of the night on the bench, which has become very cold now.

Michael waits until Florrie is safely in the train at Platform Six, and then follows her, giving June a nod.

Five minutes later, June stands, and, holding hands, suitcases in Walter's right hand, two carrier bags in June's left, they walk to and past the barrier of Platform Six. Nobody stops them or shouts at them. They walk to the middle of the stationary train, and climb into a First Class carriage.

'Speak, Roger! Speak!'

June and Walter had not slept well, nothing like as well on the comfortable seats of a First Class carriage as on the hassocks of the village church in which they had spent their first night of freedom. They had expected to be discovered by a porter, marched away by Transport Police, accused of trespassing: June had determined to say nothing except in the presence of her solicitor. That would be Clive's solicitor, of course. It would be a long way for him to come from Preston.

At twelve minutes past seven, they had begun to leave the train still standing on Platform Six, looking forward to becoming again part of the anonymity of the Concourse. From the barrier, June could see their bench. An enormous Alsatian police dog was resting its front paws on George's chest, its steaming breath arising in clouds from its panting mouth.

'Speak, Roger!'

The dog stretched back its lips, displaying a set of Ivory Castles which might have earned it a Best-in-Show at Cruft's.

George had woken as the dog's paws landed on his chest. His eyes had opened inches away from the long cold nose, the slavering red tongue and the glinting amber eyes which stared into his with the concentrated alertness which deserved a more dangerous object.

Roger spoke. First there was a growl, deep-throated and long-drawn-out. Then he lifted his head, pointed his nose towards the soiled girders of the Concourse, and achieved the top note of his snarling bark. The sound echoed back from concrete and metal. Behind the line of trailers containing mailbags, three policemen hid their laughter behind cupped hands.

George's right hand went across his heart, covering his chest. The dog, in response, took the cuff of George's raincoat between his teeth, and wrenched George's hand and arm upwards, where it remained, pointing upwards, as if George were making an appeal for help to the gods of the Concourse.

One of the three policemen, Roger's handler, ran forward three paces from his hiding place, and then stopped. Roger still held George's arm in the air, growling disappointedly, since it seemed that there was not to be a fight.

'Back! Back! Back, Roger! Heel, boy!' There was something wrong. The handler's voice sounded almost hysterical.

Roger released the cuff of George's raincoat, and the arm dropped limply back across George's chest. The dog-handler started to run.

'Come back, you stupid bloody dog!' Roger backed away, and sat, while his handler fumbled to get George's tie undone. Three buttons from George's shirt came away and rolled under the bench, as the dog-handler ripped the shirt open, and pressed an ear to George's chest. The dog's ears pricked up as he heard the buttons hit the ground. He was still on duty.

'Oh, Christ! Ambulance! Quick! Get a fucking ambulance.' There was no 'almost' now to the dog-handler's hysteria; the hysteria was positive. He had ripped the tie and collar from around George's neck, and with his mouth over George's mouth, inhaled and exhaled with desperate purpose.

June stood, at a little distance, watching. Others watched, but from a greater distance. The regulars did not care to place themselves too close to the police.

The second policeman, who had used his walkie-talkie to summon an ambulance, took over the task of giving George the Kiss of Life, and the third placed the palm of one hand on George's chest and thumped on the back of that hand with the clenched fist of the other. The first policeman was now leaning on a truck loaded with mail bags, and looking as if he were about to be sick. He didn't look to be more than twenty-three years old, and June supposed that this might be the first time his dog had killed anyone. Was there some instruction in the Police Manual that they should continue to give the Kiss of Life until the ambulance arrived?

Perhaps there was. It was fourteen minutes before the ambulance could be heard arriving, and the attempts at resuscitation continued for all that time.

The dog-handler had not been sick, and now rejoined his colleagues. 'Stupid bugger didn't stand a chance.'

'How do you know he hadn't already snuffed it?' This was the policeman with the walkie-talkie. Clearly it would be more convenient for everyone if George had already snuffed it.

'He moved his arm, didn't he?'

'I didn't see that. Did you?' Both the older policemen agreed that they had not seen George move his arm, and the one with the walkie-talkie added, 'Get yourself together, lad. He wasn't going to last long anyway.'

At this point, the third policeman noticed June and Walter. 'What are you staring at?'

'A dead friend. A dog. And three servants of the public, who all wear numbers.'

The three policemen stared at her. The young one wiped his eyes, and said, 'Jesus fucking Christ!'

June said, 'Not possible. If he existed at all, there's no evidence that he was a contortionist.' The two older policemen looked at each other. They had a right one here, but although they knew well enough how to deal with right ones of her sort in the usual course of events, this right one had the advantage of them.

'Would you like my official statement now, or shall we do that at the station?'

'We don't need it, thanks all the same.' The walkie-talkie policeman turned away, dismissing her.

'Your need wasn't uppermost in my mind. Now, the dead man's name was George. He was fifty-four. He liked alcohol, jokes, dogs and honesty, not necessarily in that order.' It came to Walter that June was enjoying herself, though the smell of danger was very strong around them. Perhaps she could not smell it. 'He told us only a few hours ago that he knew he was safe, sleeping there, as long as he moved on when required by the police to do so. I'm sure he felt confident that this request would be made by a human being, and not a dog.'

The white-coated ambulance men were carrying George's body away, covered by a blanket. 'It's a bit late for any of you to ask him now. Which station are you from?'

The young dog-handler was sitting where George had lately lain, his hands covering his face. He mumbled something, and was told to close his mouth. June waited. None of the three policemen told her what station they were from, and she did not know enough about the organization of the Force to know that the station would be Waterloo; they would be Transport Police.

'Perhaps Roger will tell me. Speak, Roger. Come on, nice little doggy. Save the lady time by telling her where to take her complaint.'

The policemen remained silent. June said, 'She doesn't wish to be unfriendly, and blab to the newspapers.' The policemen remained silent.

June waited. The three policemen waited. It was silent all around them. The whole of Waterloo station was silent. Even the pigeons were quiet, and Roger, instead of howling as the dogs in stories do when death is near, sat twitching his tail.

June made a pretence of rummaging in one of the carrier bags.

'What do you want?'

'Ten p. There's always somebody on duty in a newspaper office, and it's bound to be a long call.'

The oldest of the three policemen said, 'What do you really want?' and the walkie-talkie policeman added, 'You can say what you like. It won't do you any good or us any harm.'

'You're wrong on both counts. It will do me good, because if I don't report what really happened rather than the version you might be tempted to give, I shall feel bad for quite some time. And as for the harm to you, well, that's still for you to decide. If I make a statement to your superior officer, that may mean a small black mark on your record, a tiny hindrance to promotion. Whereas an article in Monday's *Guardian* about three policemen and a dog terrorizing an elderly bronchitic, and then trying to cover up the fact that the man died as a result, that might be really quite serious. It might mean you joining the millions of unemployed, some of whom have nowhere to sleep.'

'You really are a vindictive cow, aren't you?' said the walkie-talkie policeman.

'That has been said of me before, yes.'

June made her statement in a small office, reached by a door marked, 'Private. No admittance to the Public'. Walter waited outside, but was not moved on.

The Superintendent explained to June what a difficult job it was his men had to do. June said to the Superintendent that since the matter was now on record, she did not intend to take it further. The Superintendent applauded that decision. Speaking entirely in a friendly and unofficial way, he advised June not to frequent the railway termini of London for a while. A story of this kind was bound to get passed around, and British Transport policemen, like anyone else, were sensitive to criticism.

4

I've got a wanker on the line, who can't wait for Susan

They were asked to give their names, and their names were entered in a book, before the large blonde woman with the face of a Grand National winner, who sat behind a telephone switchboard, said, 'Would you like to go on through? Jenny will make you some coffee.' Then they were led by Jenny through a narrow passage, over the entrance to which a grubby slab of white polystyrene had been hung, so as to save the skulls of those clients who were in such distress that they failed to notice the equally grubby sign instructing them to mind their heads.

'Angela, love, can you take a call on seven? She's not still on Nine Thousand, is she? Oh, bollocks! I'll have to do it myself.' As June turned into the passage, the large woman's hands moved expertly over the switchboard, picked up the telephone attached to it, and in a voice from which almost all trace of horsiness had mysteriously disappeared said, 'Samaritans. Can I help you?'

'Through' turned out to be a central area in need of fresh white-wash and something quite radical done about the armchairs and what was left of the haircord carpet. The smell of cats was strong, and there were also many small cardboard boxes, which lined the edges of the floor, the words 'Rentokil. Poison. Handle With Care' written on their sides.

'I thought we'd come to the Samaritans, not an abattoir for mice.'

'Sorry?' Jenny's bright and smiling face held an expression composed to signify that she hadn't heard.

'Just thinking aloud.'

'Oh! Good. Yes, that's the thing to do. Do sit down.' They sat. 'Do you both take sugar?' Jenny was using her very best R.A.D.A.-trained toneful voice. She had discovered that the low arched ceiling of the crypt in which this branch of the Samaritans operated really made all those hours of practice with her diaphragm and head-resonators worthwhile. Her words sounded as if they were coming from a very expensive record-player with the bass control turned on full.

'Won't be a moment.' Jenny was peeping from behind the lid of a large urn; the steam rising from it was enough to straighten the waves in her hair. June took hold of Walter's hand, and gently applied pressure. Doors leading off this central part of the crypt had names painted on them – 'Geoffrey', 'Dorothy', 'Piers'. Were these the names of the people who sat behind the doors? Each of the doors had a little light beside it. The orange lights were all lit. She was not sure, but it was possible that from behind the door of Piers came sobbing. To which of these person-doors would she be confiding the reason for her and Walter's being here? One thing June had decided was that it would not be to this spinning Jenny, who now approached, slopping their coffee onto the blue stained haircord.

'You can tell I'm new to this. I can't even master Samaritan Rule Number One. "Make a good cup of coffee." ' Jenny smiled the smile she had practised and produced so often to those of the theatrical profession who might give her work. The smile said, 'Please like me,' and so many times they had liked her, told her so, had said in a genuine way, 'We like you. We really do,' so that her heart had leapt with joy. Then they had added, 'But not for this part,' and her heart had sunk. And they had thanked her ever so sincerely for having come to see them, and told her that she had made an impact they really would remember. 'Better luck next time.' But somehow, next time it was always the same, from panto in Carlisle to truly serious and original deodorant commercials: Jenny had improvised and done group work for the Royal Court Theatre, coming back day after day for three days, and at the end all they could say was that they really liked her and she had a quality. Meanwhile she had plenty of time to come in to the Samaritans two mornings a week.

'I should have asked if you preferred tea. We do have some bags. Will you be all right for a few minutes until someone more experienced can come and talk to you?' June nodded.

Jenny backed away towards the Reception Area, smiling as she went, and the voice of the horse-faced lady could be heard. 'Oh, you're just in time. I've got a wanker on this line, who can't wait for Susan. Sounds in a right state, poor love. It's no good me trying to cope out in the open like this; it'd scare off anyone who came in. Can you give him five minutes? You'll find he keeps losing his erection, which is making life even more complicated. See what you can do for him, there's a sweetie.'

June and Walter waited. The few minutes stretched out to more than a few. Ten minutes, then twenty, then thirty. Had they been forgotten? No Piers, no Dorothy came from behind the closed doors to speak with them. Two more people arrived, and were given coffee by smiling Jenny. One was a weeping black woman, who was also given a box of Kleenex, the other a gentleman in a dark suit, who refused the proffered coffee, and sat with his back to the rest of them, pretending to read *The Financial Times*.

More time passed. Walter and June were on their third cup. Opposite them was an old sofa, lying on it a pile of old rags and a dirty raincoat. Suddenly the raincoat and the rags moved, and a pair of feet appeared, wrapped in brown paper tied with string. Toes protruded from the brown paper, grey and bloodless, the long toenails black and curled downwards like the talons of a predatory giant bird.

At the other end of the rags there was movement. There was a nose, which had clearly lived, and above it two blue eyes, below it a pair of chapped lips at the corners of which a whitish creamy substance had dried. These features were surrounded with matted crinkly grey hair, the hairs, both of the head and the beard, seeming to be of more or less equal length.

The blue eyes blinked, then came to rest on Walter. The mouth opened with difficulty, as if the white creamy glue had been used to seal it shut.

'Where am I, Jack?' The voice was hoarse, the intonation accusing. Walter could tell that the question had been directed at him, but since his name was not Jack, turned to June for guidance.

June spoke. Loudly. 'This is the Samaritans. They say they want to help you, but I wouldn't wait if you're in any kind of hurry.'

The face winked. 'I only come here to wait in the warm. They're not supposed to let me in any more. Disbarred, I am, for disruptive behaviour, and pissing on the floor. But it's easy to get by if there's somebody new on.' His head retreated beneath the rags, and his voice was muffled. 'You'll get no money out of them.'

Jenny arrived to make an announcement, using her lower register to stress the serious and apologetic nature of her message.

'I'm terribly sorry, everyone, but we're very short of volunteers today, and it's been extra busy on the switchboard. Someone will see you as soon as possible.'

The door marked 'Piers' opened, and a man dressed as a woman appeared. He wore a short black plastic skirt, rose-pink blouse, high-heeled shoes and over-long false eyelashes, and dabbed at the make-up below his eyes with a small lace hankie held in a large muscular hand.

Could this be Piers?

'I wouldn't have minded, but I took time off work, and came all the way from Leeds, and all he says is that I'm doing it to draw attention to myself.'

An elderly lady had followed the man-woman out of the room. She had white hair, rinsed purple, and wore a twin-set and real pearls. She said, 'I know, Rosemary dear. They can be very brusque at Charing Cross Hospital, but you just have to press on, and convince him you mean business.' This lady must be Piers. As she escorted her client to the door, she said, 'Please do mind your head.' The man-woman ducked, bending almost double to make room for his beehive of a wig. The woman who must be Piers said, 'Do pluck up courage to see them at your local branch, and keep in touch.' Rosemary wobbled unsteadily up the steps in the shoes which had been purchased specially for his trip from Leeds to the Transexual Unit at Charing Cross Hospital, and then took in three very deep breaths, before opening the door and stepping out into the street.

Walter and June waited. They could hear phones ringing, and being answered. The people who answered the phones were saving lives, no doubt, but for whom?

A loud cry came from the Grand National winner on the switchboard. 'Can one of you hurry your client up, and come and take over? If I don't go to the loo in the next thirty seconds, there'll be a nasty accident.'

The black woman sobbed intermittently, and the pages of *The Financial Times* were turned. From a distance, there was a susurration of voices as the hidden Samaritans talked into telephones, talking and listening – listening sometimes to silence, sometimes to complaint, to despair, joke calls, hoax calls, silent calls, breathers and wankers, the lonely, the depressed, the schizophrenic, the fearful, pregnant, deviant, children and barren persons wanting children and other persons who had battered their children, the old and those bearing the burden of the old, the mad, the perplexed – talking sometimes easily of where to lodge or squat or to obtain legal advice or of Clubs – Clubs for agoraphobics, homosexuals, the widowed – 'Have you tried the Gay Switchboard?' 'Have you tried the D.H.S.S?' 'Have you thought of Evening Classes?' – talking sometimes uneasily of life and whether it is worth living, empathizing, always empathizing, a constant drip of empathy along the telephone wires. They came in various sizes, and sexes, and religions. They came sometimes for mornings, for afternoons, for evenings, or stayed all night, sleeping fitfully by the telephone. More were white than black, more middle-class than working-class. They made many mistakes, failed often, never knew when they had succeeded. For June, who despised so many people, they were particularly easy to despise, but it is doubtful whether she could despise them more than often they despised themselves.

'John, sweetie, do be an angel, and keep an eye on the switchboard for a moment.' The loud-voiced lady was back, refreshed, from the loo. 'We're up to our armpits in clients, and someone who shall be nameless has made a balls-up of the Rota again. Oh, and don't let Deirdre see that odd-looking couple from the north; she's not in any way right for them. Give them to Simon, and tell him to turf that old tramp out. He's not really allowed in, but it's my morning for turning a blind eye.'

The door of Dorothy opened, and a young couple with a baby came out, and were escorted to Reception by a young man with long hair, rimless spectacles and a cardboard disc marked 'Simon' pinned to his army surplus camouflage jacket. There was the sound

144

of mumbled thanks, and the Grand National winner, who seemed to have two personae, one for her fellow-volunteers, the other for clients, could be heard comfortingly giving directions for reaching a hostel, and money for the fare. A few moments later Simon had returned, and was prodding the bundle of old rags. 'All right, Shadrach. You've had a good kip. Now on your way.' Then, looking towards Walter and June, 'I'll be with you in a minute.'

The minute turned into four, which was as long as it took to persuade Shadrach that his only likely means of coming into contact with money was to pay a visit to Social Security. Then Simon turned to June. 'You haven't been to us before, have you?'

June shook her head.

'Would you like to talk out here? Or if it's private, we could go into a room.'

So they went into Dorothy, and remained there some time.

5

Shall I put 'co-habiting', then?

'Why can't you tell me where you've come from?'

'From the Samaritans. I told you.'

'I mean before that. What were you doing?'

Walter sat beside June, facing the young man to whom they were applying for Social Security. Neither answered the young man's question.

'And you're not husband and wife?' June shook her head. 'Shall I put "co-habiting", then?'

'Surely one has to have somewhere to habit before one can co-habit?' The young man put a very small white hand to his mouth, and coughed.

'You've nowhere to stay?'

'That's why we need money.' The young man already knew this, but he had been trained to ask questions so that the answers would be given in triplicate. Unreliable applicants, answering the same question more than twice, might trip themselves up, thus saving the young man the necessity of making the appropriate mark in the appropriate box on the appropriate form.

'I can't give you money or a voucher until I have some confirmation of what you've told me.' Small white-headed pimples decorated the young man's neck and chin. The blotches under his eyes were mealy. Walter knew that 'mealy' was a colour used in the description of fancy pigeons; long ago his father had shown him whole classes of mealies at a greyhound track near Preston at which the Premier Show of the Fancy had that year been held. He had not come across the word since, but now it sprang, full-feathered, into his mind as he looked at the blotches under the young man's eyes, which were of a colour somewhere between fawn, grey and blue. 'Mealy,' he said.

'Pardon?'

June said, 'And if we're not prepared to give you confirmation in return for your money or your voucher?'

The young man sighed. Inarticulate Irishmen, drunken Scots, stammering Pakistanis, these were all part of the job, but a stubborn woman really got on his tits.

'Nobody arrives in that chair from Outer Space, madam. Everyone has a past.'

'Goodness! With such wit and insight, you should go far. Does the Home Secretary know where he can contact you?'

Silence. Walter wondered whether the young man's collar was too tight. June remembered that on the way they had passed a plaque commemorating Thomas Brandon, Duke of Suffolk, who had married a daughter of Henry VII, and been granted permission to mint money at Suffolk House. She stored it away neatly in that part of her mind – it was, she thought, the largest part – labelled 'Department of Utterly Useless Information'. She looked at the clock on the wall, and waited. The young man rearranged the forms in front of him, tapped his felt-tipped pen on the counter-cum-desk, and examined the length and shape of his fingernails. Finally he said, 'Would you mind taking your friend, and going to sit on the bench over there, so that someone else can use this counter?'

June smiled graciously. 'Yes, I would mind, I'm afraid. A hell of a lot. You see, I don't think you're assisting us very well with our claim for National Assistance, and so I propose to sit here with my friend until you, or perhaps someone with a little less wit, insight and arrogance and a little more experience, age and authority, helps us.' Her voice had risen in volume as she spoke, and Walter could feel the distinct sensation of unseen people listening.

The young man coughed again before he spoke, and he also allowed his voice to become louder. 'Well, when you've told me what you've been doing, how you've been living, and where, I shall try to corroborate your story.'

'So you've said. But how?' June's acid grace was causing sweat to start up on each side of the young man's nose, and trickle down therefrom. He said, 'It's no use trying to wear me down, madam. We could sit here all day, but I'd still have to go by the book.' June wondered how many other of his female clients he addressed as 'madam'.

'Oh, come along now! You mustn't give in to paranoia. I merely want to know how you'll use any information we give you. That's not unreasonable, surely? Hello, there!'

This sudden greeting and the extra-wide flashing smile was directed past the young man and above his head. The greeting was warily returned by an older man who had appeared and been hovering behind the young man's shoulder. 'Hello! Everything O.K, Leonard?'

'Yes ... Yes, fine, thanks.'

The young man essayed a smile, which froze as June leaned forward, and whispered, 'Oh, I *am* sorry. I didn't realize you were new here. Now, where were we? Let me help you. The past ... yes, well the thing is, you see, we've buried it, Walter and I, and we don't want to dig it up again. And we certainly don't want the people we've left to know where we are. Now do you see?'

'Yes.'

'Good.'

'It doesn't help, though.'

'Why not?'

'Because for all I know, you might be claiming benefit somewhere else.'

This time it was June who sighed. 'And going to all this trouble to claim it twice?'

'It has been known.'

'And if we swear to you on Holy Writ that we haven't a penny, you're not prepared to take our word?'

'That's hardly the point.'

'But surely it is? There must be dozens of people come in here whose past can't be checked, and on whom you have to take a gamble.'

'Well, can you give me some kind of hint?'

Since this enjoyable game had now begun to go her way, June's smile was genuine this time. 'Certainly. What kind would you like?'

'Would I be right in thinking that the reason that neither of you has a National Insurance Number, and that you haven't been working is that you've both been ... been away somewhere?'

June's congratulatory nod meant, 'Getting warm.' Even Walter had become aware that a game was being played.

'Somewhere up north, I assume from your accent. Yorkshire maybe?'

'Not unless they've moved Pennines.'

'Sorry?'

'The Chain, luv. You're wrong side of t'ills. But you're doing very well. We're both from Lancashire.'

'But you have been away?'

'Aye.'

'At Her Majesty's pleasure, perhaps?'

June abandoned the broad Lancashire accent. 'Oh, no, dear, not that. At least I don't think she got much fun out of it. But then, of course, I'm not privy to what amuses Her Royal Highness. And in any case, if "prison" is the word you've been walking around, they don't have mixed ones, you know. No, think of our sabbatical from the world of commerce and industry as being more for medical than punitive reasons. The sentence was still custodial. Society was being saved from us. But it wasn't reckoned to be our fault.'

'Hospital,' said the young man, more in relief than triumph. 'You must have been there a long time.'

June nodded, and looked at Walter, who took his cue, and nodded also.

'And before that?'

Walter noticed that June's enjoyment of the game seemed to have ended, and that she was staring at the floor. Leadership, or at least the responsibility of giving answers, had passed to him. He said, 'Woolworth's. I worked for ... Woolworth's. Preston ... Lancashire ... Years. Nineteen years ... ago.'

Walter's way of speaking explained more to the young man than a life history from June could have done. He noticed the anxious glances from Walter towards June's glassy stare, and decided that he had asked all the questions which needed to be asked at this interview. In the silence that followed, he became aware of the buzzing noise made by the strips of fluorescent lighting. Perhaps a tube was about to burn itself out.

'Before that, I was a sort of housewife.' June's words, though spoken slowly, were unexpected. 'And a sort of mother.'

One of the long tubes of light flickered and almost seemed to split, before it blinked its last blink, and went out.

'Will you wait a moment, please?'

Walter waited. The young man rose slowly, and went to find the £23.07 he would later give them. Then Walter stood, and, taking June's head between his hands, kissed her on the forehead, and then pressed the side of her face against his overcoat.

6

I have felt the tearing of nails, and had my feet stamped on at Harrods

Between Gun Lane and Spitalfields Fruit and Vegetable Market in the City of London, they found Providence Row, a night-shelter for the homeless.

Above one of the doors were the words 'Women's Entrance' carved in stone, and on one of the five steps leading up to that door sat a woman. Her hair was matted in frizzy knots; her face was the colour of old parchment and was without expression. Her fingers played with stockings she had rolled down around her ankles. She ignored both Walter and June. Providence seemed to have made no provision in this woman's life.

From outside, the building represented a small prison or Army Barracks. The entrance for men was similar to the women's, and there was a third, cleaner and newer, marked 'Convent'. June counted the bodies waiting on the steps of the Men's Entrance. There were twenty-two. The time was four in the afternoon.

'You wait here with me, Walter. They're not splitting us up.'

By four twenty, five more women had arrived, and there were thirty-one men. All waited.

'He should be over there.' One of the waiting women addressed this advice to June, but her finger was pointing at Walter, who shuffled his feet uneasily.

'Don't worry, Rita. They won't let him sleep in your bed.' Rita's companion removed the cigarette from her mouth. This enabled her to laugh, cough and spit.

'Look at her, stuck up cow! It's for his own good. He won't get in.' Then, with added energy, Rita leaned towards June, and shouted, 'They only take thirty-five blokes, and there's a crowd waiting already.'

June turned on the informative Rita. 'Thank you for your concern, but he's staying with me. No one told us we'd be split up.'

'Well, I'm telling you, aren't I? I've never met a Hostel where they let you sleep with men. Not even if it's your husband.'

Walter felt as Rita did, that he should be waiting on the other steps with the men. He felt uncomfortable, surrounded by so many women. There were seventeen now, including June.

'He won't get a bed, standing there. Then you'll be split up anyway, won't you?'

'Save your wind, gal. The nuns'll sort her out.' Then, after thought, 'Ask her who sent her.'

'Who sent you here, then?' But it was at that moment that the door was opened by a small and very young nun. While the nun looked up at Walter, and smiled, and said, 'Hello!' the one woman in the queue before them rose to her feet, and, without a word or a change of expression, walked into the Refuge.

Unsurprised, the nun said, 'Hello, Margery. Have a bath, dear,' and then to Walter, 'The men are at the other door.'

June stepped forward, and attempted a smile. 'I'm afraid we're not prepared to be split up, Sister. No one warned us that we would be.'

The women behind made noises of protest, sighs, grunts, tut! tuts, and one was even driven to exclaim in a loud voice, 'Jesus Christ! Hurry up. It's fucking cold out here.' The young nun raised herself onto her toes, moved June gently to one side, and said, 'I agree, Sheila; it's very cold. If you want to bath in warm water, you'd better stop effing and blinding.' Then, lowering herself into a more comfortable stance, 'Would you mind if I let the regulars in first, and then we can talk without being barracked?'

Walter had already stood aside, and June joined him, ignoring the hostile glances from the women who filed past.

'May I see in that bag, Gertie?' Gertie opened her shopping bag, and the nun picked out of it a parcel wrapped in many layers of newspaper and tied with many yards of string. The nun untied the

string. 'Were you intending to knit yourself a hammock, dear?'
Gertie's reply was an expression of resigned hostility, as the newspaper layers were removed to reveal a bottle of British sherry, half
full.

'I wasn't going to drink it.'

'I'll keep it safe for you until you leave.'

The nun explained to June that Providence Row was a Night
Refuge, an emergency service only, that sleeping accommodation
for couples was very difficult to organize, and that most couples
accepted the necessity for the short time they were there. Clearly
the choice was separation here or another night together on the
street. And it was, as the women had said, very cold. It came to
June that she was not going to win this argument, and had better
give in.

They stood in the hall of the Women's Section, and waited. The
young nun returned unhappily. 'We've got our thirty-five men,
I'm afraid. In fact, we've turned six away. We have to turn men
away most days, after five o'clock.'

June studied the lino, and said, 'I see. Well, I'm sorry.' She looked
at Walter. 'You were right, and I was wrong. If I'd let you stand
at the other door, you'd have got in.' Walter looked at the little
nun, then back at June. He looked what he was, which was puzzled.
It was true that he had thought he should be standing at the Men's
Entrance, but he had never said so to June.

'Just a moment, please.' The young nun tapped Walter on the
hand gently, turned, and ran down the corridor in what looked
like a hop, skip and a jump.

June moved to Walter, and hugged him in affection and triumph.
She had noticed the way the young nun had included Walter in
her conversation, had referred to him, smiled at him, and seemed
at ease with him, when most other people either ignored him or
appeared embarrassed.

'Sister Rachael says we're not to abandon you to the Salvation
Army. They'll only talk you to death. We're moving Reginald into
a cubicle downstairs, and that'll make a bed free for you. What's
your name, please?'

Walter looked to June for permission to give the nun his name,
and permission was granted.

'Right, Walter. You come with me. And what's your wife's name?'

Walter's confusion multiplied, and June smiled. It was the only tactical error the young nun had made, and it was made so kindly that it could not be held a fault.

'June.' Walter pronounced the name with pride. He even managed a smile, being totally beguiled by this young woman of religion. If his mother should be watching, he hoped that she had taken note of how a lady of the church had spoken to him.

'Sister Rachael will be with you in a few minutes, June. I'll take Walter to his bed.'

Left alone in the hall, June heard the light tapping of fingers on the door of the Women's Entrance. She opened it, and a woman in her mid thirties, wearing a black cloak, smiled at her.

'My name is known here.' June stood aside, allowing the woman to move gracefully past her, then closed the door, and turned to find the woman's hand stretched out to her, the back uppermost, as if its owner expected that hand to be kissed. June shook the hand firmly, and the woman said reassuringly, 'There is no beginning, you know, and there never was an end. Honesty is too potent a medicine for this sick world.' Her tone was confidential, and she gave June a knowing wink, and seemed about to go, but, noticing June's worried expression, paused to ask, 'Weeping, sweet Veronica?'

'June.'

'Smile, flower child. Here are hot spices and sweet licorice, and rosemary for remembrance.'

'June,' repeated June, as she looked down at the palm of her right hand, into which the woman had pressed a piece of silver paper still sticky from the toffee it had recently covered.

The woman moved down the corridor and round a bend, humming a psalm, the upper half of her body held gracefully erect, while the lower half propelled her along with a little too much spring and a little too much bounce.

There was a shout. It was the shout of someone too pious to use profanity, but sounding so like a curse that no hearer would expect the shouter to be a nun.

'Out! No ifs ands or buts, Mildred. Just, out!' June heard the quick patter of sandalled feet, as Mildred came trotting back, pushed from behind by Sister Rachael.

'Please! Let me stay. I'm not very wet. Just a little damp.'

'You smell like a Scottish Off-Licence on New Year's Eve.'

'It's for the cold. I'll tell Him.'

'Do. And give Him my regards. Don't stop at the cold. Tell Him how you broke a window, and threw up over Sister Cecilia.' As Sister Rachael released one hand from Mildred in order to open the door, Mildred seized her chance, shrugged herself free, and bolted back down the corridor, shouting as she went, 'Come, cherubim, my angels bright, we'll be in Paradise ere night.'

Sister Rachael sighed deeply. 'You realize we'll never get her out now?'

'I'm sorry, but no one else seemed interested in answering the door. I was told to wait here for Sister Rachael.'

'That's me.'

Walter was shown his bed, which was in a large room containing thirty-four other beds. Two lines of ten beds, head to head, took up most of the centre of the room, and the other fifteen beds were placed around the walls. These beds were special, being separated by hardboard partitions and curtains. Walter wondered whether one had to be ill to be allocated one of these beds, for the partitions reminded him of hospital screens. However, since none of the beds was occupied, and an ill person would be in bed sooner not later than the others, he decided that the beds were kept for privileged men.

At one end of the room was a cross, seven feet high, to which was nailed a five-feet-high Christ. Walter had seen crucifixes, but never as large as this. This Christ was only a little smaller than Walter himself, dipped in plaster of Paris, and painted.

Beside the beds there were bedside cupboards, painted white, and each bed had its own straight-backed chair. Although large 'No Smoking' notices had been erected by Fire Inspectors the men smoked openly, and some of them continuously.

The young nun walked Walter round the room, pointing out items of interest. 'That cupboard's for your valuables. It can be locked.' Walter had seen this kind of tour-of-inspection at the

Hospital. Usually it was given to a mayor (or at least a councillor), some London politician or someone collecting for a new addition to the Hospital's amenities. But he was none such. He was introduced to some of the men, shook hands, and when the desultory 'Hellos', 'Pleased to meet yous' and 'How are you?'s' lapsed into embarrassed pauses, wondered if they were waiting for him to say, 'Keep up the good work.'

Finally the young nun left him, saying, 'Will you be all right now?', and Walter nodded. It was just as though they had moved him into a strange ward.

'They'll chat to you properly, I'm sure, when I'm gone.'

They did not. There was silence. Walter looked at the men. The men looked back at Walter, wondering, no doubt, what he had done to receive the privilege of being made room for. Had some of their friends been turned away? Would someone they all knew have slept in the bed he was to occupy? With the nun present, they had said, 'Hello,' and some had said, 'Pleased to meet you,' but they had not been pleased to meet Walter, and were not now, Walter could tell by the way they stared at him. Two, he remembered, had attempted a smile, and he had smiled back. Those two seemed no longer to be in the room. Everyone had a name. The nun had spoken their names. 'This is Robert ... James ... Peter ... Leslie ... Alf ... Martin ... Joe.' He remembered some of the names, but not which names went with which faces. Christopher? Herbert? Patrick? Geoffrey? Clifford? No that was wrong. There was no Clifford. He would have remembered that name. There was no one in the least like Clifford here.

Walter discovered that he couldn't move. He knew that there was nothing physically wrong with him, but if he moved, so might they. To him. Around him.

Now they were still, waiting for him to move, but he couldn't. In the room next to this there was a television. He had been shown it, and introduced to the men who were watching it. They had said, 'Hello,' without turning round, their attention being taken up by a children's programme about a magic Fruit Machine (it paid out in fruit). He had not slept on the train, and now he would not sleep here. He would have to remain standing, so that if they moved, he could move first, away from them in some direction.

And when he had to go to bed, then he must stay awake. He mustn't sleep, not in this place.

'Didn't catch your name, squire.' The voice came from behind him. Walter turned round slowly, ready to make a run for the door.

'Walter.' He had no idea which of the men had spoken.

'Friend of Gracie Fields, eh?' The speaker was a small man with a bald head, who smiled. His voice sounded almost chummy.

Walter had heard of Gracie Fields, who was a singer, but he had never met her, and certainly did not know her as a friend.

'What you doing there? Playing statues?' Walter shook his head. The bald man approached him. 'Well, speak as you find; that's what I say. Speak as you find. Don't condemn a man until you know him. Stands to reason, don't it? Got a job?'

'No.'

'Don't surprise me. Weak chest, like me?'

Walter neither shook his head nor nodded it, for his attention had become taken up by the fact that the other men had begun to move, and they were moving away from him, not towards, to go about their own business, and ignore him. Something he had said must have pleased them.

'Government! Couldn't run a raffle. Shoot 'em. Chronic waste of good money. Haven't got a fag, I suppose?'

'Don't smoke. Sorry.'

The bald man's expression changed to that of a small child being told that Christmas has just been indefinitely postponed. 'Yeah. Waste of breath. What's the point of talking without a smoke?' Aimlessly, the bald man wandered away, muttering curses on Walter's mother, the Roman Catholic Church and the discovery of tobacco.

The bald man's name was Leslie. He wore two cardigans under his jacket.

'My thirst is sore. My thirst is sore! Vinegar and gall is not a godly drink. Where is my cocoa, Sister dear?'

'You can wait.'

Mildred jumped to her feet, and danced around the room, waving

157

her arms. 'My God, my God, why has thou forsaken me?' Her energy amazed them. She seemed never to be still.

'Hanging here like a dried-out crow! Eloi, eloi, lama sabach-thani!'

'For Christ's sake, shut the row!'

She moved from a Samurai posture to one resembling an arabesque, each with equal exuberance. Her long, wavy, pre-Raphaelite hair hung down over her sore and blistered face, one moment ecstatic, the next tragic.

'It's not that you – you, my own people – don't recognize me. I can live with that. It's just that nothing changes, sisters. Nothing. They're still locking up the prostitutes of Mayfair, and playing whist for money in Church Halls. Whist Drives shall themselves be driven from the temple. How many days to Lent?'

Rita's temper, having been strained beyond endurance, broke. She had recently acquired a mug of hot cocoa, but found a more immediate use for it than to drink it. 'Fucking shit! I came here for a bit of peace.' The mug bounced off Mildred's head without breaking, but the cocoa trickled down into her wavy hair and over her forehead, reminding those present of a crown of thorns.

Silence. Then:

'With whips they shall scourge me on this body bare. Then the crown and then the cross. I have felt the tearing of nails, and had my feet stamped on in Harrods.'

Two nuns were holding Rita, and trying to pull her away, as her fist hit the sides of Mildred's face, spreading the spilt cocoa. 'Shut her up. For Christ's sake, stop her blaspheming. I'm going mad here, and you lot are laughing.' Two of the women went to help the two nuns, one taking Rita's ankles and lifting her off her feet, so that the four of them could carry her from the room. Mildred held her bruised face to the light, shook her hair back to show the other women she was smiling, and continued reciting. 'I have been made naked for all lascivious eyes to wonder at my wounds. Put to the test. Put to the fire.'

This was the point at which June emptied the bucket of cold water she had brought from the kitchen over Mildred's head, leaving the red plastic bucket covering Mildred's face.

Mildred's voice could still be heard from inside the bucket. The women laughed, and began to applaud. When the applause reached Mildred's ears inside the bucket, she removed it with a flourish, bowed, wagged her finger at the audience, laughed, and said, 'Unwise females, do not laugh at the Mad Woman of Spitalfields.'

Christopher looked as if the stuffing had been knocked out of him. His expression was one of knowing submission. He leaned against the electric storage-heater, pressed the palms of his hands to the source of warmth, and surveyed the room and its occupants with large dark sunken eyes. Everything about him was either sunken or deflated, as if the padding around his small frame, which had once filled out his clothes, was now wasted away, leaving his shirt, jacket, trousers and skin to hang, wrinkled and heavy.

He was clean. His cleanness shone. It was immediately noticeable. Christopher intended his lack of dirt not only to act as an example to others, but also as a reward for those who had put their trust in him, it being the only reward he could offer. Sister Agatha had told Christopher that the state in which he kept himself was next to godliness (he knew it), Sister Mary that he was as clean as a new pin, while Sister Rachael, who was more given to wit, had claimed that he was as clean as an old nun.

Although that Saint Christopher after whom we may suppose him to have been named was the patron saint of travellers, Christopher Considine himself never ventured further than Quaker Street to the north, Tabernacle Street to the west, Whitechapel to the east, and Cannon Street to the south. Saint Mary Axe, Bishopsgate, Worship Street, Goodman Street, Hope Place and the outside of the Stock Exchange between Threadneedle and Throgmorton Streets, where he would stand for hours, watching the faces of the stockers, jobbers and mere passers-by who came and went, made up Christopher's small world.

On cold days, he would stand with others in a Betting Shop for the warmth. It seemed to be the policy of Messrs Ladbroke, Coral, William Hill and Mecca to overheat their establishments so as to attract the cold, lonely, unemployed and homeless, not many of whom could afford to bet.

'Do you take pills?'

Walter said he didn't, for he did not imagine that the man was referring to aspirin, nor did he understand why the man should be interested in his medical history.

'Better not to.' Christopher felt someone walk over his grave, and shivered, even though he was almost sitting on the storage heater. 'You're not yourself when you're taking pills. He lives on them.' Christopher nodded to a third man, who had now joined them.

'Not any longer.'

'But you take them.'

'I don't live on them. Not now. Not at the moment, anyway.'

'You used to.'

'Yes. In the past, I have.'

'Lived on them.'

'True. I don't deny it.'

The two men talked without ever looking at each other. Walter took no part in the exchange until the second man addressed him.

'He won't eat. Says he can't bear the smell of it. Childish, isn't it?'

This second man was called Chas. He always carried a copy of *The Guardian* under his arm; a letter written by Chas had once been published in its Educational Section. He had been a teacher, would be again he hoped. He wore a brown suit and a red tie, and walked with a permanent stoop, his head down, his eyes searching the floor. A nervous breakdown was responsible for his present situation, which was the want of a situation. That and the fact that, where once there had been a shortage of teachers, there was now a glut.

'A gluttony of teachers. You wouldn't care much for the smell of them either.' He smiled. He had spoken his thoughts. It was unwise to keep everything in his head. After all, they were only words. They weren't sticks, weren't stones, but words, each with its private referents which neither Christopher nor Walter would be able to understand.

Words, as Chas knew from his reading of *The Guardian*, could explain anything away. What they seemed to be unable to do was to put him on his feet again. 'When you're back on your feet' seemed to Chas a vastly overused phrase. The nuns, who were kindness itself, said it at least once a day. His Social Worker, a girl

160

young enough to be his daughter, said it at every visit. His doctor had said it, and even his National Health psychiatrist had said it. His actual feet, those he stood and walked on, had no difficulty whatever in supporting him. It was the other end of his body which had let him down.

'My head.'

'Pardon.'

One of the symptoms of his breakdown had been an obsessive belief that he was walking on his head, or rather on his hands, head downwards. Therefore it seemed to him that 'when you're back on your feet' was an excessively thoughtless phrase to use.

In any case, he was now well. Chas was well, as well as could be expected for anyone out of work and living in a hardboard cubicle, six feet by eight, which he earned by keeping his bed dry and pleasing the nuns. Well, he did not really live there; he slept there. His days were spent at the Job Centre, the Public Library, and occasionally he too might be found in a Betting Shop, since he had discovered one which contained tall black plastic stools, on which he could sit and study *The Guardian's* Crossword Puzzle, provided he made a reasonable pretence of reading the Sports Page.

With the aid of the National Health psychiatrist, he had discovered the source of his upside-down obsession, which had consequently weakened and so died. Chas was now being encouraged to 'tail off' the tranquillizers which had enabled him to control his fears of public places, of crowds, of alcohol, Vitamin B, coffee, tea, cereals, or anything which might be eaten, drunk or inhaled to stimulate the nervous system, and particularly the brain, any stimulant, in fact, which might stimulate Chas into seeing the world as upside-down and trying to correct this view of it by standing on his head in Tesco's.

A year and eight months ago, at the age of forty-six, childless, unmarried, and seemingly unloved, he had looked up from his desk at the rows of adolescent punks who sat before him, uttered the words, 'Orwell loved shit,' and promptly burst into tears.

And the spotty punks had laughed. They had assumed it was a joke, and that his expression, which had dissolved into pain and fear, would just as quickly return to humour and confidence. It had been ten minutes before a girl had run from the room to fetch the Physical Training Instructor, ten minutes of blubbering tears and racking sobs on one side of the classroom, laughter (both hysterical and forced), elbow-jabbing, gum-chewing, shouting (wordy and wordless), missiles being thrown, pocket billiards and the stroking of after-lunch erections on the other.

Now Chas waited to be put back on his feet, to be given a chance, to be tested again before the firing-line of uninterested faces and amid the cannonade of rude noises, to stand up with a straight back and only a blackboard behind him. And not to be down and out in the City of London.

At seven forty-five, Walter stood on the steps of the Women's Entrance, waiting for June. Since he had swiftly become used to her sleeping beside him, to holding her, to waking in the morning with her there, he had slept very little, and several times he had started awake, convinced that he was still in his old bed at the Hospital, and that the happenings of the past few days had been part of a prolonged dream.

He had sat up on the side of the bed, listening to the chorus of snores and the moans of someone two beds away, who was having a nightmare, and waited for the morning, when he would return to his piece of concrete path and the wall of the Mother and Baby Unit where June would be waiting. But the morning had brought a different room, full of men who could walk, and talk, and dress themselves, unhappy men who were part of the real world, and could not be written off as Jesus's Mistakes. These men showed every reluctance to have their breakfasts and leave, even though they were free to do so. But then, they had nowhere else to go, and June wasn't waiting for them.

Walter sat down on the steps, and watched four men set fire to a wooden crate, and stand around it, staring into the smoke and flames. He watched a small boy pick up discarded cabbages, crushing them together to pack as many as he could into a string bag. Rotten fruit and vegetables of all kinds, dead flowers, paper cups, cardboard, straw and bits of wood almost covered the streets and pavements. Three women, each with a pushchair and several bags, sorted through the rubbish, picking out the best of the food. They had made an early start.

It was Her Majesty's Jubilee Year. A group of pigeons tugged and pulled at half a tomato sandwich, until a gull chased them off, its wings held high and its beak wide in a threatening screech. Behind them, a fat black woman slowly removed the pips from half a water melon she had found in the gutter.

'Let's leave what's rotten.' June laughed, as she handed Walter a pear from the ground, and found another for herself. He could tell by her eyes that she had slept, and by the way she held his hand and swung his arm backwards and forwards between them. She was happy.

Walter was delighted that she had not wanted to stay any longer in Providence Row.

From Spitalfields they walked along Commercial Street and Great Eastern Street to Old Street, along City Road to the Angel at Islington, where two pubs advertised Topless Go-Go Dancers, then along Liverpool Road, where they passed a Pie and Mash Shop selling Jellied Eels. Holding hands and singing, 'There was a man went round the town,' they walked through Barnsbury, and stopped to look at the window of a shop in which concertinas were made, then on up the Caledonian Road to Pentonville Prison, outside which a man was drilling a hole in the road. June told Walter that this was in order to assist the prisoners to escape, and he believed her. From Pentonville Prison to Holloway Prison, via Hillmarton Road, then across to Dartmouth Park, Fortess Road, until, having walked almost six miles, they came at last to the address with which the young Samaritan, Simon, had provided June, the Squatters' Advisory Centre at Tufnell Park.

There was a notice in the window, 'The Council regret that owing to the interests of Big Business, they are unable to fulfil their obligations to the homeless this year.' June read it aloud to Walter slowly, partly in order to give her time to think again. The suitcase and carrier bags did not grow lighter, and she did not wish to have to walk back to the Samaritans, who had, in any case, advised her to try the Squatters as a last resort. Perhaps the Advising Squatters would at least allow her and Walter to sit down while they received advice.

The door opened, and a man in a faded denim suit, who wore a beard and rimless spectacles, stood in the doorway, looking like someone holy out of Dostoevsky, but better dressed and fed. 'Just in time,' he said. 'Would you like to come along? We're about to undertake an occupation.'

June said, 'Could we sit down for a bit first?'

'I hate to ask you this, but would you mind breaking in again? Bruce didn't quite get you that time. He's having trouble with the light in here.'

The senior members of the Squatters' Advisory Service stared at the Australian holding a microphone. It was not the light with which Bruce was having trouble, but the lack of it. It was, in fact, dark. They were standing in the cellar of a one-time Guest House, now derelict, situated at the corner of a run-down Square between Queensway and Notting Hill. There were ten trainee squatters present, if one included Walter and June. They had between them, for the purpose of affecting entry, three hammers, two screwdrivers, a crowbar, and a long-handled wooden mallet which might once have been used for croquet.

'If you could break in just as you did then, Brucie would know this time where to put his pup. That's what us film types call a small lamp. We only have one, and it's dead critical, the placing. I hate to ask.'

The Senior Squatters' Adviser leaned his elbow against the damp wall, closed his eyes to indicate the degree of frustration he felt, and said patiently, 'We are not breaking in. We are entering an abandoned and derelict property in order to occupy it. Everything we do is legal.' The Senior Squatters' Adviser had practised rational argument and debate since the very beginning of his life, when, appraising the two people leaning over his pram, he had formulated the first two questions which defined his social position, 'Mummy? . . . Daddy?'

'Sure, sure. Right on, man.' The interviewer/director of the two-man Australian Television Film Company sensed that diplomacy was needed. They had promised the Squatters' Advisory Service a hundred pounds for information and two interviews, and to be allowed in on an actual occupation was an unexpected bonus, for which he hoped not to be charged, since the company was already running on the overdraft of his father, a pharmaceutical chemist in Canberra. 'Not break in. Right. Did I say "break in"? No, what I meant was, if we could just see the two of you again, forcing the window, climbing in, unscrewing the locks, and then see the rest of the crowd bursting in again past that corrugated barricade some capitalist pig of a landlord has put there, it'd be great for the film and Brucie would be happy. He really thinks we're on to a winner here, don't you, Bruce?'

Bruce nodded, and said, 'Great!' The two senior members, advisers both (though they did also squat, rather comfortably, near the Tottenham Court Road), considered the request, while the actual squatters under advice – Walter, June, two students of Art from St Martin's and one from the Slade, a young man from the L.S.E., a demolition worker, two unemployed secretaries and a messenger boy who had arrived that day from Plymouth – waited. If the decision should be to do it again, they would have to climb back outside, disperse in the square into little clumps of one or two, so as not to look like a mob, and wait for a handkerchief to be waved from an upstairs window by one of the advisers, as a signal that legal entry had been effected. Then they would make their way down the cellar steps, and squeeze past the corrugated iron barricade.

'It's dangerous to go out there again. Someone may have seen us come in, and phoned the police already. I wouldn't climb through a window twice in the space of five minutes; it's asking for trouble. I mean, you can't just say to the fuzz, "It's all right, officer. I'm being filmed for an Australian documentary about the homeless in London." '

Thus the Junior Adviser. He had made a point. Both unemployed secretaries giggled and the messenger boy from Plymouth nodded gravely. The Senior Adviser scratched his beard, and considered. The promised hundred pounds had not yet been handed over.

'Couldn't we just go from the people coming through that door, and then us boarding it up? That way, they wouldn't have to go out into the street again.'

'Brucie's heart wouldn't be in it. He's set his heart on getting you breaking in – effecting legal entry, I mean – through the window, and then dismantling the locks all in one shot. It's a point of professional pride with Bruce. I mean, you can see it'd be a great way to open the film. No sound. Get it? Just you two effecting legal entry, beautifully lit.'

'Great!' This was Bruce again. 'Great' and 'Jesus' were the only two words Bruce had been heard to use on British soil. Cruel friends ascribed this paucity of Bruce's vocabulary to his mother's having been frightened by an Elocution Teacher while on holiday in Earls Court. But Bruce found that these two words, with varied intonation, expressed all he ever wanted to communicate, while also excusing his inability to remember people's names and his reluctance ever to buy a round of drinks.

The Senior Adviser nodded his head. The ten trainee squatters prepared themselves to be immortalized again, while effecting legal entrance. Bruce led Walter from the line, placed him in the corridor, and proceeded to adjust the 'pup' so that it illuminated Walter's profile.

June stepped forward. 'May one inquire what that's for?'

'Bruce wants to feature the geezer in the flat cap.'

'Why?'

'No particular reason. The face is unusual.'

'Great!'

'He's not with you, is he?'

'You see that he is. We're all "with" each other, aren't we? I thought that was my point. Also, he happens to be my lover.'

Bruce said, 'Jesus!' and June stared at him. In order to mend matters a little, the interviewer/director said, 'That's what I like about English women. You're so cruel. I mean, saying a thing like that about a bloke who's missing half his marbles, that's really cruel. I love that.'

'Great!'

Walter screwed up his eyes tightly against the glare of the 'pup'. The interviewer/director said, 'He won't do that when we're rolling, will he?'

'I wouldn't be at all surprised.'

'Can he talk?'

'Considerably more than Bruce, it seems. However, he's not telepathic. If Bruce wants him to stand there like that when we make our entrance, he'd better say so.'

'Would you ask him to do that? Oh, and not to blink. It's the cap.'

'Great!'

'Not to blink?'

'The light won't look that strong on film. We're dealing with illusion here.'

'You surprise me.'

They did it all again, and Bruce seemed pleased. Walter stood on his mark, and looked around without blinking, just as June had told him. He enjoyed his starring role and the attention it brought him. June had told him that this was 'acting', and he remembered the Abbot and Costello films they had shown so many times in the Hospital, and the lady who had arrived once a month to ask the patients to help her save a baby from a tree by chopping down the tree with imaginary axes.

The ten trainee squatters rushed about the building, barricading windows and securing door. No landlord, far less a policeman, must be allowed to gain entry by means of some neglected orifice, for if a person representing the owner of a property were allowed in, then the legal entry became, in some way June did not understand, illegal, and the entrants might be as legally ejected. The squat must never be left 'open'. At least one squatter must always remain in residence to allow the others in on the pronouncement of a password. All communication with such unauthorized would-be entrants as the landlord, police or the local council must be shouted from an upstairs window, or from behind the security of a barricaded door.

Hammers were brandished, large nails and planks of wood. The trainee squatters felt like City children building a tree-house. Then came let-down.

On the first floor, they discovered an interior door secured with a Yale lock. The door also contained a letterbox. This suggested to the two Advisers that they might be looking at the door of a self-contained flat. A quick squinny through the letterbox confirmed that this was so. There were the remains of unmistakable breakfast on a table within. What had seemed to be a derelict building was, in fact, occupied, and the occupant might return at any moment, to discover entrants who had, by the mere discovery of dirty breakfast dishes, become illegal.

Could a different and unorganized group of squatters be operating in the same area, without the knowledge or approval of The Squatters' Advisory Service? The two Advisers held a meeting, moving from one room to another in an attempt to avoid Brucie's persistent camera, and arguing in whispers. The two students from the St Martin's School of Art removed one of the panes of frosted glass from the offending door, and let themselves in, discovering the door to be the entrance not to a flat, but a bed-sitting room, which had not just the air but the positive aroma of being under occupation, and by someone from the Orient.

While the two Art-students replaced the frosted glass and the wooden beading which had held it in place, and while the two Senior Advisers hid in a toilet from Brucie and his partner, Len, scratching their beards and wondering how the squat could be made secure as long as someone else was living in one room of this twenty-roomed house, a key was inserted from outside into the lock of one of the side doors. But though the key was correctly turned, the door would not open, there being a large chest-of-drawers and three trainee squatters pressing against it from the inside.

Several different keys were tried in puzzlement, before one of the trainees moved the chest-of-drawers in order to speak through the letterbox.

'This house is now an official squat.'

A round male Asian face was lowered to the level of the letter-box, and brown slightly bloodshot Asian eyes blinked back at the student of Art.

'What is this, please?'

'We're squatting.'

'What is squitters?'

'Squatters. We are. Understand?'

'No, because my key is out of order. Please open the door.'

'We've blocked it. If we let you come in, you have to accept that we're legally squatting? All right?'

'No. This is my house. We buy it to let out rooms. Many, many maisonettes. You are too early. They are not ready. Much has to be done.'

'You can say that again.'

'Please tell me what you are doing in my father's house.'

Others had joined the three. The messenger boy from Plymouth had been dispatched to fetch the two Senior Advisers from the toilet. June murmured. 'In my father's house there are many maisonettes,' and was ignored.

'This is not nice behaviour after a long day's work. I shall fetch the police to boot you out.' The Asian eyes were removed from the letterbox, and Asian footsteps could be heard retreating from the door, making for the rush-hour crowds and (it had to be assumed) the police of Queensway.

Under the superintendence of the Senior Advisers, they made an orderly evacuation of the squat, and waited on the pavement outside to explain to the police. The Senior Advisers waited, the students of Art and the unemployed secretaries waited, the young man from the L.S.E., the demolition worker, the messenger boy from Plymouth, Walter and June waited; Brucie and Len waited. No policemen appeared, nor did the Asian gentleman return.

After forty-five minutes' waiting, the group was smaller. Bruce and Len explained – which is to say that Len explained while Brucie interpolated either the word 'Great' or the word 'Jesus' in support – that since they had only been able to film half a squat, they should only pay half the money, and, the pubs being open, left with their equipment. No police arrived. After an hour and a quarter, only Walter and June, the student from L.S.E. and one of the Senior Advisers remained. June was turning over in her mind the prospect of approaching the Salvation Army.

'So that's it, then, is it?'

' 'Fraid so.'

'That's all the advice you have left, is it? Squatters' Advisory Service! Jesus!' June was not above borrowing a word from Brucie when it suited her. She took Walter by the arm. 'Well, Walter, having spent all afternoon being unpaid film stars for these people, you and I are back on the streets again.'

'Me too.' The young man from L.S.E. added his grievance to June's. 'Not very good public relations.'

'Don't you have any friends you could stay with?' The Senior Adviser kicked the kerbstone with his left sandal, and wondered if this lot were about to commit the ultimate solecism of asking for money.

'Don't know anyone in London yet. One reason I wanted to squat.'

'The Y.M.C.A. –'

' – was full last night. Full by lunchtime.'

They waited, while the Senior Adviser tried to think of words with which he could take his leave of them. Why should he always be the one left holding the baby?

The young man from L.S.E. said, 'Isn't there any room at any of the existing squats?'

The Adviser shook his head, and June realized that at any moment he would simply apologize, and leave them standing there.

'What do you usually do when something like this happens?'

'It doesn't.' The Senior Adviser smiled, and shrugged his shoulders.

'You mean, up to now everything's gone smoothly?'

'Well, no, but if there's a hitch, people usually have somewhere else to fall back on.'

The young man from L.S.E. looked at June, then at Walter, and finally at the Adviser, and said, 'Well, we three haven't. Are you just going to piss off, and leave us stranded?'

The Adviser sighed, thought, removed his hands from his pockets, looked first up, then round about, but never straight at them.

'I'll make a phone call.'

'My name's Graham,' said the young man from L.S.E. to Walter and June, and they shook hands.

They were reminded yet again that this was an Emergency Squat, a place for temporary accommodation, for one or two nights at most, a doss, no more. 'It's not fit for a pig to live in really, but it's better than a draughty doorway.'

June's thoughts went to pigs in draughty doorways, and the

words, 'Evenin', all,' came involuntarily to her lips. No one else saw the joke.

Inside the house was the now familiar smell of damp rotting wood, flaking plaster and musty fabric. The Senior Adviser said, not for the first time, 'I don't think the floors upstairs are safe. I'd stay down here.' Seven stair-treads were missing, and the banister rail was broken. He pushed open the door of the ground-level front room. A pair of very old tennis shoes lay on their sides in the centre of what had once been oak-stained floorboards. June said, 'Looks as if the pig left in a hurry.'

Together, Walter, Graham and June surveyed the room which would be their home, at least for one night or two.

The Senior Adviser switched on the light, and they blinked. 'Good. That's still working.'

A jagged piece of broken mirror had been propped up on the mantelpiece. They were reflected in it, looking like three prospective purchasers and a hovering and over-anxious estate agent.

'The loo's under the stairs.'

'Won't the water have been turned off?' Graham's spectacles caught the reflection of the bare sixty-watt bulb hanging from a cord in the ceiling.

'It was, but we turned it back on again. The stopcock's in the back garden. Well ... yard really.'

June pointed at the light-bulb, and asked, 'Who pays for that?' This question amused the Senior Adviser greatly. He tittered, and toyed with his frizzy beard.

'Some questions are best not asked. We just manage to keep in dispute with them, and refuse to pay. They've had so much bad publicity lately, with old-age pensioners freezing to death, that they're reluctant to cut anyone off. But it's one reason why nobody can stay here very long.'

Around the edge of the room were five stained single mattresses. Someone had started to paint the walls tangerine, but had stopped when either paint or enthusiasm had run out. A purple poster advertised a Squatters' Benefit Bop – 'Keen and the Mustard Gang. Live !'

In one corner of the room, resting on the floor, was the frame in which the strings of a baby-grand piano were set. No other part of the piano could be seen, and June assumed that it had been burned. On top of the piano was a very old Underwood typewriter, and by it a number of white cards on which cryptic messages had been printed, one of which read, 'Beware ! Savage hamster at large. Please jam door shut. Ta.' June twanged on the strings of the baby-grand with her thumbnail, and attempted to depress the keys of the typewriter, but they were all stuck. Walter sat down on a pile of bricks which had once served as a coffee table, and inspected a pub ashtray.

'If the police come, simply tell them it's a civil matter between you and the landlords, and that the landlords will have to summon you to a civil court.' The Senior Adviser had decided that Graham looked the most responsible of the three.

'Do we know who the landlords are?'

'The local Council, but it's the same thing; you're given twenty-three days on average to get out. If they don't intend to start work on the place, they don't usually hurry you. By occupying, you're keeping the rats out.'

Walter dropped the ashtray, and it broke.

'Not to worry. Plenty more where that came from.'

June found a roll of dusty faded posters, on one of which were the words, 'Re-use Paper. Save trees.'

'According to the Electricity Board's charter of eighteen ninety-three or something, they're legally bound to supply every occupier where there's an outlet. So, when you do find somewhere more permanent, don't let them come on funny with you.'

Walter had collected every piece of the broken ashtray, and was holding them in both hands, wondering what he should do with them.

'More permanent?'

'A more permanent squat. You buy a rent book from Woolworth's, and fill a bit of it in to prove you're bona fide occupants. Then you take it to the Gas and Electricity, and ask them to re-connect you.' June made a loud *twang!* on the strings of the baby-grand. 'You'll be liable for rates, of course; there's no way round that; but you tell them you didn't realize. Those of you who aren't students' – the Adviser was looking in June's direction but not at her – 'should be eligible for a bit more Social Security, as house-

172

holders. Unless, of course, you're just slumming, and have an enormous private income.'

Graham's eyes were impassive. The pieces of broken ashtray were no longer reflected in his glasses, for Walter had placed them on what was left of the mantel. The Senior Adviser realized that someone with Graham's accent might indeed have a private income; clearly Walter and June did not. 'You're at L.S.E., then?' he said.

Graham nodded. 'And you?'

'Salford Polytechnic. Used to be. I wanted to do Social Work, you see.' If Graham did see, he didn't appear to be saying. 'The Sociology Department at Salford – it's pretty well known, you know. One of the best really.'

'Really?'

'In the north.'

'Yes.'

The Senior Adviser did not know why he had begun to feel in some way inferior to Graham. He was, after all, the Senior Adviser; it wasn't up to him to prove anything.

There was a period of silence, during which June held the nylon net window-curtains open slightly. They felt greasy, and were the colour of the slates on the roof opposite.

Graham said, 'Well, thank you, I think we can manage now.'

'I haven't shown you the kitchen.'

'We'll find it.'

The Senior Adviser found himself being shown to the door of a squat in which he had become a visitor. Graham said. 'Oh, by the way, where do *you* live?'

'Just off Tottenham Court Road. We have the whole block of flats.'

'Good address.'

'Yes. We've been there some time, of course.' Why did he keep saying 'of course'? 'Done quite a lot to it. Painting, carpentry – you know, improvements.' Why did he feel the need to impress a trainee squatter who, properly considered, was no more than a pain in the arse? It was Graham who should be ingratiating himself if he wanted to be helped to a better squat. The Senior Adviser reverted to generalities in an effort to remind himself of his own importance. 'London's full of empty houses and flats, if you know where to look. Disorganized Councils who've bought them and can't yet afford to pull them down and rebuild. Speculators waiting for the next property boom. It's also full of people with no place to live, of course.'

'Who owns the flats you're in?'

'Some fuddy-duddy trust handles them. They're part of the estate of some old woman, who can't afford to do anything to them, and isn't allowed to pull them down.'

'Perhaps she should sell.'

'Well, that's difficult, of course, when she's got squatters.'

'Of course.' Graham smiled. The Senior Adviser found himself saying, 'If anyone should move out, I'll certainly . . .'

'Let me know? I'd be very grateful. We must have a jar very soon. Goodbye.' Graham closed the door, and the Senior Adviser shuffled down the steps, feeling like a toad who had failed to turn into a prince.

In the kitchen, June was reading the graffiti on the walls. 'DON'T SEND ANY MORE TO SHERMAN STREET. THEY'VE HAD ENOUGH,' were the words she read.

7

My hobby's a secret, girl, but I'll give you a clue.

At Eltham Street, just as in the Hospital, Walter woke at six, or just after. It was a habit, a routine he had followed for almost twenty years. Now that June was beside him, and they were in their own place (for all that they shared it with Graham), he slept as well as he had used to do in the ward, but by six thirty he was out of bed. Since he no longer had Clifford to clean and dress, or any other patients to help and organize, there was plenty of time to be used or killed before June woke. He would never wake her, and would move around slowly and carefully, knowing that she was a light and poor sleeper. Also the privacy of the time he had while she did sleep was important to him. Privacy in a hospital hardly existed; finding it was like a privilege for good conduct. Before the hospital, his mother had allowed him privacy only when he was actually sitting on the W.C. and even then he was timed. Now he was his own man – his own man and June's man – and in the early mornings, no one watched him, or even stood outside the door of the toilet, listening.

His first action on waking was to smell the air, lifting his head, and breathing it in deeply. To have done that at the Hospital, in a ward full of incontinent persons, would have been thought strange behaviour even in someone labelled as mentally handicapped, so that Walter had saved his deep breathing for those times when he was outside the grounds of the Hospital. The first time he had been allowed to be part of a crocodile of Jesus's Mistakes, the line of men had passed a group of seven rhododendron bushes, and Walter had smelled the same smell he had smelled twenty years earlier, walking through a park in the rain, his father's arm around his shoulder.

Every morning now he remembered that first walk outside the Hospital, and the earlier one with his father, and every morning he looked up, just as he had done at seven years old, and the memory of his father's face, looking down at him, owning him, accepting the fact that Walter was his, belonging to him and part of himself, gave Walter a sensation too complicated for him to be able to describe. There was happiness in it, and security, the exchange of love, and belonging, and it filled him so full and bubbled up so zestfully inside him that he had to walk about the room, smiling and hugging himself and whispering under his breath, 'Thank you, Jesus.'

That was just one of the reasons Walter needed some moments of privacy. He knew that here, in the real world, such a demonstration of so much feeling would be considered strange. He himself thought it strange, but he knew that the comfort he found in these moments was something he was meant to have. Jesus meant him to have it. He had given it to Walter in exchange for Walter's parents, and even now that Walter had June, Jesus continued to give it in proof to Walter that his mother had been right, and that Jesus did love him. Therefore Walter could not be one of His Mistakes, since mistakes are forgotten and not cherished.

Another part of Walter's morning ritual was to check and count his clothes, making sure they were all there. This had been an essential part of his routine ever since he had first been allowed to wear and be responsible for his own clothes at the Hospital. There, if anything should be missing, it had been left to him to find and chastise the guilty party. After a while, nothing ever had gone missing.

Now, if he mislaid anything, it would prey on his mind for days, and he would refer to it over and over again, telling himself and June when he had last seen it, testing his memory for any sign of weakness by recalling what they had eaten that day, to whom they had spoken, and what they had both been wearing.

After counting his clothes, Walter would examine them for stains or tears, and scrutinize each button to make sure that none was loose. To lose a button would upset him greatly. How would one go about replacing it? Finding new buttons to replace old was a hit-or-miss operation, and in Walter's experience, mostly miss. Newly bought buttons might not match, and that would be as bad as wearing a garment which was one button short. Odd buttons looked wrong. They would attract attention. People in the real world did not wear mismatched buttons.

On the fourth day at Eltham Street, one of the buttons on his jacket broke. It just split into two pieces. Walter felt as if he had lost a close friend. He sighed and worried over it all day, sometimes just standing and staring at the two pieces of button in his hand. He asked June if she had ever endured such an experience, and could she possibly explain to him why this strong and healthy-looking button should suddenly split in two? Could it have something to do with the rain? Had the wet weakened it, did she think? He had worn the jacket over eighteen years, had lived with this button, touching it and its companions several times a day on those days on which he had worn the jacket. Yet none of the other buttons had split. Could he have been wearing a faulty button all that time without knowing it?

The cleaning of his boots every morning took between twenty and twenty-five minutes. Something else he had learned at the Hospital was that if he organized his time, he never needed to rush.

He became frustrated by the fact that in London it was possible to get dirty merely by walking about. June would watch him wriggling inside his clothes, as if the grime of London had coated his skin, and was sending him mad with irritation. Skin which had been kept scrupulously clean for almost twenty years in the Hospital now seemed to attract dirt as a fly-paper attracts flies. Almost every time they passed a Gents, Walter would excuse himself, and go inside to wash his hands and face.

'Do I look all right?' Walter would ask June this question several times a day. He was afraid that he would 'let her down', and also that people would be able to tell from his appearance that he had come from the Hospital.

For some time he was reluctant to approach any of the real people of the real world in which he and June now lived. He would sweat, clear his throat, and begin to shake, if June gave him money, and asked him to buy the bus-tickets. In shops, he would stand by the door, ready to open and close it for other customers while June waited to be served. Gradually she encouraged him to stand beside her at the counter, placing an arm around his waist in moral support, and holding tightly to his jacket to prevent him from shuffling away. The way in which shop assistants would glance at him dismissively and refer automatically to her, infuriated June. Every time this happened made it harder the next time to persuade him to do the talking.

'My husband has the money,' June would say defiantly, and she would attempt to outstare the assistant until notice was taken of Walter. Sometimes this provoked knowing smirks, nods, winks, even titters, and once a heartless guttural belly-laugh from a large West Indian bus-conductress.

'If he's your husband, honey, my name's Ian Smith.' Sycophantic commuters laughed their first laughs of the day. 'That's right, children. Start the day with a laugh, and get it over with.' June wanted to punch the shiny black face, expressing so much self-confidence, to break all the gleaming white teeth and hear them drop to the floor. 'This is not colour prejudice,' she would say. 'That I feel such rage at all towards someone of your colour is the very opposite. I am treating you as an equal, you bitch, and how do you like this bunch of fives?'

What she did say was, 'Does London Transport pay you to be insulting, or is that just your hobby?'

The black head was tossed back, and the whites of the eyes flashed. 'My hobby's a secret, girl, but I give you a clue. It begins with "s" and ends in nine months, less you careful.'

More commuters laughed, and June could see that Walter had become positively frightened. She would never again pretend that they were married.

And time passed. Her Majesty's Jubilee ended, and 1978 began.

178

PART FOUR

Walter Alone

I

Now just holding his hand is like taking an animal to the vet's to have it put down.

'How did you get here? Where have you come from? Hospital or prison? Where have you been before that? Where did you sleep last night? Have you any money? Any possessions? None at all? How have you been living? What was your last job? Can you read? Write? Spell your own name? How much money did you say you had? Do you expect me to believe you? Do you suffer from any of the following? Epilepsy? T.B? Migraine? Asthma? Bronchitis? Piles? Dizzy spells? Gonorrhoea? Athlete's Foot? Eczema? Verrucas? Boils? Tennis Elbow? Constipation? Acute or Chronic? Alcoholism? Colour Blindness? When did you last see a doctor? How old are you? What's the colour of your eyes? What religion? Why are you arguing? Are you now or were you at any time? Having a nervous breakdown? I was. Can you drive? Type? Subtract? Tie your shoelaces? Mend roads?'

'Will you? Take any job offered? Only one you have done before? Paint white lines? Be prepared to wear a clean tie? Underwear? Promise not to pick your nose or break wind in front of customers? Be civil? Look happy? Feel happy? Be happy? Never give in to a nervous disorder? I did. Over it now. Valium is my Saviour. Lo, though it lead me into the shadow of death, I shall not fear.'

Walter's unhappiness was total. A physical thing.

'*You're watching me all the time.*'

He had moved forward, slowly placing one foot in front of another, without aim or destination. He had come to this place, the Reception Centre.

'Simply because I sit this side of the desk, and you that, doesn't mean that there is a class, cultural, intellectual gap between us. We're all on your side, you know. A desk is not a symbol; it can be moved. But then where would we put our elbows? Your cap? My forms? Biros? Worry-beads? Your identity bumf, if you had any?'

'*I can't stand being watched. Things don't always last, Walter. Feelings change.*' And he had watched her, his head lowered, and his eyes fixed on hers. '*I never plan too far ahead.*' She had waited. '*It's just not wise. Not wise for me.*' Her eyes had flickered, and she had known that he had seen the suitcases.

'My point is a simple one, Walter. I'm you; you're me. So? I'm in work; you're out. Ergo, I have a mortgage, which you have not. I'd have been a gentleman of the road, Walter, but for faulty equipment. Flat feet. Bitter disappointment. Am I putting you at your ease? I do hope so. It's what I'm here for.'

'*If you'd been able to read, I'd have left you a note. That's what people usually do when they can't face a situation.*' Once, only once, he had asked her outright, very simply, as if asking what she had had for lunch, 'Why are you so nice to me, June?' and she had laughed, and hugged him, and told him that it was because she loved him. Now she had turned her head away.

'Don't ride, I suppose? Horses, I mean. No? Daughter got onto it. Can't get her off. Sex. All that rippling dog-meat under her crutch. Where were we?'

Walter moved his mouth, and the sound of a fart in a bath of soapy water came out. Among the bubbles could be heard the words, 'I need somewhere to sleep.' Now he had spoken.

The man took off his spectacles, and held them at a distance to study the lenses. It was all right; they were still there. He spoke gently. 'Of course you do; of course you do. I'm the Prevention of Abuses Officer. I have to find out your reasons for leading an unsettled life, why you have this wanderlust. Then I point you in the right direction.' He replaced the spectacles on his nose, and picked up another sheet of paper. 'Now we come to the Warning List.

Haven't given me a false name, have you?' Walter shook his head. 'Not wanted by the C.I.D., are you, for any little peccadillo? Murder? Rape?' Walter said that he was not wanted by the C.I.D. 'How about constantly deserting your family? Refusing to keep them?' Walter said he had no family, and, without thinking before he spoke, the man said, 'Good.'

He had no family. He was not wanted by anyone.

'If you agree to be helped, you could become a resident. A Gate Man. For just fourteen pounds thirty-five from your Social Security, we'll arrange real security. Some of our residents have been here thirteen years. Some of them were born into institutions. It's all they know, and who's to say they're wrong? They come up to me, and say it to my face, "I wouldn't last five minutes on the outside, Mr Saunders. I'm all right for another month, aren't I?" They know where they are here. There's a TV Room, and a film show once a week. The psychiatrist visits us twice a week, and the doctor once a day. All reasonable care. Their only duty is to look after the Casuals' clothing, whereas the Casuals have to clean out the Centre before they leave. Everything has its price, Walter, even freedom. If you have a drink problem, spit it out.'

'I know how you're looking at me. Your eyes watch me. It's as if you're standing on one leg hunched up, with your feathers all ruffled like one of your bloody pigeons, waiting for its neck to be wrung. My nearness is all you have to live for. The responsibility's too much for me.'

'Drink problem.'

Walter attempted to summon up what would pass for attention.

'Don't hug it to yourself. Sobriety is your best friend, more precious than rubies. Unless you can believe that, you'll never give up alcohol. We have a hundred and twenty men here at the moment with the very same problem. We have A.A. Meetings, a Sick Bay; we try to feed them up, and stop what we call "Stink Thinking".' The man became suddenly fierce. 'Why are you looking at me like that? I'll batter your head in.' Walter jumped as the man seemed to lurch across the desk towards him. 'Things like that. Remarks of such a nature.' The man relaxed, having given his performance. 'All that aggression, we have to get rid of it. I mean, take you. You're all screwed up inside, aren't you? I can tell. You need to talk to someone.' Walter nodded. 'The Catholic faith asks too much of me, Walter. My wife's a slut and my children are bastards, and I wouldn't say that to just anyone. I've been to Hell and back. I know. I've seen men with maggots in their boots.' He was wiping the sweat from his forehead with the palm of his right hand. 'It's cold and lonely out there, isn't it? Did you know that one of our Casuals was found battered to death in a derelict house near here? And there was another man, a householder, strangled in the park.'

'*You make me feel bad, Walter. If I stayed with you because of that, it wouldn't be any good, would it?*'

'Carry a heavy torch with me when I go out. It's the only way.'

Behind the man's head, there was a Notice Board. 'BOXING CAN CAUSE BRAIN CANCER. FILM SHOW WED 6.00. MEETING FOR MENTALLY HANDICAPPED CHRISTIAN FORUM NEAT APPEARANCE REQUESTED.' Below the Notice Board was a glass cabinet, in which were cups and shields awarded for success in various sports.

'If you'd left it any longer, you might not have found us here. We're supposed to be phased out by 1980. Smaller settlement units; can't see it myself. Where would they put them? Who'd want fifty or sixty assorted Jocks and Micks, pissing up against their garden wall, while they waited to be admitted to the house next door?'

'*You can cope now.*' He had watched her, twisting the string handles of the carrier bag between his fingers. '*Shop and cook. You're a good cook. You'll be all right, won't you?*' Her mouth had trembled, and she had screwed her eyes up tightly. '*Hard bitches like me don't always have a soft spot. You shouldn't – Oh, Jesus fucking Christ!*' She had moved to him quickly, hugging, kissing and stroking his face, her lips moving over his ears, his nose, his eyelids and eyebrows, and he had seen that her own eyes were closed, and felt the dampness of her tears, tears she had left to dry on his face.

Then she was gone, with the door left open and the room completely still and strange to him. And he had stood, twisting the handles of the carrier bag, not knowing if he would ever be able to let go of those two pieces of grey string, not knowing if he would ever move.

The furniture and all the objects of the room had seemed all at once to rush into his head, fighting each other for a good place there, shouting, every object and particle of an object shouting in the spaces of his head, 'Don't go!' as he should have shouted.

But Walter had only whispered it. 'Don't go.'

'Shout! Scream! Weep!' cried the objects in his head.

He had moved quickly to the door, had been able to do so much. 'June!' One word. Too late. It had echoed round the room, and then there had been silence.

Almost silence. He had sat still, holding the carrier bag, and listened to the quiet noises the room made. At first there had only been the noises of complaint from floor and furniture, then, after much longer, he had become aware of noises from outside in the street, and he had thought of the people outside. They outside, he alone in the room, sitting there, frightened and angry that he had not touched her, hadn't reached out when he could have done, hadn't held her when she rushed to him. Then had come the realization that he had no idea where she was, and might never know, a..d that at some point he would have to stand up, move, walk about this room. Then he had lifted the back of his right hand to his mouth, and had wept.

He had wept.

He had walked.

He had walked as if his mother were trying to teach him to walk again, unaided, to walk as a good boy walked, not held, but with difficulty. When he had not been a good boy, his mother had said, 'You break my heart, Walter,' and he had known that a broken heart must be a painful thing. Now as Walter had walked (unaided – oh, without aid of any kind), pain had been everywhere except where he knew his heart to be.

He had walked out of the room and into the street, and pain had rung like a single church bell inside the joints of his limbs as he had moved. It had pushed at his forehead from inside, and had churned around in the base of his stomach, as though someone had been scraping the insides of his belly with a large soup-ladle.

He had moved. Unaided. Walking for the sake of it, not daring to stop. Walking would make the time pass. 'Time waits for no man, Walter, and certainly not you,' his mother had said. Not for Witless Walter, dribbling and giggling Walter, Parrot-Face Williams, who had tried to pretend to be part of the real world, to feel and give love, cook, and buy goods from shop assistants. Real people, had he continued to walk in front of them, would have noticed, crowded about him, stopped the traffic, written to the newspapers.

So, although he had not been able to stop either walking or weeping, Witless Walter had, after some while, found an alley, destitute of real people, containing only dustbins, and there he had leaned his forehead against the bricks of the wall, and had continued to weep.

He had remained in the alley seventeen days. For seventeen days, he had not spoken to anyone, and came to believe that he had forgotten how.

He had told the difference between day and night by the changes in the light and in the temperature. The nights were colder. Even so, he preferred the nights, preferred darkness, as long as there had been no voices, no sounds of people talking, laughing, singing. Walter and June had sung, had held hands, and sung about the little man who had walked round the town, and got no bread with one fish-ball.

In the darkness, without human sounds, he was just like everyone else. Even the voices inside his head seemed to rest at night, as if they too were tired, and had run out of questions about June, about Walter and June, about why June had gone and where. Since his mind must know that he could not answer these questions, Walter wondered why it should ask them. His mother had told him that there was always a right answer, hidden behind all the wrong ones; he had only to reject all the wrong answers, and the right would be left. That would please her. He would get a tick and not a cross.

June had never marked or corrected his answers to questions. She had encouraged him to talk and to communicate his thoughts. As his confidence had grown, and he had discovered that he enjoyed talking, enjoyed the experience of people listening to him, giving him their full attention, he had stored up thoughts to tell June when the right moment came. Working out what words he would use to express these thoughts had given him pleasure. He would wait until he saw the expression in June's eyes which meant that she was thinking unhappy thoughts about Baby John, or enduring frightening ones, and then he would start, sometimes taking her by the hand, and making her sit by him. There had been no waiting to be asked questions, no being pressed to speak, no shyness or stumbling or tripping over parts of words or forming sounds that seemed to come out wrongly. He had talked, and she had listened, often laughed, or smiled, and squeezed his hand. Walter had made words he had never used before, words he had heard and stored away in his mind. There had been no darting flickering goldfish in his head; his thoughts had been clear.

In the alley, his thoughts were not clear. He drank from an overflow pipe, and ate from dustbins, and once a dog had pissed on his broken shoe. In the alley, Walter wept and thought persistently of June.

Once she had said, 'Come here,' and he had gone to her, thinking that she was frightened and wanted him to hold her, but instead she had pointed to their two reflections in the mirror, and had said, 'Every morning we must stand here, and look at ourselves for a moment, to remind ourselves who we are. It's all there in our faces; every second we've lived so far is marked there, all those years remembered in one single expression. It's a miracle that we're both here now.'

And he had looked at her, and seen how beautiful she was. If what she said was so, the years had made her beautiful.

There passed at the end of the alley a very small boy, walking behind his father, and holding onto the hem of his father's coat, while the father carried shopping. Walter and his father. And the smell of rhododendrons strong, all about the alley.

There passed four drunken men, swaying and gliding. The shop at the end of the alley was still lighted, and sold food, and one of the men unzipped and passed water against the shop window which contained pork pies, while his companions laughed and applauded, and Walter had, for one moment, a very clear vision of the pies sitting there behind the glass, and the man's steaming water splashing on the glass which protected them.

He knew there were pies. He had been four times to the end of the alley, and seen them.

People passed the end of the alley, and some even walked down it. One such was the woman whose dog soiled Walter's shoe. Lovers passed, some walking hand in hand, as he and June had walked. Time passed. Walter lay on his side in a foetal position, so that the whole of him was tucked inside a small doorway. He closed his eyes, and tried to rub the world out of his mind. When he woke, he would draw it again. On a large blackboard with white chalk, he would recreate the world in sharp white lines which everyone could understand. Then he would be able to see it clearly, and fit himself into it.

Walter set himself to imagine the drawing he would make of himself, fitting into the blackboard world, but the self he saw was empty, an outline drawing of a man with a hat on.

Seventeen days of alternating light and darkness, comparative warmth and hard cold, weeping and thinking, people passing, of June, and Walter and June, and perpetual hammering questions asked by a mind which knew it could not supply the answers. *I must have food, or I die.* He had uncurled, and set himself again in movement, and walked out of the alley, and come to the Reception Centre, the Spike, and must now endure the forms and invariable procedures of the Spike, and the people of the Spike, who were so clearly of the real world.

2

*We smell the same now, so don't go getting
confused. June's the one over there.*

Walter was told by a man in a beige overall to take off all his
clothes, and did so slowly. He was to undergo the process known
as 'Being Put Through'. All clients of the Spike, the lost, the
lonely, the homeless, drunk or sober, clean or dirty, must be 'Put
Through' on their arrival, and if, for any reason, even to buy a
packet of cigarettes, they were to leave the building, on their
return they would be 'Put Through' again, to strip, and shower,
and stand about naked, waiting for their clothes to be fumigated.
Only the Gate Men, the semi-permanent residents, were not obliged
to endure this nightly ritual.

Naked, elderly and not-so-elderly men stood around Walter,
hugging their sallow and sagging dugs. All were shivering. Their
testicles looked ridiculous, hanging low in long-forgotten and
deflated pouches like old abandoned pieces of luggage, and putting
Walter in mind of untreated tripe, yellow before being bleached.

'Come on!' The man in beige had his arm out, waiting for
Walter's clothes. Walter removed the last piece of his clothing, his
stained underpants, and, avoiding the eyes of the shivering men,
screwed them up quickly, and stuffed them into the pocket of his
jacket, while the man in beige sighed a heavy sigh.

Every article of Walter's clothing, including his boots, was held
up to a powerful electric light and closely examined, before being
placed in a machine which looked like an oven. Once the Spike

189

had used steam, which had shrunk the clothes of its clients, who would leave in the morning with wrists and ankles protruding from shortened sleeves and trouser-legs. Time passes. Everything gets better. By the time of Her Majesty's Jubilee Year, so recently over, ten c.c.s of Ethyl Tomile had replaced the steam.

Naked, Walter discovered that his arms had grown and huge hands no longer belonged to him. If his skin had had pockets, he would have hidden them there. As matters were, they swung at his sides, as he rocked backwards and forwards, and studied the water under the duckboards beneath his feet, enduring the stares of the elderly and some not-so-elderly irregulars.

A large bar of strong-smelling soap was placed into his right hand, and he was led to one of the showers. The irregulars stood aside to let him pass. They had seen it all before, had sworn never to come here again, and here again they were.

He felt the warm water hitting the top of his head, and trickling down his body. He was forty-eight, being given a bath, as back in the Hospital, Jesus's Mistakes were given baths. Walter was not one of Jesus's Mistakes, but a person of the real world, who had loved and been loved. Yet he did not protest, for he knew that, in places such as this, it is always the sanest who seem most mad.

'Why are you so nice to me, June?' She had laughed, and hugged him. 'Because I love you.' And she had been looking at him. 'Because I love you.' She had looked at him, been able to see him clearly, what he was, and she had said, 'Because I love you,' had said it to him, Witless Walter, of whom his own mother (now with Jesus) had once said, 'You must be the ugliest person in this town, Walter, and you spent nine months inside me.'

Water. Warm water on a naked body, watched by other naked bodies, as he had watched, seen them, both of them together on a stained mattress, and the bath in the middle of the room still full of water, watched through a crack in the door, had watched Graham and June making love.

Memories. Nothing made sense.

'Sense is different things to different people, Walter. Don't let them force their sense on you. If you think something makes sense, that's all that matters.' June had told him that, but then later, 'If you'd been able to read, I'd have left you a note. Feelings change. Things don't always last.'

And she had turned her head away. 'You'll be all right, won't you? You can cope now.' What should he have answered? What was the right answer?

Once the right answer would have been to put his arms around her, and she would have hugged him to her. 'Hold onto me. It's a bad day.' But on that afternoon, as he had watched through the door, it was Graham who had held onto her in a different way from Walter, and she had laughed in a way Walter had never made her laugh, and Graham had done things to and with her which Walter would never have dreamed of doing. It had been almost as if it were not his June he was watching, not his June but a larger, stronger June, who laughed differently, moved differently, did things with Graham she had never done with him, was not the same June as she who slept with Walter, and loved him, and was good to him.

'You're very good with him.'

'Good? Goodness doesn't come into it. I took him on when I needed someone, and he was the only one there. Now he's the only person in the world who can make me feel guilty.' And Walter, looking through the crack in the door, had seen the marks and bruises around her nipples. Later, when he touched her, his June had flinched, and said, 'I'm sore, Walter.'

'Every time he uses my name, I get that heavy feeling of responsibility. Constant sidelong glances for approval! I know he's wondering why I stay with him. He still half expects to wake up, and find I've gone.' The noises she made were noises of both pain and pleasure, and the boy was biting the bruises he had already caused.

'Help Graham to empty the bath, love.'

Walter had looked down at the soapy bath-water, and then at Graham, who was tucking his shirt into the top of his trousers.

'I had a bath, and then Graham used my water.'

'Saves on the electric.' The newly dressed Graham grinned, unaware that Walter knew that they didn't pay for electricity.

'We smell the same now, so don't go getting confused. June's the

191

one over there.' It had not made sense, but June and Graham had laughed all the same.

Graham and Walter had emptied the water from the zinc bath into the back yard, and hung the bath on a nail. Then Graham had gone back to his books, and Walter had sat watching June.

'All right, love?' To his surprise, Walter had discovered that he could nod his head in the same way as he always nodded his head. What thereafter had surprised him even more was that June should have kissed him on the forehead, and ruffled his hair in the way she had always done, and that he had actually been relieved that she had done so. She was very good with him.

Walter slid the strong-smelling soap over his body as carefully as he had soaped Clifford's body every day for nineteen years. His love for June would remain a secret; in a place like this, it would help to have secrets. He would not allow himself to be sad. *'I once told him I loved him. It spoilt everything. Now, just holding his hand is like carrying an animal to the vet to be put down.'*

'That's enough.' The man in beige was shouting at Walter above the noise of the showers.

If he had banged the door or coughed, as he should have done, they would have had to stop. If he had gone into the room, they would have sat up and covered themselves. But he would not have known what to say, how to act. Instead, he had stood as still as he could, and watched.

Now, as he remembered (and had remembered so often), he saw only parts of what he must have seen then, only sections of the two bodies, which bit, licked, stroked, rubbed, twined and inter-twined. Hands – Graham's, then June's – how greedy and grasping they looked. Her face, and the pleasure on it. The bruises on her breasts. Her legs, wrapped round the boy, and her blue-white ankles crossed over each other at the base of the boy's back – ankles Walter had once thought so small and fragile. The boy's bottom, pumping in and out, in and out, and June's eyes, sometimes closed, sometimes wide open as she had made a sound that had seemed almost as if she were cold, had been shuddering from the cold, yet she was not cold, but beaded with sweat all over. And lastly, as the boy withdrew himself, and lay on his back beside her, the part of him which had been inside her, resting against his left thigh, and glistening with body-fluid.

'That's *enough!*' Walter was given a towel to wrap round his waist. 'You're the first I've seen enjoy it.' He was instructed to sit on a wooden bench, and wait his turn to be examined by the doctor.

Though the doctor's manner was of total disinterest, his inspection was not perfunctory. Heart, chest and stomach were listened to, the penis squeezed, the anus stretched and peered into by the light of a small torch, and the same torch illuminated the inside of Walter's mouth and ears.

'Piles and halitosis.' A note made. 'When did you last have a bowel movement?'

Walter looked at him, and the doctor sighed. 'Shit! When did you last move your shit?'

Walter could not remember. It had not been uppermost in his mind.

'Can't remember.' A further note. Then the doctor removed from their cellophane wrapper a pair of sterile gloves made from the finest rubber, and, with the help of a lubricant, placed something up Walter's back passage. 'Now don't go to sleep until you've had a really good shit. Understand?'

Walter nodded. He did not understand why the doctor thought it necessary to speak in such a loud and distinct voice. Surely all the towel-wrapped men on the wooden bench outside the door would have heard.

'Through there! Next!'

As Walter moved past the lines of seated men, some of them looked up, but to his surprise, none of them laughed at him, or even smiled. Every one of the irregulars looked as apprehensive as Walter himself, and was so, for, apart from their extreme modesty (many clients of the Spike have run out of the building on being told that they would be required to undress) and dislike of being touched, anything the doctor might have to tell them would certainly not be good news.

The doctor made out a card for the Index, on WILLIAMS, Walter', and under the heading 'General Impression' where usually he might have written 'Poor', or 'Very Poor', or 'Critical', he printed the words, 'Not to be Bred From'.

The irregulars sat wrapped in the blankets with which they had been issued, drinking their soup and eyeing each other over the rims of their mugs.

The Officer in the white coat, whose job it was to ration out the soup, had seen it all before. He was an old man. Nothing was new to him. Bad breath, stale wind, the noisy supping of soup, eyes watching other eyes in uneasy silence, they all made up an evening which was just one among many. He had disliked most of the evenings which were past, and had no doubt that he would continue in the same frame of mind.

'Do you have a smoke on you, John?' A middle-aged Glaswegian with long hair and sideburns of the most busy and extravagant kind had posed the question. 'Come on, boy. Don't be keeping them for yourself.'

The elderly Officer's eyes were bright with anger, piss-holes in the snow of his aged skin, but he did not reply.

'Jesus!' The Glaswegian looked about him at the other irregulars, and began to sing:

> 'Roll out those lazy, hazy, crazy days of summer.
> Roll out the soda, and pretzels, and beer.
> Roll out those lazy, hazy, crazy days of summer.
> I wish to fucking hell I wasn't here.'

He moved his head from side to side. 'Bloody unsociable country, this. The only person I've spoken to for over a week, and you haven't a tab for me to smoke.'

This provoked the old man into speech. 'I'd be ashamed to be in this place if I were the age of some of you. Taking charity! I was born in one war, and fought in the other.' He became lost in his own memories. His life spent in servitude was to be repaid by an old age served in solitude. He spoke to few, and was seldom spoken to. He shopped for himself, and cooked for no one else. When he listened, it was to the B.B.C. His radio licence was a prescription against insanity. 'It's all too easy. Doesn't pay to work these days.'

The Glaswegian was on his feet, and holding the old man by his white coat. 'Listen, you bugger. I used to work a fifty-two-hour shift before I started to take a dram. I had a family and five wee ones. I used to pay more income tax to your stupid government than any of this lot put together. So just you be careful when you talk to me about taking charity. I've paid for these mangey blankets and this piss you call soup.'

He dropped the old man, having shaken him so fiercely that the old man's upper plate fell from his mouth, and landed on the floor close to Walter. As the Glaswegian left the room, banging the door as he went, Walter picked up the false teeth, and handed them back to their owner, relieved to notice that they were made of a kind of plastic, and had not broken.

The old Officer took the teeth from Walter's hand, wiped them on his spotlessly clean handkerchief, placed them where they belonged, and continued to talk, as if making up for all the years he had been unable to answer the B.B.C. back. He spoke of his life between two wars, and his service in the second, and of a man named Percy, who broke wind constantly because of his nerves, and had hanged himself in a disused barn and been nibbled by rats. But the irregulars were no longer listening.

They had all been given bed tickets by the Bed Officer. These had then been exchanged for three blankets each. Some of the irregulars had asked for more blankets, and been refused, even though, of the nine hundred beds in the four blocks of the Centre, only six hundred were ever used.

In Walter's dormitory, there were forty bunks in two layers. Each was numbered, made of iron with steel springs. A rubber mattress, two inches thick, and a striped pillow, grey and greasy with dirt, covered each of the numbered bunks. The allocation of beds by numbers was important. If the police were to call during the night, to collect an irregular whose conduct had been more than usually irregular, the Duty Officer would know exactly where to find him.

Someone had removed Walter's pillow, in order to have two.

'Did you hear about the Irish G.C.E?' The relief of having got through so much in order to get here – filling in Form 3C with the Interviewing Officer, the undressing, delousing of clothing, compulsory bathing – seemed to have made one of the not-so-elderly irregulars light-headed. 'Question. England won the Second World War. Who were the runners-up?' The older tireder irregulars kept themselves apart, mumbling to themselves or to some imaginary companion.

'Question. Who's buried in Grant's Tomb?'

Walter lay on his numbered top bunk, using his hands as a pillow, and staring at a ceiling which had once been painted cream. He would not remove a pillow from another bed. He was not a Mistake, but someone in the real world, a free man in a Reception Centre into which he had freely walked in search of food, warmth and rest, which were his due.

He had never been alone before, except for that time he had spent in his mother's bedroom with the pigeons, and she lay there, unmoving and looking increasingly strange, while he waited for Jesus to make up His mind whether Walter's mother was to stay with Him or come back to Walter. He had often felt alone, but except for that once and now, had never been it. He remembered Clifford. Clifford was not like any person whom Walter had met in the real world, but he was a person, a human being, and Walter had looked after him. Was Clifford still a person, or had he been buried in the cemetery near the Hospital? Perhaps he had expected Walter to return, and had not allowed anyone else to look after him.

Here, now, Walter was looking after nobody, and nobody was looking after him. He had nobody to please except himself, and nobody had to please him. There was no need here to worry at the sound his voice made, no need to make sense, to practise sentences inside his head, to have thoughts and to express them.

He could have talked well now, if there were someone to listen, or listened well were there anyone to talk to him. June had taught him how to listen and how to talk, but since she had left him, both talking and listening were useless.

An idea came into Walter's mind, and it seemed to have sense in it, for it would explain why so many of the people he had met talked to themselves. The only reason Walter now had for talking would be to keep in practice, and not forget how, so that when he met June again, he could speak to her, ask her questions, tell her what had happened, explain. He must talk. Practice makes perfect. He must practise on the only person constantly available to him. Himself.

'You *can cope now. You'll be all right, won't you?*' That's what he would do now. He would be all right. He would cope.

He had watched her. She had said she couldn't stand it, and she had gone away. He would find her, and promise not to watch her. Ever.

'I warned her. It was him or me. I told her to choose.' The man in the bunk below was thinking aloud. He jerked himself over from his left side to his right, letting out a mirthless laugh as both the steel springs and the iron frame of the bed rattled. 'She laughed, didn't she? Thought I wouldn't go through with it, didn't she?'

Walter knew better than to proffer answers. This man also was practising talking to someone.

'Couldn't stay with the two of them there. Creep!' A moment's pause. 'Smarmy bugger too.' The man rolled over again, and Walter held tight to the sides of the bunk.

' "You'll never go. Like your comfort, don't you? You like the little comforts I give you." Comfort! Once a bloody fortnight, with the dog watching! Creep! She'll not be smiling now. He'll have left her, shouldn't wonder. One whiff of that cheesy smell behind her ears, and he'll be off. Sebaceous cysts, my toe-rag! Shouldn't wonder! Musk under her armpits and African Violets between her legs.'

Walter closed his eyes to try to block out pictures which were beginning to form, but soon the man began to practise talking again, this time in a petulant whimper. 'He'll have had her by now. Got it all the way up. Had her on the rug where we ... had her with the dog watching.' The man was moaning and grunting quietly into his pillow, and Walter's bunk, as well as his own, was rocking backwards and forwards gently. The man was masturbating, using his free arm to rock the bunks. Walter waited for the climax. Afterwards, the man would probably sleep.

'FILTHY COW!'

'Shut your bloody noise.' Shouts from the nearby bunks, as the man below Walter gasped. 'Bet she opened like a cesspool to him.

Bet he never even touched the sides. Made the dog sick, shouldn't wonder.'

An angry irregular from the next bunk jumped out, slid barefoot across the adjoining tiles, and shook the man below Walter by the scruff of the hair. 'You get on with your fucking wanking, will you, and shut your filthy mouth.'

As the angry irregular returned, grumbling, to his bunk, a very old irregular in one of the bunks nearest the door began to cough, and having begun, could not stop. He climbed painfully out of his bunk, and opened a window to stand by it, gasping into the cold night air like a wizened goldfish, and clinging to the iron window to hold himself upright.

No one moved to help him. The old irregular was dying; Walter was sure of it. The other irregulars waited, not for him to close the window and return to bed, but for someone else to make a decision. Each of them knew *he* would not. The old irregular was not part of them, nor they of him. If his heart stopped, it would not spoil their sleep.

At last the coughing stopped. The old irregular's hold on the window loosened, and he fell to the floor. No one moved. Then Walter lowered his feet to the floor, and went to find someone on duty.

Two men in beige took the old irregular's body away. They would take it to the Sick Bay; he might not be dead. But Walter had no doubt that the old irregular was gone, and where. What puzzled him was why Jesus made it so painful to get there.

Five minutes later, the irregular in the bunk below had started to whimper again. 'All right in here. This is the last place she'd come looking.' Walter ignored him. He had come to a decision. He had been at fault, first hiding his tears in the alley, then coming to this place. His place was with June. He would go back to the squat, and find her.

3

Where are you pigeon ?

'Can you tell me where I am, please?'

'Coldharbour Lane.'

'I want to go to . . .' Walter searched his memory. 'Eltham Street.'

'Where's that?'

He knew he could do it. He could call up the words, and form them. June had made him memorize the complete address during their first days at the squat. 'W Four.'

'You'd be best on the Tube. Get the Victoria Line from Brixton, down there. Tell them the address you want before you buy a ticket. They'll look up what station you should get off at.'

Walter thanked the woman, and walked in the direction she had indicated, since it would be rude to go in any other. But he could not take a Tube, because he could not pay for a ticket. He knew the name of the Tube Station nearest the house. It was called Turnham Green, and was on the District Line.

He must get there before dark. At the Tube Station he would find someone else to ask, someone who would know how to get to Turnham Green Station. They would be more likely to know where that was than where his road was.

But when he spoke to the man who was issuing tickets at Brixton Station, Walter was told that he was miles out of his way. Even if the man had known which way to point, which he hadn't, it was too great a distance to walk, but Walter could buy a ticket which would take him there for sixty pence.

Walter thanked the man, and left his company. Studying the map outside the station, he conceived an idea. He traced the route with his finger. Not counting the one at the beginning and the one at the end, there were thirteen stations between himself and Turnham Green. If he made a list of them in order, he could walk from one to the next, and thus find his way home. Ever since he had written words on the wall of the Mother and Baby Unit for June to read, he had always carried at least one pencil in his pocket. He found an empty cigarette packet in a litter bin, turned it inside out, and wrote his list, beginning with Stockwell, Vauxhall and Pimlico, and ending with Ravenscourt Park, Stamford Brook and Turnham Green.

June would be waiting. She would be waiting for him now, pacing the floor and looking through the window. She would rush to the door, and put her arms round him. She would kiss him, covering his face with kisses. He would laugh, and she would cry, hug him and cry. *'Please put your arms round me. We're both cold.'* She had said that to him in the church, wiped his face dry, and they had made love on the stone floor. *'Look at me, Walter. Don't pretend it's not happening.'* It had happened. She had shown him how. He had seen his own reflection in each of the dark shiny brown conkers, which were her eyes. He had seen Walter. It had happened.

Walter leaned over the side of Vauxhall Bridge. He felt giddy and faint. The food he had received at the Spike had been insufficient to nourish him for such a journey, for there had been days of hunger to make up for. The muscles of his legs seemed to be pulling him down into the pavement. His knees shook. He held tight onto the parapet, knowing that if once he fell, he might not have the strength to get up again.

Then he had crossed the bridge, holding onto the wall and walking sideways, and was sitting on a bench, looking at the Thames which moved like oil, although it was not yet night. He had heard Big Ben strike noon. The sight of the moving water and his own weariness combined to drag him towards sleep. Sleep was what he did best (his mother had told him so bitterly), and his next best was laughter, when he had learned as a child so long ago to laugh first before other people laughed at him, so that they could all be laughing together.

Walter was out of practice at laughing, but to sleep now would be very easy, to lie on the bench, to float, cool oil lapping at his ears, making the sound he had once heard in a sea-shell. To lie in it, be covered by it, his eyes closed, the oil-like water carrying his weight, to drift past bright green sea-weed, where goldfish played hide and seek! But June would not be there.

He was walking again. His legs ached, his knees wobbled, and his left foot was bleeding. He could feel the warm blood sticking to what was left of his sock. The nail in his left boot was digging deeper into his second toe. But they were his boots, moving with his feet inside them, and what was his could be commanded. Once Walter had been scared of being in charge of his whole body. No longer. He ordered his feet to walk, to go on walking; if they didn't get a move on, he would make them run.

Walter commanded, and his feet disobeyed. They slowed down. Even a child, an invalid, a cripple, a one-legged man with a wheel-barrow could walk faster. He could walk on his hands, and get to Turnham Green in half the time. Every moment he wasted in slow-ness and resting was a moment in which June might decide not to wait for him any longer.

'I've got to get away. Will you come with me? I can't do it on my own.'

He was crossing the Earls Court Road when he fell. The time was twenty-five to five. The rush-hour drivers hooted, and leaned out of the windows of their vehicles to shout abuse at him. This traditional greeting, given by London drivers to children, the blind, pregnant women, nuns, the halt and the lame, lasted longer than usual because Walter, having fallen, did not get up.

At St Stephen's Hospital in the Fulham Road, they gave Walter something to wake him up, cleaned and dressed his injured toe, and questioned him.

'Do you know where you are?'
'Earls Court. West Kensington next.'
'Where have you come from?'

'Gloucester Road.'

'Where were you born?'

'Baron's Court.'

'What's your job?'

'Hammersmith.'

'What did you have for lunch?'

'Ravenscourt Park.'

'What's your name?'

'Stamford Brook.'

'What are you going to do?'

'Turnham Green.'

'Can you tell me ... ? Have you ever ... ? Do you know ...?' In so far as he did know, he told them whatever he could, and having been told, they went away, and talked about him behind a screen. Then they returned, and informed him that he would be pleased to know that they had decided to allow him to stay in their hospital overnight. They were stretching a rule, they said, since all he really needed was rest and quiet, which they supposed he could come by easily in Turnham Green. However, since he had experienced a shock, and was in discomfort, they had found him a bed.

They stood back, as if for congratulation, which was not given.

Was there, they asked, anyone he would like them to inform of his whereabouts, anyone expecting him at home?

Walter thanked them kindly, but said he could not stay. He had to meet someone, and that someone would be waiting. He got down from the high bed in Casualty, and made his way unsteadily to the door. At this, the Evening Duty in Casualty at St Stephen's Hospital adjusted their bedside manners, and proclaimed that, if he insisted on leaving in that condition, he would have to sign a form relieving them of all responsibility.

Walter printed the name 'Walter' in block capitals. Then he became agitated. He couldn't remember his surname. They were waiting and watching him. What was it? He knew it well enough; it began with the same letter as his first name. His initials were 'W.W.' He had already printed the second W, but what came after that?

He was sweating, and his head was full of goldfish. If only he could stop them moving, he would be able to think properly. He screwed up his eyes tight, then opened them again, and the room was spinning, and so were the watching faces. Faces dressed in white span and merged. Six eyes of different colours, different shapes, and at different heights, whirled round above ten noses and eleven mouths, then turned to their partners, bowed, dosie-doed with three raised eyebrows, and all the time Walter's name was on the tip of his tongue, and there it remained. He must concentrate. It was Earls Court, then – was it South Kensington? no, he had passed South Kensington – was it . . . ? He visualized his list, and the words came clear. 'West Kensington': that was it.

Slowly, carefully, Walter printed ' W E S T' on the form. It was not his name, but it was a word; it began with 'W', and he could spell it; it would do.

'Right, Mr West.' Someone was talking, and he must listen. 'You do realize we'd much rather you stayed here overnight? You don't look at all well.'

Walter nodded, and said, 'It's dark. She'll be frightened.'

He stepped out into the Fulham Road, and looked at the evening traffic crawling along, bumper to bumper. The lighted lorries, buses, cars and taxis, all evacuating exhaust fumes and filling the air with noise. The lights dazzled him, and he felt sick again. He could tell it had been dark for some time. She would have closed the flimsy make-do curtains, and would be lying down, listening to music from the radio. He looked up to see whether there was a moon, and six young men wearing Chelsea scarves collided with him, stepping on his injured foot, and sending him down to the pavement.

'Mr West!'

'Sorry, mate.'

'Mr West!' He was helped to his feet.

'You all right?'

'Mr West!'

'Don't hang about, Merve. Old Bill'll think you've started something.'

Walter realized that he was walking again, but could not tell in what direction. Someone was holding his arm, and he was walking, being led. Then a door was opened for him, and he was inside. It was warm. He was back in the Entrance Hall of the Hospital.

He had only travelled twenty yards. His hand was being held by a young nurse, and she was speaking to him. What was she saying?

'There's a floodlit match at Chelsea tonight. Nobody's safe on the streets. You'd never get a taxi, even if you had the . . .' She would not say 'money'. 'Are you sure you won't stay overnight? We could phone whoever it is you're worried about.'

Walter shook his head very slowly. Such strange things were happening to him that it was not safe to try to move quickly any more.

'All right. You wait here, and we'll get an ambulance to take you home.' The young face was close to his. 'It won't get you there as fast as the Tube, but it'll be a lot safer. All right?' He could not move, even his head. 'Turnham Green, isn't it? I'll tell them at the desk. They'll come and get you when it's time, so please wait. Don't wander off again, will you?'

She was gone. He would be there before bedtime. June would wipe his face dry, and he would tell her he was sorry for having watched her. From now on, he would look at her only when she was laughing, and then she would be happy, and not mind. It would be all right. All right now. June would hold him. And she would touch him on the face with her lips.

'Are you sure this is the road? All these houses look derelict to me.'

Then they saw a light. There was a light on in the house, shining through the flimsy curtains just as Walter had imagined it.

'She's waiting up for you, then.' Walter almost fell from the ambulance in his haste to get to the front door. 'Mind how you go on that foot.'

He was giggling to himself, chuckling and giggling like a baby. Everything was as he had supposed. She had come back; she had waited. He must stop himself laughing, pull himself together, wipe that smile off his face, and remember not to stare at her. He was a man now, not the boy who had baled rubbish at Woolworth's.

Walter looked in through the window at a point where the curtains failed to meet. He was looking at their room. There were some things he remembered, others not. The furniture was the same. But there was food on one of the mattresses. He and June had never put food on the old stained matresses. They had kept it in the kitchen. Now he could see the remains of a sliced loaf in its paper, a carton of eggs, a jar of coffee exactly like the one in which they kept their money.

There was no answer to his tap on the window, but if she were in the kitchen, she wouldn't hear. He played 'their tune' on the knocker, the tune which told whoever was in the house that this visitor was not the police or council, but one of their own.

He waited, then tried the knock again, then remembered where they had hidden a spare key after having once locked themselves out. He went to the back of the house, and found the key where they had hidden it in a flowerpot under some earth. She was not in the kitchen. Yet there would not be a light on if she had gone out.

Walter let himself in by the back door. In the kitchen greasy plates were soaking in the yellow plastic bowl they used for washing up. Two small pieces of bacon rind floated on top of the water. June always ate her bacon rind, even when it had 'Danish' written on it.

In the lighted living-room, he examined the remainder of the sliced loaf, which was fresh, and noticed that wood had recently been burned in the grate, but he could find no clothes or anything of June's.

There had been no light in Graham's room, and was not. He paused outside, lifted his fist to knock, then changed his mind, and walked about the hall. He tapped with his good foot against the skirting board, so as to be heard walking, and coughed three times. Then he shouted 'Hello' four times up the stairs, even though none of them ever went there, the stairs being unsafe.

Finally, he tapped on the door of Graham's room, and entered. There were blankets on the bed, and some text books on the floor. Had Graham left them behind?

Then he heard a key being turned in the front door.

'I went out for a drink. Couldn't stand this place any more.' Graham had drunk a great deal many more than one drink. 'Where did you get to, then?' Walter didn't answer. 'June and I thought you'd stay here.'

They were waiting for the kettle to boil. 'I'm sorry about what happened, but we really were in love.'

Walter looked at the kettle. What steam did was to escape from the kettle. Yet when it had escaped, it was no longer steam.

'She said she was sure you'd come back here, looking for her, and you have. She was very good about people, if not so very good to them.' Graham heaped two and a half teaspoons of Instant Coffee into each mug. He had never been able to remember that Walter could only drink coffee if it was very weak.

'No sugar for you, I'm afraid. Don't take it myself, as you'll remember, so didn't buy any. Not being as certain as she was that you'd come. Cheers!' Walter was handed a cup of strong sugarless coffee, and they moved into the lighted room, and sat on separate mattresses.

They sat in silence until Graham had drunk half his coffee. Finally he spoke. 'You'll be wondering.'

He waited for a reply, but got none.

'We went to another squat. Lots of people there. Much better than this place.' He thought. 'Must get out of here.' He thought again. 'Where was I? Oh, yes. Well, there was this girl I knew from college. Upset June. We had a row. Several, in fact. Then she did a bunk. June did. Never trusted anybody, did she, not even you?'

Walter realized that Graham was more than slightly drunk. When the light did not glitter on his spectacles, it could be seen that his eyes kept closing. Also his hands shook.

'I knew she had enough Valium for a couple of weeks, so I didn't run after her.' Silence. Graham's head was still. Was he staring into space, or had he closed his eyes again?

After a while, Graham's head dropped forward, and in an almost inaudible voice, he asked, 'What shall I do? Can you tell me?' Walter could not, and did not, but after a while, as the silence persisted, he realized that he was sitting close to the sliced bread. He had forgotten how hungry he was. But to get any bread, he would have to ask.

'I've got to work. Somehow. It's all there is really.'

'Can I have some bread, please?' He had spoken for the first time since Graham's arrival.

'Sorry?'

Walter indicated the sliced bread. 'Can I?'

'Yes, of course. There's butter and something ... something to put on it ...' But Walter already had four slices in his fist, rolled into one, and was eating. 'I remember there was something to ... Oh Christ!'

Walter stopped pushing bread into his mouth, and stood up. He supposed that he was standing because Graham was crying. He had stared wide-eyed at Walter eating, and then burst into tears, holding his spectacles between his thumb and index finger, biting at the back of his hand, and blubbering like a baby.

The crying became more extreme, more abandoned. Walter found that he was standing with Graham's arms around his neck, supporting most of Graham's weight.

Between the sobs, there were words. 'There's something ... you should see ... upstairs. Come upstairs.'

But no one ever went upstairs. The stairs were not safe.

Graham controlled himself, and found a torch. There were no lights upstairs. Going on all fours, and carefully avoiding the stairs without treads, they reached the landing of the first floor of the three-storey house.

Graham opened the door of one of the rooms. 'The floor's safe in here. It's been tested.' The beam of light from the torch swung round the empty room, and came to rest, illuminating a patch of wall close to the floor. Graham stood with his hand on the door-knob, while Walter clutched at his slices of bread, which had gained some dust during the climb.

'Go and look on the wall. Over there.'

Walter crossed the room cautiously, and bent down to look at the patch of wall in the circle of light. Someone had scratched writing on the wall with a nail.

'Can you read it?' Walter shook his head. Graham came over to him slowly, and stood behind him. Then he began to sob and whimper, making whining sounds like a dog, as he read aloud what was scratched on the wall.

'First day. I think. Can't move my legs or arms. Cried wolf but nobody came. Know you'll come back. Second day. Where are you, Pigeon? It's so cold. Third day. Please hurry.'

207

The beam of light moved from the wall, and zigzagged about the ceilings, floor and walls of the empty room, as Graham made his way back to the door. 'She came back here. It'd been very cold. She went all over the house, looking for things to burn – lino, wood, anything. She went right to the top of the house, striking matches to see her way.' He swung the beam of light so that it pointed to the ceiling, a large part of which had collapsed. 'She was lying where you are. Died in the ambulance. Internal bleeding.'

Walter placed the fingers of his right hand near his boots, and felt the floorboards.

'Better go down.'

They stood in the hall.

'I suppose she scratched that on the wall in case I didn't get here in time. I've used up all the Valium I brought for her. Got to get out of this place. Always felt there was something wrong with the house. Staying here won't bring her back. Really loved her, you know. Told me she had a baby up north. Wonder what'll happen to it.'

Time passed. They stood together in the dimly lighted hall. 'What will you do now?' Walter did not answer. 'I've got some money, if you want to go back up there, up to that hospital you came from.' No reply. 'She talked about you in the ambulance. She was very fond of you.' Graham waited for a response, and got none. 'I've got to work. Somehow.'

They were still standing in the hall. 'Funny name she called me – "Pigeon". Never called me that before. How will you manage?' No reply. Graham moved back into the lighted room. 'If there's anything else you need ... I mean, there's more to eat if you want it.'

Walter remained in the hall. He had left his bread on the floor upstairs.

4

*Don't let me disturb you. Thought I'd give you
something for a pillow.*

The clouds were wispy and red, yet the ground was iron-hard
beneath the snow, which had remained frozen into whatever shape
had last been pressed into it. Many of the footprints had been there
for weeks.

Walter lay on the snow in Gunnersbury Park, hardly denting it.
Above him the red sky reminded him of Hell. The snow which
pressed against the right side of his face, numbing it, was white
and as cold as Heaven must therefore be.

Christmas had gone. He would be too late to wish Jesus a Happy
Birthday. Walter himself had never had a birthday party. He
wondered how many candles there would have been on Jesus's
cake.

His body shivered, but the snow against his face had stopped
the aching in his head, and would cool the hotness of his skin. He
was sweating, but the sweat would freeze into a block of ice all
round him, and he would be allowed to sleep for ever, since there
would be no one left behind to wait for Jesus to decide. And Jesus
would not turn him away. His mother had promised that he would
go to Heaven if he were good, and he had not been bad. She had
promised that they would meet together in Paradise, and there
would be no reason for Jesus to feel embarrassed since Walter was
not one of His Mistakes.

'What's it like, then?'

Walter blinked.

'Sleeping in the snow. What's it feel like?'

Grey dots floated down towards him.

There was a boy standing over him. A teenager.

More grey dots floated down like confetti, some landing on Walter's face. He brushed them aside.

'Must try it some time. Kipping in the snow.' The teenager was holding something in his left hand, and picking at it with the fingers of his right. The something was moving. Struggling. Walter saw that there poked out from between the fingers of the left hand the leg of a bird. 'Try anything once.'

The bird's leg withdrew quickly and reappeared as the teenager plucked. What was floating down on Walter were not grey dots, but the tiny grey breast-feathers of a bird, which was being plucked alive by the youth who stood over him.

'Always wanted to do this. See what it felt like.' A tail-feather floated down towards Walter.

Slowly Walter attempted to get to his feet, but the youth casually placed one of his own feet on top of one of Walter's hands. 'Don't let me disturb you. Thought I'd give you something for a pillow. Feathers.' There was no humour in his voice. He did not even look at Walter, but continued to pull out the feathers of the struggling bird as if he were unwrapping a parcel in the contents of which he was only minimally interested.

It seemed to give him no particular satisfaction to contemplate the raw purple skin of the bird, covering the network of veins and the projecting bones, or the bird's heart, beating faster, so large a pulse within so small a frame, getting faster and faster and faster, as each feather fluttered to the ground and panic grew with each successive pain.

'Don't even make a noise.' A beak appeared above the youth's thumb. It was opened in a silent scream. Walter knew that pigeons make no sound when they are in pain.

'Shit itself stupid when I picked it up.'

Now the bird was hanging from the youth's hand, and fluttering as he held it by one wing so as to make his choice of which flight-feather to pluck. Walter shouted, 'Don't!'

The youth looked first at Walter, and then upwards at the sky.

For a moment, Walter felt relief, believing that the youth was about to release the bird, and throw it back into the air.

The moment passed. The youth returned his gaze to Walter. A smile illuminated the youth's face. 'It's only a poxy pigeon. Too many of them. Spread disease.' And resumed plucking.

How could the bird understand that fingers of the same human kind from which in the past it had received bread and stale cake could now tear at its flesh? Using his free hand, Walter made a grab for the youth's ankle, and tugged as hard as he could.

The youth lost his balance, and toppled backwards. The pigeon fell chest first onto the snow, and was still. The youth swung back his right leg in preparation to kick the dying bird towards one of the sixty goal posts which stand in Gunnersbury Park. Walter made a dive for the pigeon, and clasped it, before the youth's shoe landed against the back of his hand. Then a second kick, intended for the groin, landed on Walter's right thigh. Walter was on his feet before the third, and the youth was retreating backwards like a boxer, jumping up and down, and laughing.

'It's bloody dead. Like you. Bloody deadbeat!'

At first Walter believed him. The bird was so still, the lower lids of its eyes almost closed. It seemed as if the layer of film which covers a bird's eyes in death was already present. Then by accident, his fingers touched the bird's raw breast, and its beak opened in another silent scream of pain.

It was still alive. Only he could save it. He could feel the bird's heart, beating against his fingers, thumping, thumping hard against them, as if trying to burst out.

Slowly Walter unbuttoned, and tucked the pigeon inside his shirt and up under his vest, until he could feel its heartbeat against the skin of his chest.

His own heartbeat would calm it, and their combined warmth would renew its wish to live.

Buttoning up his clothes against the bitter wind, he began to walk, and as he walked, he spoke gently to the pigeon which lay against his heart. 'I've no food for you. You should taste hemp seed. You'd like that. You should have tares and linseed, maple peas and maize.' His voice was like the sound of a fart in soapy water, but how should the bird know that?

211

Then he remembered the remainder of the sliced bread he had left on the floor of the room in which June had lain waiting for his return, and he changed direction.

'You'll be all right with me. We'll both be all right.'

He was walking again. He was talking again.

5

Finis

That is the end of the story of Walter, and as for June, she was never more than a part of it, and found at last by accident what she had so often tried to bring about deliberately.

He is still alive. He has returned – well, he has been returned to the Hospital; they have accepted him.

He watches television and the weekly film show. Sits. Speaks if someone speaks to him, but not much, and not always in a concentrated way. He never speaks of pigeons.

Only at night, in his dreams, the pigeons fly. Russian High-Fliers and Birmingham Rollers, Turbits, Long-Faced English Tumblers, White-Lace Fantails, Norman and Marlene, Marge and Lionel, Freda the favourite of all favourites, Clarice, Edna, William and Amy, they fly high in the air, swoop, glide, tumble and recover, flying forever in wide circles, clapping their wings as they wheel above the solitary figure looking up at them from below. All night they cut the clean air for their delight and his.

And when he awakes, his cheeks are wet with tears.